BOOK FIVE

EVIL
THIRST

For my sister Ann, who is a vampire

1

I am a vampire. For centuries I believed I was the last vampire on Earth, that I was the most powerful creature in existence. That belief gave me great self-confidence. I feared nothing because nothing could harm me. Then one remarkable day, my supposedly dead creator, Yaksha, came for me, and I discovered I was not omnipotent. A short time later another vampire appeared, one Eddie Fender. He had Yaksha's strength, and once again I was almost destroyed. Yet I survived both Yaksha and Eddie, only to give birth to a daughter of unfathomable power and incomprehensible persuasion – Kalika, Kali Ma, the Dark Mother, the Supreme Goddess of Destruction. Yes, I believe my only child to be a divine incarnation, an *avatar*, as some would describe her. In a devastating vision she showed me her infinite greatness. The only problem is that my daughter seems to have been born without a conscience.

Actually, I do have three other small problems.

I don't know where Kalika is.

I know I must destroy her.

And I love her.

I don't know which of these dilemmas is worst, but together they make a very dangerous combination. There is another child who has recently been born to rival my daughter. I don't know the child's first name, but he is the son of my friend, Paula Ramirez. The power of this child is still a mystery to me. I only know that a tiny vial of his blood was able to bring my closest friend, Seymour Dorsten, back from the dead. I don't know where Paula and her son are either. I don't know if they're with Kalika. If they are, I do know they are both probably dead. Above all else, my daughter wants this child.

But why? I don't know.

I am beset with problems.

They seem never to stop.

I stand outside the Unity Church in Santa Monica, Seymour Dorsten by my side. Three months have passed since we were last in Santa Monica, on the pier. On that day Kalika first chose to spare Seymour's life, but then threw a stake into his spine while he thrashed in the ocean water below us. She said she did so to make a point.

'Do you really need to know?'

'Yes.'

'The knowledge will cost you.'

The question I had asked was who Paula's child was. Killing Seymour was her answer to the question, a very curious answer. Had Kalika not killed Seymour, I never would have thought to use the child's blood on a dead person. I never would have known just how special the child was. Yet Seymour does not remember any of this. The shock of being impaled has dimmed his memory of that night's events. He remembers being thrown off the pier and into the water – that's it. Of course he is still pressuring me to make him a vampire. He thinks then we will have great sex, or at least *some* sex. I don't sleep with him because I am afraid it would destroy our delicate balance of love and insults.

For the tenth time Seymour wants to know why I have dragged him to a New Age lecture. It is entitled: The Birth of Christ – an Egyptian Prophecy Fulfilled. The speaker is to be a Dr Donald Seter, founder of the New Age group, the Suzama Society. I want to attend Dr Seter's talk because of two incredible facts he has publicly announced. On a radio talk show he stated that Christ has been reborn – his birth took place on the exact day Paula's child was born. Of course he makes no mention of Paula and does not know to whom the child was born. The second fact is his claim that he has in his possession an ancient Egyptian scripture that supposedly gives details of this rebirth.

I would immediately discount the latter claim if the date had not been so personally coincidental, and if I had not happened to have known the original Suzama when I was in Egypt almost five thousand years ago. At one point Suzama was my teacher, and I know for a fact she was clairvoyant.

Yet I have never heard of the Suzama scripture before.

I wonder where Dr Seter obtained it, and how accurate it is.

But these things I can't explain to Seymour without telling him that he was brought back to life by the blood of a three-hour-old Hispanic infant. I feel there is a reason for his memory block, and I hesitate to tamper with it. Besides, I am afraid he might not believe me if I told him the truth. Who would? It is difficult to contemplate God and His Son and immaculate conceptions without feeling like a potential fanatic. Especially since Paula was not – in her own words – a virgin.

'We could be at a movie,' Seymour says. 'We could be having dinner. Besides, this whole Christian thing bores me. They have been waiting two thousand years for him to show up. If he was coming back, he would be here already.'

'Krishna promised to return,' I say. 'He said he would not be recognized.'

'He won't be bringing his flute?'

'I think he will return in humble surroundings.'

Seymour studies the poster outside the church announcing the lecture. 'You *are* history. What can you learn from this joker?'

4

I have to let something slip or Seymour won't attend. Actually, I'm not sure why I've brought him, but I suppose I know that at some point I'll have to open my heart to him and ask his advice. I always have in the past. I want him at the lecture so that he'll have all the facts when I need his advice.

Yet I hesitate before speaking. Every time I bring him deeper into my life, I bring him closer to danger. Still, I remind myself, it is his decision to stay with me, even after he has seen what my daughter can do. He at least knows that I am searching for her, even if he doesn't realize I am also desperately seeking Paula and her child. Yet Paula hasn't called the number I gave her to call. She should have tried to contact me two months ago, a month after I said goodbye to her. It worries me that Kalika may have gotten to her first. I am at Dr Seter's lecture in the hope that he can give me some clue as to where they might be. It is unlikely, I know.

'Dr Seter says he has a copy of a scripture Suzama wrote,' I tell Seymour. 'She was a real person, a revered priestess of the Church of Isis, a high adept in ancient Egypt.' I pause. 'I knew her, I studied with her.'

Seymour is impressed. 'What did she teach you?'

'How to bring the white light above my head into my heart.'

'What?'

'She taught primarily esoteric forms of meditation. She had many gifts.' I grab his arm and drag him towards the church door. 'I will tell you more about her later.'

On the way in there is a registration table and a donation basket. I throw a few dollars in the latter. A young man in a dark blue suit and a red tie stands near the door greeting people. Actually, there are a number of people similarly outfitted – young, handsome people, males and females, wearing navy blue clothes and shiny faces. They are Dr Seter's followers, I realize, but I hesitate to make the judgment that the man has formed a cult. Not all New Age groups, or Christian groups for that matter, signify sects. Besides, I don't care if he has formed a cult or not. I just care if he knows what he's talking about.

The young man greeting people pauses to say hello to me.

'Welcome,' he says. 'May I ask how you heard about our lecture?'

'On the radio,' I say. 'Yesterday night. I heard Dr Seter's interview.'

'KEXT?' he asks.

'That was the one,' I say. 'Have you known the doctor long?'

'I should say.' The young man smiles and offers his hand. 'James Seter – I work for my father. Have since I can remember.' He pauses. 'And your name?'

'I'm Alisa. This is Seymour.'

'Hi,' Seymour says, shaking James's hand when I'm through with it. But James Seter only has eyes for me.

'Have you read Dr Seter's book?' he asks me.

'No,' I say. 'I was hoping to obtain a copy here.'

'They will be on sale after the lecture,' James says.

'Fascinating reading, if I do say so myself.'

'What allowed your father to predict so accurately the birth of Christ?' I ask.

'The Suzama scripture. It contains very detailed knowledge about the next coming of the messiah. It predicted Christ's coming the first time very accurately.'

I smile. 'And you believe all this?'

He nods. 'Suzama had a great gift. Studying her words, I have never found her to make a mistake.'

'It sounds like a remarkable document,' I say. 'Why haven't modern archeologists, linguists, and theologians had a chance to study it?'

James hesitates. 'My father will address all these questions in the lecture. Better to ask him. His knowledge of the scripture is extremely comprehensive.'

'Just one last question,' I say. 'Has he brought the original scripture with him tonight?'

'I'm afraid not. It's a priceless artefact. We cannot risk it at a public lecture.'

I detect no deceit in his words, and I have a sharp ear for it. Also, there is an ease in his manner, a naturalness. He does not act like a fanatic. His dark eyes continue to study me, though. I think he likes me. He is remarkably handsome, and cannot be more than twenty-two years old.

After muttering my thanks and taking Seymour's hand, I step into the church and search for a seat. The place is crowded but we manage to squeeze in near the front. The audience is remarkably diverse, made up of old and young, tramps and professionals. I am disappointed I will not have a chance to study the scripture. I am certain I would know if it were authentic. Suzama had a fine hand for hieroglyphs. I remember her work well.

Dr Seter enters five minutes later.

He is a small man with white hair and an unassuming manner. As he walks toward the podium, I estimate his age at seventy, although he appears less than sixty. It is his vitality and bright grey eyes that make him seem younger than he really is. He wears a medium-priced grey suit and expensive black shoes. He is not so handsome as his son, though. Indeed, I suspect he is not the biological father, that James is adopted. There is a scholarly air to Dr Seter that I find interesting. The lines on and the planes across his face show intelligence and extensive education. I see all this in one penetrating vampiric glance.

James Seter comes forward to introduce his father. He lists a number of academic achievements. Dr Seter has Ph.Ds in both theology and archeology, from Harvard and Stanford respectively. He is the author of numerous published papers and three books. For the last decade, James says, his father has been studying the Suzama scripture and bringing the knowledge contained in it to the world. James does not mention where his father obtained the scripture, probably to leave his father something of interest to discuss. The introduction is brief, and soon Dr Seter is at the podium. His voice is pleasant, although somewhat reedy. He starts by welcoming us and thanking us for coming. Then he pauses and flashes a warm but shy smile.

'It is quite a claim for one to make,' he says, 'that one knows that the messiah is in the world. That he has been born on such and such a day in such and such a country. Had I attended this lecture as an observer ten years ago, I don't think I would have sat through the introduction. For as my son James has pointed out, I come from a fairly rigourous academic background. Until ten years ago, I never thought of the second coming or even, quite frankly, much of Christ himself. This may come as a surprise, since I hold a doctorate in theology. But the truth of the matter is my studies of religion were purely academic. I was an agnostic. I neither believed nor disbelieved the world's religions, yet I found them fascinating.

'Now this is where I may lose half of you. In fact, when I first began to lecture on the Suzama scripture, it was normal for a quarter of my audience to get up and leave at this point – my introduction to the scripture. Since those days I have managed to decrease that number by initially asking all of you to please set aside your doubts for the next few minutes to listen to what I have to say. You can form your judgments later. There is plenty of time, believe me.'

Dr Seter paused to sip from the glass of water on the podium. Then he cleared his throat and continued.

'The Suzama scripture comes from the culture of ancient Egypt. Carbon dating and an analysis of its hieroglyphic style place it back approximately five thousand years, in what is commonly called pre-dynastic Egypt. I did not find the scripture in Egypt, but in a country in Western Europe that I cannot reveal at this time. The reason for this secrecy may be obvious to some, and despicable to others.' He pauses. 'I took the Suzama scripture back with me to America to study, without the permission of the country where I found it. In that sense I am guilty of stealing, but I make no apologies. Furthermore, as long as I refuse to name the country from which I took it, I cannot be legally prosecuted for the act. But with my background, I felt I was best equipped to study the scripture.

'Now many of you may feel that is the height of egotism on my part. By keeping the original scripture to myself I immediately bring into question its authenticity. What reputable scientist would do such a thing? If you had told me ten years ago that I would be guilty of this behaviour, I would have said it would not be possible. I would have said that every ancient artefact belongs to the world. Nothing should be hidden away and kept secret. That is a basic scientific credo. And yet I have hidden this document. Why?

'Because I believe the Suzama scripture contains information that could be dangerous if publicly revealed. Dangerous to whom, you might ask? To the Christ himself, as an infant, and to the public as a whole. For Suzama, a powerful clairvoyant of her time, has set down information that might allow one to find the Christ before his time. Also, the scripture contains information on powerful forms of meditation that are, in my estimate, dangerous for the inexperienced.

'Who am I to decide what knowledge is too dangerous for mankind to receive? I can only say in my defence that I have experimented personally with many of Suzama's instructions, and almost lost my life in the process. From my point of view, it would be the ultimate in irresponsibility to throw all of the Suzama material out there.

'Then why should you believe anything I have to say? Why should you even believe there was a Suzama? Well, you don't have to believe me. I don't ask that you do. But as a measure of proof I have turned over numerous slides of the original scripture to eminent archaeologists. Because I have not allowed them access to the original artefact, they are unwilling to state unequivocally that the Suzama scripture is authentic. But many of them are willing to certify that as far as they can tell it is the real thing. A list of these experts is recorded in my book.

'What does this long dead woman have to say about the birth and rebirth of the Christ? For one thing Suzama states that Christ has not come just once, but at least four times in our history: as Lord Krishna of India, two hundred years before Suzama's birth, as Adi Shankara of India, five hundred years before Christ's birth, and finally as Christ himself. The Suzama scripture predicts each of these births, and says that the soul of all these great prophets and masters was identical. Furthermore the text predicts that this same infinite soul took birth in a human body recently, in the last three months. The exact date is given, in fact, as last March fifteenth, and the child was destined to be born here, in California.'

A loud stir went through the audience. Dr Seter pauses to have another drink of water. He deserves one, I thought, after the mouthful he had just said. Clearing his throat once more, he continues.

'What proof do I have that Suzama knew what she was talking about? If I accept her scripture as authentic, a product of ancient Egypt, then I am forced to accept that she has had a pretty good track record so far. But beyond that is the inner validation the material has given me. Following her prescribed instructions, I have been given an intuitive insight into the hidden meaning behind certain of her verses. Now I see many eyebrows rise with that statement. Are her instructions and her predictions presented in an obscure form? So obscure a form that their meaning is open to interpretation?

'The answer to both these questions is yes and no. Suzama is often specific when it comes to dates. She says when Shankara and Christ were to be born. But as far as esoteric practices are concerned she can be very subtle. A study of her text requires a study of one's own mind, and it is this last point more than any that has stopped me from letting the whole of the scripture become public. Scientists demand that knowledge be objective, empirical, when the very nature of this type of study, the search for the soul, for the God, is in my mind almost entirely a subjective exploration.'

Dr Seter pauses and scans the room. 'I never like to lecture too long without taking questions. I will take some now.'

Many hands shoot up. Dr Seter chooses a middle-aged man not far from where we are seated. The man stands to speak.

'How did you manage to find this religious text in the first place?' he asks. 'What led you to it?'

Dr Seter does not hesitate. 'A dream. I simply dreamed where it was and I went and dug in a certain spot and found it.'

The man is stunned. 'You're not serious?'

Dr Seter holds up his hand as a murmur goes through the crowd. 'Believe me I would like to give another answer. Unfortunately another answer would not be true. This is how I found the scripture. There was no research involved, no tedious digs lasting decades. I found it as soon as I started looking for it.'

The man continues to stand. 'So you believe God directed you to it?'

'I believe somebody directed me to it. I don't know if it was God himself. Actually, Suzama never speaks of Christ or Shankara as God. She calls them masters, or perfected beings. And she believes we are all evolving to the same heightened state of perfection.' Dr Seter pauses. 'It was an especially vivid dream, unlike any I had ever had before. It would have had to be for me to act on it, I assure you.' A pause. 'Next question.'

He chooses a young woman at the back. Even before she speaks, it is clear she has a chip on her shoulder.

'What if I were to say that you made this all up? That the Suzama scripture is a complete fraud?'

'I would say that's not a question.' Dr Seter pauses. 'Do you have a question?'

The young woman fumes. 'There was only one Christ. How can you dare to compare him to these heathens?'

Dr Seter smiles. 'It is questions like this that reaffirm my decision not to make public everything I know about the Christ's birth in our time. Each of the others I spoke of was a great spiritual leader in his time. Had you been born in India, even today, you might follow their teachings. It is largely because you were born in this country that you are a Christian.' He pauses. 'Don't you agree?'

The young woman is uncomfortable but remains defiant. 'I hardly think so. You twist the teachings of Christ, comparing them to these others.'

'Frankly, I think I compliment all of them by comparing each to the other. But that is beside the point. I never asked you to believe that the Suzama scripture is accurate. I am merely saying that I believe it is, based on my research and personal experience. If you believe it is a fraud, fine. But the text warns that those who profess to worship the Christ will be the first to dismiss him when he returns.'

I approve of the manner in which Dr Seter deals with the young woman's insolent attitude. I have never appreciated religious dogma. It seems to me only a more insidious form of racial prejudice. Yet I am not sure if I agree with Dr Seter when he says the three spiritual leaders were one and the same being. Having known Krishna personally, I have trouble reconciling many of Christ's teachings with Krishna's, although I suspect the early disciples of Christ distorted what their master said. At the same time I am familiar with Shankara's work, particularly his commentary on the Brahma Sutras, which I have studied over the centuries. I agree with the Eastern claim that Shankara was the greatest intellect who ever lived. Yet his style of teaching was very different from either Krishna's or Christ's. For one thing, he never claimed to be anyone special, either the son of God or God himself. Yet he worked many recorded miracles.

Nevertheless I find the doctor's words fascinating. I raise my hand and catch his eye, using a fraction of the great power I have in my eyes to rivet a person's attention. He immediately picks me. I also stand as I ask my question.

'You say Suzama gives exact dates as to the births of these various avatars,' I say. 'Yet the solar calendar was not used in ancient Egypt until two thousand B.C. Suzama surely must have used a lunar calendar when presenting her dates. How did you translate one to the other?'

'No translation was necessary. The dates are not expressed in terms of a lunar calendar but a solar one.'

I am disappointed in his answer. 'But you realize as an archeologist how unlikely that is. It almost certainly means the scripture you have found is either from a much later period, or that it is fake.'

Dr Seter is not dissuaded. 'As an archeologist I was *surprised* she predicted the birth of these masters in terms of a solar calendar and not a lunar one. Yet if we accept as true her profound intuition, then we must also accept that she would understand that in the future her lunar calendar would not be used. Actually, at least to my mind, the fact that she did not use a lunar calendar supports her claims.'

'Did she mention any other avatars besides the three you mentioned?' I ask.

Dr Seter hesitates. 'Yes. But she says they are of a different line.'

'Does she mention Isis for example?'

Dr Seter is taken aback. 'I did not discuss that in any of my books. But, yes, it is true, Suzama was a high priestess of a group that worshipped Isis.' He pauses. 'May I ask why you ask that question?'

'We can talk about it another time,' I say and quickly sit down. Seymour leans over and speaks in my ear.

'You're drawing attention to yourself,' he warns.

'Only enough to make him want to meet me afterward,' I reply.

'Do you think he's telling the truth?'

'He is definitely *convinced* he is telling the truth. There is not a shred of deceit in him.' I pause. 'But that is not the same as saying he is right. Far from it.'

There followed dozens of questions.

'How did Suzama describe California?'

Answer: 'At the other end of the great continent

across the ocean, where the sun always shines.'

'What kind of family was Christ reborn into?'

Answer: 'A poor broken family.'

'What nationality will the Christ be?'

Answer: 'Brown skinned.'

A lot of people didn't like that answer. Of course it would have made me chuckle, except Paula's baby had brown skin, like his mother.

Toward the end there was one question that disturbed me, or rather, Dr Seter's answer did. He was asked if the reborn Christ was in any danger, as an infant. Dr Seter hesitated long before responding. Clearly the Suzama text contained a warning of some kind.

'Yes,' he says finally. 'Suzama states that the forces of darkness will bend even the will of the righteous to try to find the child and destroy him. She further states that it is the duty of the old and powerful to help locate the child and protect him.'

My hand is up in an instant.

'Does Suzama describe the form these forces of darkness will take?' I ask.

He pauses. 'No. Not really.'

It is the first lie he has told all night. Curious.

The old and powerful?

Who on the planet is older and more powerful than I am?

17

It is my desire to have coffee with Dr Donald Seter this very night, and to increase my chances of success I send Seymour away. He's only too happy to try to catch a late movie in Westwood. Seymour, I feel, may hold me back because I plan to reach the esteemed doctor through the son, James Seter. Picking up a copy of Dr Seter's book, *The Secret of Suzama*, on the back table for a mere twenty bucks, I stroll over to where bright-faced James is saying goodbye to people. He stands near the exit and thanks people for coming. Such a nice young man, with a firm handshake, no less. He lights up when he sees me.

'Alisa,' he says. 'Your questions were very interesting.'

'You remember my name. I am flattered.' I pause. 'I am perhaps a little older than I look, and a little more educated. I have made a thorough study of ancient Egypt, and would enjoy chatting with you and your father about the Suzama scripture.'

He doesn't take me seriously. 'I'm sure that would be fun and informative, but my father has to catch a plane for San Francisco tomorrow morning early.'

I catch his eye, put an ounce of heat behind my words. 'Maybe you could talk to him about me. He expressed an interest in my knowledge of Suzama's connection to Isis.'

James blinks a few times. He must have a strong will; he does not immediately jump at my suggestion.

'I could talk to him. But as you can see he is not as young as he once was. I worry about tiring him unnecessarily.'

I do not want to push James too hard. There is always the possibility I might damage him in some way. Since my rebirth as a vampire, I have found the power in my eyes particularly biting. I use it in small doses. But I do not want Dr Seter to just walk away. I decide to let a portion of my ancient knowledge drop, but in the form of a lie. Making a drama of it, I pull James Seter aside and speak in hushed tones.

'Your Suzama scripture is not the only one in existence,' I say. 'I have another one, but I think it is different. I would be happy to trade information with your father.'

James pauses a moment to take this all in. 'You can't be serious?'

I speak evenly. 'But I am. If your father will meet with

me, I would be happy to talk to him about it.' I pause. 'He will know within a minute whether I have discovered something authentic.'

'He will want to question you before spending time with you.'

I shake my head. 'I will not talk here about what I have found. But please assure your father that I'm not a crackpot.'

'Where do you want to meet?'

'There's a coffee shop three blocks from the ocean near Ocean Avenue and the freeway. I can meet you there in, say, half an hour.'

That is the coffee shop where my beloved Ray came back to me, where he in fact returned to life. He appeared just after I shot two men to death after they'd tried to rape me. I was covered with a fine spray of blood at the time, a fitting ornament for dark delusions. I have not been back to the coffee shop since, but for some perverse reason I want to go there tonight. Maybe another phantom will appear to spice up my life. Yet I hope not. The pain of the last one is still an open wound for me. Just the thought of Ray fills me with sorrow. James is studying me.

'When you came here tonight,' he says, 'you acted like you had no knowledge of Suzama. Why?'

I reach out and straighten his tie. 'If you knew what I know, James, you would make a point of appearing ignorant.' I pause. 'Tell your father to come. I will be waiting.'

* * *

A half hour later I sit in the coffee shop across from Dr Seter and his son. They have come alone, which is good. Actually it is good that they have come at all, but I suspect son dragged father along. The doctor doesn't look at me as if he expects to receive any divine revelation from me. But he does seem to be enjoying the apple pie and ice cream I've ordered for him. When you're a cute five-thousand-year-old blond, you can get away with murder.

'James tells me you're a student of archeology,' Dr Seter says as he forks up a heaping piece of pie. He has taken off the tie he wore to his lecture but otherwise he is dressed the same. His manner is relaxed, a scholar enjoying himself after giving a lecture he has obviously given a thousand times before. Briefly I wonder about his motivation for publicizing the Suzama scripture. I don't think he can be making much money from doing so. The cost of his book is nominal and he doesn't teach any high-priced seminar. He seems like a nice man with no hidden agenda.

'I am a student of Suzama,' I say seriously. 'I was not boasting when I said I possess a manuscript of hers.'

Dr Seter is amused. 'Where did you find this manuscript?'

'Where did you find yours?' I ask.

'I have explained why I am reluctant to reveal that information.'

'I have the same reluctance for the same reasons,' I say.

He returns to his pie. He thinks I am a nice girl with nothing to say.

'Then I guess we'll just have to enjoy the food,' he says politely.

I open his book to a photograph of a portion of the Suzama scripture. I point to the hieratic writing on the ancient papyrus.

'There are probably only two dozen people on Earth who can read this at a glance,' I say. 'You are one of them, I am another. This line says, "The secret of the Goddess is in the sixteenth digit of the moon. Not the moon in the sky, but the moon in the high centre. It is here the ambrosia of bliss is milked by the sincere seeker. It is only there the knowledge of the soul is revealed."' I pause. 'Is my translation accurate?'

Dr Seter almost drops his fork. 'How did you know that? I don't translate that line in the text.'

'I told you, I am a student of Suzama.'

James interrupts. 'How do we know someone else didn't translate the line for you?'

'Because I can give you information that must be in the portion of your scripture that you keep hidden, as it is in mine. For example, I know of the four-word mantra Suzama used to invoke the white light from above the head, where the moon digit is really located. I know how the first word relates to the heart, the second to the throat, the third to the head. I know how the breath is synchronized with the mantra and that on the fourth word the divine white light of Isis is brought down into the human body.'

Dr Seter stares at me, stunned. 'What is the four-word mantra?'

I speak seriously. 'You know from your scripture that it is only to be revealed in private, at the time of initiation. I will not say it here. But you must realize by now that I know a great deal about Suzama's secret meditation practices. Therefore, it should be easy for you to believe that I must have access to another scripture belonging to her.' I pause. 'Am I correct?'

Dr Seter studies me. 'You know something, that's for sure. Frankly, I would be very curious to see your scripture.'

'You have to show me yours first,' I say. 'I will be able to tell if it is authentic.'

'How?' James interrupts.

I smile for him. 'I will compare it to mine.'

'Do you believe your scripture is identical to mine?' Dr Seter asks.

'No. Yours speaks of a danger to the new master. Mine does not address that point.' I add, 'You lied when you said your scripture did not specify what the danger is.'

Dr Seter sits back. 'How do you know that?'

'It doesn't matter. It's true.' I pause. 'Tell me how the danger is described?'

'I'm afraid that's not possible,' James says. 'Only inner members of our group are given such information.'

'Ah,' I say. 'This inner group you have organized, what's its purpose? To protect the child once it is found?' By their reaction I see I have scored a bullseye. 'Isn't that rather presumptuous of you? To think the messiah needs your protection?'

Dr Seter is having trouble keeping up with me. Still, I have his full attention. 'What if the scripture itself says he will need protection?' he asks.

'Does it?' I ask.

Dr Seter hesitates. 'Yes.'

He is telling the truth, or at least the truth he knows.

'Father,' James interrupts. 'Should we be talking about these things in front of a stranger whom we have just met?'

Dr Seter shrugs. 'Isn't it obvious she knows as much about Suzama as we do?'

'But I don't,' I say again. 'I know different things about her. I am working with different source material. But back to your group, and how they will be used to protect the child. How exactly is that going to work?'

'Surely you can understand that we can't divulge the inner workings of our group,' Dr Seter says. 'Not the way the government is scrutinizing every spiritual group in the country, searching for the next crazy cult. Please, let's try to keep this on an academic level. I would like to see your material, you would like to see mine. Fine, how can we work a place and a date to exchange information?'

'I told you,' I say. 'You have to show me yours first. If I am convinced it is authentic, I will show you what I have.'

Dr Seter is suspicious. 'Why not have a simultaneous exchange?'

I smile warmly. 'I will not harm your material. I'm sure when you show it to me there will be a dozen of your well-dressed boys and girls gathered around.' I pause. 'I suspect you travel with it. Why don't you show it to me tonight? I will not have to study it long to reach a conclusion.'

Dr Seter and James exchange a long look. 'What could it hurt?' the doctor says finally, testing the waters.

James is unsure. He continues to study me. 'How do we know you don't work for the FBI?'

I throw my head back and laugh. 'Where will you find a FBI agent who can read hieroglyphics?'

'But you are curious about the purpose of our group?' James persists. 'These are the kinds of questions the government might ask.'

I catch James's eye and let my power out in a measured dose. 'I am not from the government. I represent no one other than myself. My interest in the Suzama material is motivated only by the highest and best desires.' I pause and catch the eye of the doctor as well. 'Let me see it. You will have no regrets.'

Dr Seter touches his son's arm as he nods in answer to my request. 'We don't exactly travel with it, but it's not far from here.' He pauses. 'It's out in Palm Springs.'

'Palm Springs,' I mutter. What a coincidence. One passes through Palm Springs on the way to Joshua Tree National Monument, where Paula supposedly conceived her child. I have been meaning to go out there for some time.

'James can show you the scripture tomorrow morning,' Dr Seter says, checking his watch. 'It's too late to see it tonight.'

I stand. 'But I'm a night girl. And I would like you to be there, Dr Seter, when I examine it. If you please? Let's go now.'

He is taken aback by my boldness and gazes up at me. 'May I ask how old you are, Alisa?'

I smile. 'You must know that Suzama was not very old when she wrote your scripture.'

Dr Seter shakes his head. 'I didn't know that. How old was she?'

'I take that back. I'm not sure how old she was when she wrote it. I only know she died before her twentieth birthday.'

I don't add, like me.

Some, of course, consider vampires the walking dead.

3

Before heading for Palm Springs, I leave Seymour a message on the answering machine in our new home in Pacific Palisades. We stay in regular contact. It's a promise we keep to each other. I have left him before in the middle of the night without explanation and have promised never to do it again. Also, my daughter, Kalika, still walks the streets, and it is impossible to tell when she will come for us again. Seymour and I, we cover each other's backs. But I feel in my heart it will not be long before I see Kalika again. A part of me senses that she has yet to find the child, but is searching constantly for him. I have to wonder if my intuition about her is attached to the psychic thread that connects all mothers to their children.

Dr Seter and James drive ahead of me on the long

road to Palm Springs. They have an old white Volvo, I a brand-new red Porsche. James is behind the wheel. I keep only fifty feet behind, just off to their right in the fast lane. They would be surprised to know that I can hear them as they speak. Yet it is only when we have been on the road an hour that they finally begin to talk. Before then Dr Seter had been slipping in and out of sleep.

James: 'Why are we doing this?'

Dr Seter: 'Do you think we should just ignore her?'

James: 'Not at all. I'm as curious about her as you. Remember it was I who insisted upon the meeting. But I think we should investigate her background before letting her see the scripture.'

Dr Seter: 'What harm can she do to it? She will not be able to translate a fraction of the hieroglyphics without hours of time. I don't care how well versed she is in the field.' A pause. 'She must be older than she looks. It takes years to learn to read the way she did.'

James: 'I'm sure she's older than she looks. Notice she didn't actually tell you her age?'

Dr Seter: 'What are you saying? That she has mastered Suzama's practices and managed to reverse her age?'

James: 'It's possible. She knew enough about the high initiation.'

Dr Seter: 'That's what startled me about her, too. There are few people in our group who know about that.' A pause. 'She must be telling the truth. She must have another text.'

James: 'I agree. But she's evasive. I don't trust her. I want full security when we show her the papyrus.'

Dr Seter: 'Of course. You've called ahead? They know we're coming?'

James: 'Yes. The whole group will be there.'

Dr Seter: 'Really? Why? We don't need all of them there. The others should be on their way to San Francisco.'

James: 'I told you, I don't trust this girl.' A pause. 'But I have another reason.'

Dr Seter: 'What?'

James: 'I wonder if Alisa has direct knowledge about the child.'

Dr Seter: 'Now you're speculating.'

James: 'I'm not so sure. She seemed particularly concerned about the child being harmed.' A pause. 'Maybe I say that backwards. I wonder if she already knows about the Dark Mother.'

I almost drive off the road. They are talking about Kalika.

My daughter? Did Suzama brand her as evil five thousand years ago?

Dr Seter: 'I didn't get that impression.'

James: 'Can I say something really off the wall?'

Dr Seter: 'It's a long drive. We may as well discuss every possibility.'

James: 'What if this Alisa is working for the Black Mother?'

Dr Seter laughs: 'She hardly seems the type, do you think?'

James: 'Consider. She looks like a twenty-year-old, but she appears to have the education of someone who has studied for thirty years. Also, her manner is curious. Notice the way she catches your eye, and then says things you have trouble resisting.'

Dr Seter laughs some more: 'I never noticed that. I think you are the one who is having trouble resisting her.'

James: 'I don't know. I just hope we're not leading her to the child by letting her study the scripture.'

Dr Seter: 'But there's nothing in the scripture that points to where the child is at this time, except perhaps still in California.'

James: 'To us maybe. But she may find clues in the text we have missed.' A pause. 'I pray to God we're not doing anything to endanger the child further. From the descriptions I have read of the Dark Mother, I wouldn't want anyone, friend or foe, to run into her. I think that kind of evil lives to kill.'

Dr Seter: 'But you know, son, we have spent the last ten years preparing to meet her.' A pause. 'It's inevitable, if we're to believe half of what we've read.'

James: 'Do you really think we're the ones chosen to defend the child?'

Dr Seter: 'I wouldn't have bought so many automatic weapons unless I did.' A sigh. 'I'm more worried that Alisa may be from the government than that she represents the Dark Mother.'

James: 'Then why show her anything?'

Dr Seter: 'As I said, it can cause no harm. She will not

have time to translate the portions of the scripture we don't want her to translate. And she will find nothing in our centre the government would be excited about.'

James: 'I hope you're right.' A pause. 'She is incredibly beautiful.'

Dr Seter: 'I noticed.'

I find their private conversation fascinating.

The centre they have referred to is a large house in an area clearly zoned for both business and residential properties. There are many cars parked along the street as we pull up. Like Dr Seter, I am surprised that James has directed the whole group here, especially when they have a lecture the following night in San Francisco. Yet James's intuitions about me are shockingly accurate. He wonders if the Dark Mother has sent me. How would he feel if he knew I am the Dark Mother's mother? I would have a hard time convincing him I'm on his side, not hers.

Yet the one thing I have learned by eavesdropping is that the Suzama Society is there to protect the child, not harm it. Still, the reference to automatic weapons disturbs me. It is true that they might come in handy should Kalika show up, but I know guns in the hands of true believers seldom get pointed in the right direction at the right time.

What is the source of James's excellent intuition? Perhaps it is a result of following Suzama's meditation practices. I found his reference to reversed aging intriguing. Is James older than he looks? I remember

Suzama's often saying that aging is a product of lower consciousness, and immortality the gift of highest consciousness.

Dr Seter and James welcome me warmly as I climb from my car.

'Did you have a pleasant drive?' Seter asks.

'I listened to loud music the whole way,' I say, gesturing to all the cars. 'Is there another lecture here tonight?'

Dr Seter glances at James. 'Many in our group have returned here to collect supplies for the remainder of my tour,' the doctor explains. 'I have to fly to the East Coast after my San Francisco lecture.' He gestures to the house. 'Please come in. Would you like some coffee?'

'Thank you, no. I am wide awake.'

'That's right,' James says, moving up behind us. 'You're a night person.'

Inside there are two dozen navy blue suits, half and half, pants and skirts, male and female, all young and attractive. I don't get the uniform thing, especially around Dr Seter, who seems so laid back. Perhaps it is James's idea, although he seems far from a fanatic. The group studies me as I step into the huge house. The place is orderly, the furniture traditional, every corner clean and dust free. There is a faint odour of fried chicken in the air, mashed potatoes, and broccoli. They are not vegetarians, even though Suzama was.

Staring at the innocent faces, I wonder if they practise using their automatic weapons deep in the desert when no one is around. Simply to own an automatic weapon is to invite a felony charge, jail time. Dr Seter must be convinced the enemy is at hand to go to such extremes. Of course, who am I to judge? He has not fed the enemy another person's blood in the middle of the night just to get her to stop crying. My dear daughter – my how fast she grew and how strong. She can kick my ass in a fight. That, I know from experience.

The memory of Eric Hawkins, Kalika's personal snack bar, is never far.

'Oh God, I'm bleeding! She's cut my neck! The blood is gushing out! Help me!'

But I could not help him. I was only able to use him.

A young woman about my apparent age steps forward to shake my hand. 'My name is Lisa,' she says. 'You're Alisa?'

'Yes.'

'We hear you can read hieroglyphics?'

'Hieroglyphics and comic books have always been favourites of mine,' I say. There is a murmur of laughter. 'Where are you from, Lisa?'

'North Dakota. I met Dr Seter there last year—'

'Lisa is our accountant,' Dr Seter interrupts. 'I call her boss.'

The group laughs. They obviously love the man.

I am led down into a basement. Few homes in Southern California have basements, and this one is special, to say the least. As James closes the door behind us, I notice that it has a rubber seal all around it. Almost immediately I notice a change in the air pressure, and

I understand why. They are worried about dust and dampness and the effect they would have on the scripture. The air in the basement is carefully filtered.

Six of the group have followed me into the basement, including James and Dr Seter. A young man named Charles steps to a vault at the far end of the basement. In the centre of the room is a large white table with brilliant overhead lights and a double ocular over-size microscope at one end. There are also a couple of magnifying glasses and loupes sitting handily by. Charles spins the steel knob on the vault, dialing the combination. His body is between me and the knob but I listen closely and in a moment I know the combination, R48, L32, R16, L17, R12, L10.

The vault pops open. Charles lifts out a pale yellow sheet of papyrus wrapped in acid-free tissue paper and carries it to the table to set down under the bright lights. The scripture is a foot across, two feet long. A rush of excitement makes my heart pound. Even through the covering tissue paper, I smell ancient Egypt!

I recognize the hieratic writing.

It is tiny, carefully crafted.

It is definitely in Suzama's cursive.

Dr Seter gestures for me to examine it closer after he lifts off the tissue paper.

As I bend over the table, he has no idea I am about to read it much faster than he would read a large-print book. Yet James stands close beside me, his eyes on mine.

I begin to read.

I am Suzama and my words are true. The past and the future are the same to my illumined vision. You who read these words are warned not to doubt what is recorded lest you fall into error and lose your way on the path. I am Suzama and I speak for the truth.

The lord of creation is both inside and outside creation. He is like the sap in the flower, the space in an empty room. He is always present but unseen. His joy shines like the sun in the sky, his will swims like a fish beneath the ocean. He cannot be known by the mind or even the heart. Only the inner silence recognizes him.

He is both male and female and he is neither. To speak of him as one or the other is only a manner of speaking. In order to protect the righteous and destroy the wicked, he takes birth again and again throughout the ages.

His most recent birth was as Sri Krishna in the land of the Pandu brothers. Then and there he slew demons and granted realization to the worthy. His life lasted 135 years, from 3675 to 3810. He will be remembered as the divine personality.

His next birth will be as Adi Shankara in the land of the Vedas. Then and there he will make available the knowledge of the Brahman, the highest reality. His life will last 32 years, from 6111 to 6143. He will be well remembered as the divine teacher.

His subsequent birth will be as Jesus of Nazareth in the land of Abraham. Then and there he will embody and teach perfect love and compassion. His life will last 108 years, from 7608 to 7716. He will be well remembered as the divine savior.

* * *

The scripture ends there. I look over at Dr Seter.

'Where's the rest of it?' I ask.

'You do not need all of it to judge its authenticity,' Dr Seter says.

'That doesn't answer my question,' I say.

'The rest of it is in the vault,' James interrupts, close to my right side. 'But we decided it wouldn't be a good idea to bring it all out tonight.'

On the road, I was briefly separated from them by a distance of two hundred feet. At that point they had their radio on and their windows up. Even I, with my supernatural hearing, could not hear what they were saying. They must have made this decision at that time. Naturally, I am disappointed not to see it all. Yet I am thrilled by what I have read. Already I am convinced the scripture is authentic. The papyrus even feels as if it is five thousand years old. I stroke it gently, making James jump.

'Don't do that,' he says.

I withdraw my hand. 'I know how to handle such things. I did not harm it in any way.' I pause and look at the doctor. 'It is my belief that this scripture is authentic.'

Dr Seter is taken back. 'You can tell that by such a brief study?'

'Yes. This portion matches what I have. I take back what I said earlier. They're almost identical.' I pause. 'It would help us if I could see the rest.'

Dr Seter is apologetic. 'Alisa, surely you understand what an act of good faith it was for us to show you what we have shown you. Now it's only right, before we reveal any more, that you show us at least a portion of what you have discovered.' He pauses and smiles. 'I think that is fair. Don't you?'

'Very fair. May I have a day or two to deliver the material to you?'

'Certainly,' Dr Seter says. 'James will not be accompanying me east. You can bring what you wish to show us here and he will have a look at it.'

'Fine,' I say. 'But you must look at it yourself, Dr Seter.'

'But I have told you about my commitments on the East Coast.'

'What I have to show you will make those commitments seem unimportant.'

Dr Seter is troubled. 'I am not willing to cancel any of my lectures until I have more proof.'

'I will give you such proof before you leave for the East. Where will you be staying in San Francisco?'

'At the Hilton by the airport,' James says. 'You can leave a message there. We'll return your call promptly.'

I offer Dr Seter my hand. 'I look forward to meeting you again soon.'

The doctor is surprised at my sudden departure. 'But you've said hardly anything about what we've shown you.'

I keep my tone light. 'It's what you haven't shown me that I would have a lot to say about.'

James touches my arm. 'I'll walk you out, Alisa, if you'd like.'

I smile. 'I would like that very much.'

Outside James is a study in politeness.

'I hope you can understand our caution,' he says. 'We just met you tonight. While we're all impressed with your understanding of the Suzama material, we still have to take things one step at a time.'

'No problem,' I say as I open my car door. 'I doubt that I would have been nearly as open as you and your father have been.'

James smiles. 'Actually, Alisa, you haven't been very open.' He pauses. 'You can at least tell us where you found your material.'

'In India.'

He frowns. 'Are you serious? Where?'

'In Sri Nagar.'

He nods. 'I know where that is. In the Himalayas. What were you doing there?'

'I had a few dreams of my own.' I pause. 'How old are you, James?'

'Twenty-eight.'

'You look much younger. I am twenty-five, for your information.'

'You look much younger,' he says. 'Do you practice anything Suzama taught?'

I smile. 'A personal question. I don't know if I want to answer that.'

'Come on,' he insists.

'I'll tell you what, I'll make a deal with you. Tell me what you practise and I'll tell you what I practise.'

He gives a sheepish grin. 'You're a clever young woman, Alisa. I don't know if it's smart to share too many secrets with you.'

Before I climb into my car I place my palm on his chest. I catch his dark eyes once more, and for the first time I notice how deep they are, how beautiful. There is more to him than meets even my penetrating eyes. A soothing warmth sweeps over me, for him, as well as for his father. Beneath my soft hand his warm heart beats faster. He may not trust me, but I know he likes me, maybe even wants me.

It is strange how I suddenly want him. Since Ray, I have not really desired any man. Even with Joel and Arturo, it was more my love for them that bound me to them. Yet, out of the blue, James has me all hot and bothered. Seymour would be incredibly jealous.

'Secrets are what make us all interesting,' I say, and give him a light peck on the cheek. 'Have fun in San Francisco. I will call you.'

He grabs my arm.

'There is something unusual about you, Alisa,' he says in a gentle voice. 'I'm going to figure out what it is.'

I laugh. 'And tell the whole world?'

He smiles, but when he speaks there is a seriousness in his voice. 'I have a feeling few in the world would believe me.'

4

The time is well after one, but I do not drive straight home. Being a vampire, I find one in the morning not unpleasant. Also, since my rebirth as a vampire, I have found I need little rest, an hour's nap here and there. Even when the sun is high in the daylight sky, my powers are hardly affected. Once again I attribute this to the fact that I used primarily Yaksha's blood to bring about my transformation.

And a few drops of Paula's child's blood.

I, like Seymour, have the influence of it in my life.

I drive to Joshua Tree National Monument, and when I arrive the moon is high in the sky. The park is large, and I have no idea where Paula sat when the brilliant blue light came out of the sky and blessed her. Only that she sat on a bluff watching the sunset. After the blue light left and the sun rose the next morning, the surrounding Joshua trees were larger.

'The Joshua trees around me – they were all taller.'

'Are you sure?'

'Pretty sure. Some were twice the size they had been the evening before.'

I park in a spot that catches my eye and get out and walk across the desert. The moonlight, as it pours over me, seems to seep into the crown of my head, and I am reminded of the time in the desert outside Las Vegas when I escaped a nuclear explosion by filling my body with moonlight and floating high into the sky. As I prowl the sandy terrain among the Joshua trees that stand like sentinels from another age, I feel my step lighten. It is almost as if I can bob off the ground, and that possibility fills me with excitement. To fly up with the stars and escape the prison of my problems. My bare arms begin to glow with a milky white radiance. I can almost see through them.

Then I see the place. My recognition of it is immediate. I do not even have to take note of the tall surrounding trees to confirm my belief. I simply know it is the spot. A feeling of tranquility, of sanctity even, radiates from the place. It draws me forward. Clearly something momentous occurred here. In a minute I am standing atop the bluff where I am convinced Paula conceived her child. I lift my arms to the stars.

'Suzama!' I call. 'Show me what you saw!'

There is no answer, at least no obvious one. Yet I am suddenly overcome by a wave of fatigue, and I sit down to close my eyes and meditate with the rhythm of the breath and the secret mantra. Soon white light is pouring, not from above, but from a place inside me, and I am lost in memories of nights of wonder and terror at the feet of a tender clairvoyant, who saw not only the birth of God, but the death as well. There was, of course, a reason Suzama died so young, and perhaps I was a part of that reason.

When I arrived in Egypt, it was fifty years after the death of Lord Krishna, fifty years into the dark age, what was to become known as Kali Yuga. Following the trail of adventurous merchants, who traveled the Far East thousands of years before Marco Polo was born, I arrived in an Egypt that to my eyes was infinite in splendour and riches. Truthfully, it overwhelmed me, although I was also relieved to be out of India, where Yaksha was in the midst of a bloody rampage to destroy every living vampire, as part of a vow he had made to Krishna.

The bright sun was hard on a young vampire like me. Riding into the enchanted city on the back of a camel, I had to keep my head covered with many layers of cloth. The sun burned into my brain, sapping every ounce of my strength. Yet the sight of the Great Pyramid, four times larger than the present-day pyramid that bears the same name, filled me with wonder. Covered with shiny white ivory and capped with glistening gold, it stole my breath away. All I could think as the bright rays heated my already boiling blood was to escape into its dark interior, rest, and try to forget the many trials of my journey. I thought it more than a coincidence that one of the first people I met when I entered the magical city was Suzama herself.

She was far from a high priestess that day. Only sixteen, with long dark hair and eyes as bright as they were kind, she wore a slave's simple garment. I saw her bending over the bank of the Nile to collect water in a large clay jar. On my exhausted camel, moving slowly towards her, I thought she seemed to stiffen. She glanced over her shoulder at me, almost as if she felt me approach. Later she was to tell me that she'd already had many visions of my coming. As our eyes met, my heart beat faster. I could remember no dream I'd had about her, but I knew her face was one I would never forget awake or asleep.

Suzama was not merely beautiful, although she would have been considered attractive in any age or place. Her allure came from the marks that austerity and pain had stamped on her young beauty, marks that made her enchanting, not repulsive. It was as if she had witnessed a thousand lives of suffering and come to a realization that transcended mortal acceptance. She was both saintly and sensual. Her lips so generous, she had only to smile to make you feel kissed. I loved her when I saw her, and until then I had never loved anyone on sight, except for Krishna himself.

She offered me a drink from her jug.

'I am called Suzama,' she said. 'Who are you?'

'Sita,' I answered, giving her my real name. I drank

the water hungrily, and splashed some on my dusty face. The Nile was cool and sweet in those days. I don't know what has become of it now. 'I am new here.'

But Suzama shook her head. 'You have always been here.' Then she touched her heart and I saw tears in her eyes. 'I know you, Sita. You have great power.'

This was my first sign of her power. Suzama knew things from inside herself, not from outside. Indeed, later, I came to believe the entire world was a dream to her. Yet paradoxically it could still cause her intense pain. Her deepest feelings were enigmatic, dispassionately unattached, but at the same time passionately involved. When she took my hand and led me in the direction of her family, I felt I had been touched by an angel. Yet I did not know that for the next three and a half years, I would hardly ever leave her sight. Her mystical mission had not yet begun, but soon it would hit like a bolt of lightning. And I would be her thunder.

5

The next morning I have been only seconds in my expensive and exquisitely furnished tri-level home in Pacific Palisades when the phone rings. Upstairs I hear Seymour snoring peacefully, yet the call makes me anxious. Our number is unlisted. Who would know to call? And so early in the morning?

I pick up the phone and hold it close.

'Hello?'

There is a pause. Then the soft voice, the gentle inflections.

'It is I,' she says.

The blood freezes in my veins. 'Kalika.'

'Yes, Mother, you remember me. That is good. How have you been?'

'Fine. How are you?'

'Wonderful. Busy.'

'You haven't found him yet,' I say. 'You're not going to find him.'

Kalika could be smiling. 'You are wrong. I haven't found him but I am going to find him. You are going to help me.'

'I hardly think so.'

'You think too much. Your thoughts blind you. I told you I'm not going to harm the child. I'm your daughter. You should believe me. I believe you even when I hear you lying to me.'

'Where are you?' I ask.

'Not far. I'm high up. I have a view. You would enjoy it.'

'How did you get this number?'

'It wasn't difficult.' A pause. 'I saw you last night at that boring meeting. I saw you talking to those people.'

If possible, my blood grows colder. Just by meeting and talking to people, I put them suddenly in danger. It does not seem fair that I should love someone who causes me such grief. Yes, I am chilled by Kalika's call, and grateful for it as well. How hopeless mothers are.

'Those people are no concern of yours,' I say harshly.

'I think the doctor is a nice man. But I see you like the son. Handsome devil, isn't he?' A pause. 'Is it appropriate for a daughter to comment on the company her mother keeps?'

'No.'

She laughs softly. 'Nothing is as it seems. Black can appear white when the light is blinding. But white loses all lustre at the faintest sign of darkness. Why trust them when you can trust me?'

'Because you are a coldblooded murderer.'

'Oh. We all have our faults. When did you become so judgmental?'

My tone is bitter. 'You know when.'

'I suppose. How is Seymour?'

'He's dead.'

'That was his corpse at the lecture last night?'

I sigh. 'He's fine, no thanks to you.'

'See. I can be merciful. I am a mother as well, you know.'

'You called Paula. You faked my voice, and even so she did not call you back.'

'That is true,' Kalika says. 'But Suzama would know how to set up a meeting with Paula. She might have spelled that out in her book. You knew her, didn't you?'

I hesitate. 'Yes.'

'And you still think fondly of her. But to this day you do not know what destroyed her.'

'She was destroyed in the big earthquake, along with the Setians. Her death is no mystery to me.'

'But who were those Setians? You stared them straight in the eye and did not recognize them.'

'I knew they were evil, in the end.'

She mocks me. 'But too late to save Suzama.'

'Why do you talk about them? Or are you just up to your old tricks? The master manipulator trying to confuse the issue. If you want to come for me, fine. Come now, I tire of your games. You don't scare me.'

Kalika is a long time answering. While I wait for her next words, I listen closely and hear in the background, not far from where Kalika is, the splash of water. My daughter must be near an open window, standing on a balcony perhaps. There is definitely a swimming pool in her vicinity. It is far below her I believe. There are many people in it, children playing with a ball, laughing and shouting, and more serious athletes swimming serious laps. I hear the latter turn in the water as they finish each lap and push off the walls. I count the strokes, and there are many of them. It is a large pool. There are not many such large pools in the Los Angeles area. I should be able to get a list of them.

Kalika finally speaks.

'I do not want to harm you, Mother. I am here for the child. But if you stand in my way, I cannot promise you that you or your darling Seymour will survive.' She adds, 'That is not a threat, merely an observation.'

'Thank you. I feel much better. Why did you call?'

'To hear your voice. For some reason your voice carries special meaning to me.'

'I don't believe that,' I say.

'It is true.'

'And the other reason for your call?'

'If I tell you that it will spoil all the fun.' A pause. 'Is there anything I can do for you, Mother?'

'Leave Dr Seter and his people alone. Leave the child alone.'

Kalika hesitates. 'I'm afraid I can't do that. Is there anything else you want?'

I slump against the wall, exhausted. 'You know, Kalika, the night you were born was hard for me. The delivery was agonizing and I lost a lot of blood. I almost died, and even when I held you in my arms and looked into your eyes I was scared. Even then I knew you were not normal, not even by vampire standards. But despite all that a part of me was happy, happier than I had ever been in my life. I didn't realize this until later. I had wanted a daughter and now I had one. God gave you to me, I thought, and I thanked him for you.' I have to take a breath. 'Do you understand what I am saying?'

'Yes.'

'You are what you are. Your nature is to kill, and I understand that because I'm a killer as well. But over the centuries I have learned to control that instinct. Now I only kill when it is necessary. You can learn to do the same.' I pause. 'That is what I ask of you. Only that.'

She considers. When she speaks next, her voice is particularly soft. It is almost as if she is speaking inside my brain. And I find her words strangely moving.

'I can do that for you, Mother. But my list of who can live and who must die is vastly different from yours. The phantom, Ray, was one of your illusions, one of your *mayas*. Your desire to have your child Lalita reborn is still a maya for you. You refuse to let it go. That is why you were given me as your daughter – one of the reasons. But anyone who sees through the veil of maya cannot fathom the divine will. The veil is stained and the absolute is without flaw. One cannot reveal the other. In the same way, I am your own daughter but you cannot fathom me.'

I have to shake myself to resist her subtle spell.

My memory reminds me that she is using me.

'Was torturing Eric to death part of God's will?' I ask.

She speaks matter-of-factly. 'I did what I did to Eric to inspire you to tell me the location of the child.' A pause. 'Besides, he was not well. He was going to die anyway. His next birth will be more auspicious.'

I snort. 'Of course he was not well! You had been drinking his blood night and day! He died in horrible pain, in your hands!'

'So he did, and he stained my dress.' She laughs again. 'Goodbye, Mother. Don't think about what I have told you. It will only confuse you more. Just have faith in your darling daughter. It is the only thing now that can save you from suffering much greater pain.'

Kalika hangs up the phone.

6

As Seymour comes down for his breakfast, I am sitting at the kitchen table. I have made him bacon and eggs and toast, his favourite high-cholesterol meal. He has on a brown robe and is fresh from a warm shower. He smiles at me as I pour his hand-squeezed orange juice from the other side of the table.

'One day you're going to make somebody a great wife,' he says.

'Thank you. One day you're going to make a girl have a nervous breakdown.'

'You worry about me too much. I just went to the movies. God knows where you were.' He picks up his fork and tests his eggs. 'Did you get me the morning paper? You know I can't enjoy my food unless I'm fully informed on current events,' he jokes.

I speak seriously. 'I am your morning paper.'

He butters his toast. 'What's the matter? Did Suzama predict that I am the next messiah?'

'The scripture is authentic.'

'You saw it?'

'A piece of it. Suzama wrote it.'

He puts down his butter knife. 'But how come you never saw her working on it?'

'I was with her most of the time, but not every second. She could have written it on any number of days.'

'But she didn't talk to you about it? And you were her best friend?'

'She never talked about it to me. But Suzama kept her own counsel. I doubt if she spoke to anyone about the scripture. But she left it in a place where it could be found – at a time she wished it to be found.'

Seymour considers. 'How did you talk Dr Seter into letting you see it?'

There is an edge to his question.

'Are you asking if I slept with his son?'

'I noticed you were talking to him after you told me to get lost.'

'I didn't tell you to get lost. I told you to go have fun.' I pause. 'I convinced both son and father that I have a similar scripture. They want to see it soon.'

'Great. We can make one up this afternoon. We can make papyrus and age it in the sun, then you can give me a lesson in drawing hieroglyphics.' He pauses. 'It wasn't a very inventive lie.'

'It served its purpose.' I frown. 'I will have to give them something substantial to make them let me see the remainder of the scripture.'

'Why don't you just give them me to use as a human sacrifice?'

'Stop that. They are not such a bad bunch.' Then I have to smile. 'But they are busy practising with automatic weapons in the desert.'

'They sound like a nice all-American cult.'

'No, I don't think they're that, but they really do have guns. I heard the Seters talk about them when they didn't think I was listening.' I pause. 'But those guns might come in handy.'

'Why?'

'Kalika called.'

This shocks him. 'When?'

'A half hour ago.'

'Did she call here?'

'Yes.'

He has lost his appetite for his breakfast and sits, staring out the window, his face pale. In the distance is the blue Pacific. Only he and I know how red the water can run when it is diluted with blood. Yet I remind myself that Seymour doesn't remember exactly what Kalika did to him. The time has come, I know, to tell him. Many things.

'How did she get our number?' he mutters.

'Who knows? She gets what she wants.'

'If she has our number she has our address. She could be on her way here now.'

I shake my head. 'If she just wanted to kill us, I don't think she would have called first.'

'Why did she call then?'

'She said she wanted to hear my voice.'

'Like Hitler used to call home to talk to mom?' he asks.

'She hasn't found the child. She wants me to help her find him.'

'But you don't know where the kid is.'

'She knows that. Still, she seems to feel I can lead her to Paula and the baby.'

Seymour is puzzled. I can see the question coming.

'You must have some idea what is so special about this child?'

I pour myself a glass of orange juice. I have drunk blood only three times since my rebirth as a vampire, and none of my snacks were any the worse for wear in the morning. I suspect, towards the end of his life, that Yaksha did not need blood at all to survive. Still, it tasted good to me, the warm red elixir, better than the orange juice I now sip.

'This child could be the one spoken of in the Suzama scriptures,' I say softly.

Seymour stares at me. 'You've got to be kidding?'

'No.'

He is annoyed. 'That's ridiculous. All right, I believe in vampires. I believe in you. I even believe in your bad-tempered daughter. But I don't believe that Jesus was just born in a hospital in Los Angeles. I'm sorry but I can't. It's too weird.'

'Do you remember what happened to you after Kalika threw you off the pier?'

He hesitates. 'Yeah. The water was freezing and I got hypothermia and passed out and you came to my rescue.'

'Where did you regain consciousness?'

'Up in the mountains. The next morning.'

'You were unconscious for a long time, don't you think?'

'So? What does this have to do with this kid?'

I speak carefully. 'Seymour, you did not simply pass out in the cold water. Kalika did not let you go so easily. She threw something at you, a sharp stake. It was shaped like a spear.' I pause. 'She threw it so hard it stabbed through your spine and out through your stomach.'

Seymour stands. 'That's not true.'

'It is true. I jumped off the pier and helped you to shore, as I told you. But you were on the beach less than a minute when you finally lost consciousness.'

He is agitated. 'Then how did the wound disappear? You told me you didn't give me any of your vampire blood.'

'At the time I intended to give you my blood. But I was afraid to pull out the stake. I thought it would kill you.' I shrug. 'So I left it in.'

He is breathing hard. 'You're not answering my questions.'

I stand and step to his side and put a hand on his shoulder.

'You lost too much blood. Even I couldn't save you.'
I pause. 'You died that night on that beach.'

He forces a smile. 'Yeah, right. I'm Lazarus, back
from the dead.'

'There was a vial of the child's blood. I stole it from
the nurse who was caring for the baby at the hospital. I
had that vial with me when I took you up to the
mountains.'

'Why did you take me up there? You never explained
that.'

'To cremate your body. You must remember that
when you woke up you were lying on a huge pile of
wood.' I squeeze his shoulder. 'Seymour.'

He jumps back and trembles. 'That's not possible.
You're making this story up. I couldn't have been dead.
When you're dead you're dead. God damn it, Sita,
don't lie to me this way. You're scaring me and I don't
like it.'

I am patient. 'Just before I lit the wood, a strange
feeling swept over me. I was looking down at you and I
was holding this burning lighter and I couldn't stop
staring at your face and thinking how you shouldn't be
dead. Then I remembered the vial of blood, and I took
it out of my pocket and poured some over your wounds
and some down your throat. Then I walked away and
stood behind a tree and prayed to God that everything
would be all right.' I move to his side again and put my
arm over his shoulder. Both our eyes are damp. 'And
you were all right, Seymour. It was a miracle. You were
sitting there and everything was perfectly all right.' I

kiss the side of his face and whisper in his ear. 'I wouldn't lie to you about this, you know. I don't lie to those I love.'

He is still shaking. 'But I don't remember any of this.'

'Maybe that is part of the miracle. Maybe it is for the best.'

He looks at me with a sad little boy's face. 'She really killed me?'

'Yes.'

'And that baby's blood brought me back?'

'Yes.'

He is awed as well as shocked. 'That must mean . . .' He can't finish.

'Yes.' I bury my face against his chest and dry my eyes on his robe. 'I can't let my daughter get to him or to Paula. I just can't. I have to stop her and the only way I can do that is to kill her.'

Seymour strokes my hair. Now he comforts me. We make a fine pair.

'Can she be killed?' he asks.

I raise my head. 'I think so. Even Yaksha could be killed.'

'But she is more powerful than Yaksha. You said so yourself.'

I turn away and look at the ocean out the window.

'She must drink blood to survive,' I say. 'She has needs that only mortal flesh can fulfill. A portion of her must be mortal. She must be vulnerable.'

'To the fire of automatic weapons?' He is recovering

from the shock. His inner strength never ceases to amaze me. But he is a believer now, even if he won't admit it. Perhaps Lazarus argued that he had never been dead. For God's sake, Jesus, it was just a bad cold. Yeah, well, why do you smell so bad, Laz?

I continue to stand with my back to Seymour.

'I have thought of enlisting their aid,' I say. 'But to do so I would have to tell them an awful lot, maybe even what I am. I might have to give them a demonstration.'

'You don't want to do that. They'd kill you after they killed Kalika, just to be on the safe side.' Seymour considers. 'Kalika is described in their scripture?'

'That's a perceptive question. Yes. But they haven't let me read that portion of the scripture. I only know of their knowledge of Kalika because I eavesdropped on their conversation.'

'Did they call her Kalika?'

'The Dark Mother. It is the same difference.' I grimace. 'They have a horrible opinion of her.'

'No doubt. Especially if Suzama was as accurate as you say.' Seymour scratches his head. 'You can't tell them that you're a vampire and knew Suzama personally. You would have to drink some blood in front of them to get them to listen to you after that, and then they would go running for their guns. But if you're able to describe Kalika in clear enough terms, they might believe you enough to check her out. How many of them are there?'

'Two dozen, which is a small army if they have the guns I think they do.'

'You can give them some of your high-tech weapons.'

'I've thought of that as well,' I say.

'The only problem is that you don't know where your daughter is.'

'That may not be true.' I explain how Kalika spoke of her wonderful view, and the large pool below her. Yet this tip only seems to disturb Seymour.

'She mentioned the view,' he says. 'She went to the trouble to stand out on a balcony when she spoke to you. She knows all about your phenomenal hearing. And she probably knows how few places fit the description of her current residence. Does this add up to something in your mind?'

'A trap, of course. She might be lying in wait for us.'

'She might be lying in wait for the entire Suzama Society. If she was watching you last night, she might suspect you will turn to them for help.'

'I don't know if she takes them seriously. She called last night's lecture boring.' I pause. 'Plus she promised she wouldn't kill unless it was necessary.'

'Oh, that's a relief. I feel a whole lot better now. The Mother of Darkness promises her vampire mother she's not going to get rough unless she gets pushed around. If I understand you correctly, the Suzama Society thinks it is their destiny to kill Kalika. Well, your daughter's not going to stand around and let them fill her full of lead.'

I shake my head. 'Kalika is many things, but I don't think she would have said such a thing to me unless it was true.'

'By that reasoning you should believe she has no intention of harming the child.'

'No. Obviously she intends to kill the child. She has killed to try to get to him. She is not some starstruck devotee who wants to gaze upon him in wonder. But her promise to me was something else. In fact, she asked if there was anything she could do for me.'

'Still, the Suzama gang will have to hit her hard and quick if they're to survive.'

'Agreed. But should we go to them for help? Should we risk their lives? Do we have the right?'

He shrugs. 'It's their decision.'

'Don't be so flip. No matter what you or I tell them, they won't understand how deadly Kalika is until they come face to face with her.'

'I meant what I said. Their decision would not be flip. This is something these people believe in. They have dedicated their lives to it. Also, if all this is true, look at what's at stake? If this baby is the Big Guy then the world needs him. Kalika must be stopped, and I have to say no price is too high to stop her.'

I nod sadly. 'You said something similar when she was just a baby.'

'Yes. And you wanted to give her a chance to see who she turned out to be.' He pats me on the shoulder. 'I'm sorry I have to put it that way. I just think we have to get a hold of all the firepower we can. Let's try to track down Kalika today. If we find her, and we live, then we'll go talk to Dr Seter. He'll listen. It's just a question of how far you have to go to persuade him.'

'Is there anything I can do for you, Mother?'

There is pain in my voice as I speak next.

'This child is special, there can be no question about that. But to me, Kalika, even if she is evil, is special as well.' My head hangs heavy. 'I don't know whether to pray for success or failure.'

7

A local realtor informs me that there are only a dozen places in Los Angeles that fit my description of a tall apartment building with a large pool. The one with the largest pool is in Century City, at Century City Park East. Seymour and I decide to go there first. The place is exclusive, with twin towers that rise twenty stories into the sky. There is valet parking, a gym, and a tennis court beside the wonderful pool. I let the valet take the car, but I don't immediately head for the woman at the reception area.

'I appreciate what you said about this being a trap,' I say to Seymour, who insisted on coming so that he could serve as lookout. 'But the chances are she doesn't know we're here. I don't want to walk in and request her by name.'

'Chances are she's working under a different name. Did you bring a picture of her?'

'Yes. I have several of her taken when she was fully grown. But I don't want to tip our hand. If we quiz the woman at the desk, and show her Kalika's picture, she may tell Kalika someone was looking for her. These people are trained to do that. I would rather check out the underground garage first. If Kalika has a car, it will probably be new and I should be able to smell her on it.'

'She could be out,' Seymour says.

'It is a possibility. But I want to do this first.'

So we head underground. We're dressed properly, like rich sophisticates, so no one pays any attention to us. On the second garage level a new white Mercedes catches my eye. From where I am standing, forty feet away, I don't smell my daughter. Yet there is something about the car that draws my attention. I wonder if the vehicle is emitting *vibrations*. Certainly my daughter has a very powerful aura.

A moment later we have our hands on the car.

'If this is hers,' Seymour says, 'she has good taste.'

'I need to smell the interior,' I say.

Seymour points to a tiny flashing red light inside. 'Don't set off the alarm.'

'I see it,' I mutter as I flex my palms over the driver's side window. Very slowly I begin to push the window down. A crack appears and I let go and stick my nose close to it. There is a faint musky odour, which, according to the Vedas, is Kali's smell. But I don't need my knowledge of the Vedas to remember what my own daughter smells like. The odour fills me with nostalgia for her, but I don't know why. Ray and my darling daughter never allowed us to have a normal family life. He was a ghost and she was a demon. I glance at Seymour. 'This belongs to her.'

He is not as happy as he was a moment ago. He may not remember the stake through his back, but he was there when Kalika opened Eric's throat. I carefully push the window back up and wipe away the faint impressions my palms have made on the glass.

'We'd better get out of here,' he says.

I study the number at the front of the parking spot. 'Eighteen twenty-one. It must be her suite number. We need to stake out this building.'

'Not down here,' he says quickly.

'No. We'll cross the street to the high-rise office building and find an empty office that has a view of the valet parking area. When she leaves, I'll break into her condo and search it.'

He swallows. 'Do we have to do that?'

'You don't have to do anything. I'll do it.'

'But then you'll think I'm a coward.'

'I know you're a coward,' I lie.

He is insulted. 'Is that why you won't sleep with me?'

'No. It's because you're still a nerd. Let's get across the street.'

Back outside we cross Olympic Boulevard and enter one of the triangular towers that overlooks the condo towers. This commercial building has forty floors, twice what the condo towers have. A glance at the office listings in the main lobby tells me that 3450 and 3670 and 3810 and 2520 are empty. I steer Seymour toward the elevator. We are alone as we rise up to the thirty-sixth floor.

'Maybe she never goes out,' he says. 'We could wait all day for her to leave.'

'You're free to go to a movie if you like.'

'That's not fair. You're a vampire. You don't have to fear her the way I do.'

'You will recall that last time I tried to attack her on the Santa Monica Pier, she grabbed my foot before I could touch her and snapped my ankle.' I shake my head. 'She can kill me as easily as she can kill you, if she chooses.'

'But you do think a bullet in the head or in the heart will stop her?'

'Who really knows?'

Suite 3670 appears empty. I listen at the door for a moment before breaking the lock, stepping inside, and closing the door behind us. Suite 3670 directly overlooks the condo towers. We have a clear view of the valet area. If Kalika comes down and asks for her car, or simply gets it herself, we will know. Briefly I scan the portion of the eighteenth floor that faces us. It is possible I can see 1821, but I can't tell without examining the interior of the building or seeing a floor plan. Yet all of the condos on that floor have closed vertical blinds, so even if I was staring directly at her place, it would do me little good.

Seymour and I sit down on the floor and take up the watch. Actually, it is only my eyes that are of any use. This high up, Seymour wouldn't recognize his own mother if she came out of the building across the street.

An hour goes by. Seymour gets hungry and goes for a sandwich. While he is gone I see a beautiful young woman with long dark hair come out of the condo tower. She hands the parking valet a dollar after he brings up her shiny white Mercedes. I am staring at the Dark Mother, the scourge of Suzama's prophecies, my own daughter.

'Kalika,' I whisper to the glass. 'What do you want?'

She climbs into her car and drives away. I am out the door in a flash. I run into Seymour on his way back with a sandwich for me. One look at my face and he is a mass of nerves. I raise my hand.

'I want you to stay here,' I say. 'I'm going into her condo, and you'll just get in my way.'

'But you'll need a lookout,' he protests.

'No.'

'But I can't stay behind and let you take all the risks.'

I decide not to be too quick to crush his brave initiative. Also, I am not in the mood to argue.

'All right,' I say. 'But if she rips your head off don't blame me.'

He throws the sandwich in the garbage and we grab an elevator.

This time, at the condo tower, I have to speak to the receptionist, but I purposely keep the conversation short and silent. Catching her eye through the glass, I press her with my fiery will and mouth the words: '*Open the door.*'

A moment later the door swings open.

Suite 1821 is naturally on the eighteenth floor. I do not want to break the lock because I still hope Kalika will know nothing of my visit. With a couple of pins I have brought for just this purpose, I quickly pick the lock. The door creaks open. Seymour stands behind me, the colour of a hospital bed sheet.

'It's more fun to write about this stuff than do it,' he says.

'Shh,' I say as we step inside and close the door. 'Stand on the front balcony and keep a lookout for her white Mercedes.'

'What are you going to do?'

'Look for evidence of her state of mind.'

Kalika owns, or rents, a two-bedroom corner condo. She has twin balconies and glorious views of the city. The place is elegant, the plush carpeting new, the white paint fresh. Her furnishings are few but tasteful. She seems to prefer traditional to modern, but nothing she has is old-fashioned. There are no magazines in the living room or dining area, yet she has a rather large TV, and I wonder how many channels she subscribes to and what her favorite programs are.

While Seymour stands outside on the balcony, I step into her office, the first bedroom on the right. She has a desk, a computer, a fax machine. Her drawers are unlocked and I rifle through them. Not entirely surprisingly, I find several maps. Most of them are of California, blow-ups of Big Sur, Mount Shasta, and Lake Tahoe. She has travel books on these areas too. There is also a guidebook on Sedona, which is located in Arizona. In another drawer are more books on these same places, but these are not typical travel guides. They contain personal accounts of the spots. I scan the books – I can read over thirty thousand words a minute with total comprehension. Quite a few of the stories describe how powerful the *vibrations* are in each place. I am fascinated because Kalika appears to be doing a lot of research on spots that have been New Age retreats for the last couple of decades.

'Do you like these places?' I whisper to myself. 'Or do you think the child will be drawn to them?'

I move into my daughter's bedroom. Her queensize bed is neatly made, covered with a hand-made quilt from China. In the corner, on top of a chest of drawers, a white silk cloth has been spread, almost as if a small altar has been set up. There are only a few books and a small Shiva Lingam set beside a brass incense holder in which a stick of musk incense has recently been burned.

The lingam is a polished grey phallic-shaped stone with three red marks on it. The shape and the markings are natural to the stone, I know. When I was a child, still a mortal, five thousand years ago, our tiny village had a Shiva Lingam. The rocks are supposed to contain the energy of Lord Shiva himself, Mahakala, who is the spouse of Mother Kali and the supposed destroyer of time at the end of all ages. Geologists describe lingams as the offspring of meteor crashes. In either case, they are highly magnetic. Brushing my hand over the stone, I feel its charge.

Kalika has three books beside the lingam: the *Bhagavad-Gita:* the *Upanishads*, the *Mahanirvana Tantra.* The Gita is the gospel according to Krishna, the *Upanishads* are collected stories of divine knowledge from ancient rishis, and the *Mahanirvana Tantra* describes Kali in her different avatars, and details her various modes of worship and innovation. All this reading material is entirely spiritual in nature. But try as I might, I cannot understand what that means. If I should be relieved or frightened. It is an old and regrettable truth that more people have been killed in the name of God than anything else.

I am picking up her copy of the *Gita* when Seymour bursts breathlessly into the room. 'Her car just drove up,' he says. 'She wasn't gone long.'

I replace the book in its exact spot. 'It will take her a minute to get up here. Come, we have time.'

Back out in the hallway, however, standing in front of the elevators, I begin to have doubts. As Seymour starts to push the down button, I stop him.

'Even in the garage basement,' I say, 'she might note the elevator going up to the eighteenth floor. She is shrewd – she might consider that more than coincidence.' I pause. 'Let's take the stairs.'

'I just want to get out of here,' Seymour says with emotion.

Halfway down the stairs I stop Seymour. Straining my ears to listen far below, I hear someone climbing up the stairs. The person is in no hurry and it could be anybody. But I don't like the fact that this person stands in our path, and that I can't see who it is – each floor is partitioned off. Seymour watches me anxiously.

'What is it?'

'Someone's coming up the stairs.'

'Is it she?' he gasps.

'I can't tell.' I pause. 'I think it is a woman. This person has a light step.'

'Oh God.'

'Shh. She is far below still. Let's grab the elevator.'

In the elevator, Seymour starts to push the button for the lobby, but I stop him for the second time and push the button for the second garage level. Seymour throws a fit.

'Why did you do that?' he asks.

'It is the last thing she'll expect us to do, if she thinks we know where her car is parked.'

'But for all we know she's still in her car.'

'Relax, Seymour. I know what I'm doing.'

I hope. When the elevator *whooshes* open, I am tensed for an attack. But none comes. We appear to be alone in the underground garage. Signalling for Seymour to remain where he is, I step lightly into the garage and stretch my sensitive senses to their limits. There is no sign of Kalika. I signal to Seymour to join me.

'Let's just get our car and get out of here,' I whisper in his ear.

He nods vigorously. 'I am not cut out for this crap.'

8

I call Dr Seter in San Francisco but end up speaking to James, who acts happy to hear my voice. Perhaps it is not an act, but he does want to know if I am ready to show them my scripture. I tell him I have something even more important to show him. After making an appointment to see him and his father at the Hilton, after the lecture, I book a flight for San Francisco. As the plane lifts off the ground, Seymour nods to the manila envelope in my hand.

'What's that?' he asks.

'Newspaper clippings. Proof.'

'I won't ask.'

'You'll see soon enough.'

We do not attend the lecture because I have a slight fear that Kalika will be there. We are waiting in the lounge area of the Hilton when Dr Seter returns to the hotel. The elderly doctor looks fatigued from his travels and lecture, but James is as bright faced as ever. I introduce Seymour as an old friend and they take seats across from us. Dr Seter orders a scotch and James a Coke. Seymour munches on the pretzels and sips cranberry juice.

I have nothing to eat or drink, not even a few drops of blood. I fear there may soon be enough blood flying to satisfy my most perverse thirsts. I wonder if Kalika still kills her victims, how many she hunts a night.

Dr Seter studies me with tired eyes. For the first time I listen to his heart beat in his chest. He has clogged arteries, cardiac arrhythmia. He must know – I sense he is experiencing a tightness in his chest even now. Yet he smiles warmly before he begins to speak. He is a charming man.

'James tells me you have something exciting to show us,' he says.

I stare at both of them for a moment.

'I know where the Dark Mother is,' I say. 'I need your help to kill her.'

This gets their attention. Dr Seter takes a moment to catch his breath. James glances at him anxiously, but I don't know if his anxiety is concern for his father's health or concern for the confrontation. Finally the doctor manages to speak.

'How do you know about the Dark Mother?' he asks. 'You said your scripture did not speak of a particular danger to the child.'

'It speaks of her in general terms,' I say. 'And I know this young woman.' I open the manila envelope I have brought with me. 'I have chronicled her behaviour. But perhaps you have as well. She's been in the papers lately.'

First I give them clips from the *Los Angeles Times* of the series of brutal murders that were committed last December. Crazy Eddie Fender and his gang of nasty vampires were responsible for these crimes, but the murders are of such bizarre nature – heads torn off, bodies drained of their blood – that I feel they strengthen my case. Next I show them clippings of the major shoot-out the police had with a gang of terrorists in downtown L.A.: three helicopters downed and dozens of police killed by a tiny but invincible force. Of course, I was responsible for those deaths. The police and FBI had the bad judgment to chase after me and Joel for our vampire blood.

I show them clippings of the Nevada nuclear explosion, and finally give them articles on Eric Hawkins, who was kidnapped from the park while playing basketball with friends. He was not found until weeks later, his throat scissored open by what appeared to be sharp fingernails. Yes, the words of the city coroner have made it all the way into the article, and they are surprisingly accurate. Naturally, it is only this last death Kalika was responsible for but now is not the time to reveal that. Dr Seter and his son study the clippings for several minutes and then the doctor frowns at me.

'I don't see what this has to do with the Dark Mother,' he says.

His voice is without conviction. I suspect that either he or James has been collecting similar clippings. The possibility strengthens my position and I decide to hold nothing back. I lean forward slightly as I speak and my tone is deadly serious.

'The Dark Mother is vampiric in nature,' I say. 'The original serial murders in L.A. all bear a vampiric stamp. This is when the Dark Mother moved into the Los Angeles area. Notice the dates of the murders, how they cease right after the terrorist shoot-out with the police. Yet these terrorists have never been found, never been identified. The media says it's because they escaped, but the real reason is that these terrorists never existed. In fact, the only one the police ever spoke about definitively was a young woman who was able to move extremely fast.'

'We have read about her,' James says, glancing at his father.

'Then there is the nuclear explosion in the Nevada desert,' I continue. 'Once again the media and the government drew a connection to terrorists, but here, too, they failed to identify the terrorists. Because there weren't any. For a brief time the Dark Mother was a prisoner of the military camp where the explosion occurred. But even with all their guns, all their tanks and soldiers, they couldn't contain her and she broke free and destroyed them. She went underground after that, yet she didn't leave the Los Angeles area. Note the description of Eric Hawkins's supposed kidnapper and compare it to the descriptions the police gave of the young woman who helped mess up downtown L.A. You will see they match. That's because all these events originate with one young woman who is not really a human being at all.' I pause. 'I know her name. I know where she lives. She may know I know this, I'm not sure. She won't remain where she is long. If you want to destroy her, you'll have to strike at her tonight. And don't look so shocked. I know you've prepared for a long time to do exactly this.'

Dr Seter is so taken aback by my words he can't speak. James takes up his role. 'How do you know these things?' he asks. 'You didn't read about them in an ancient scripture.'

'I had a friend in the FBI who leaked parts of this information to me. He came to me originally because his agency was researching the Suzama material. This friend is now deceased – he died in the Nevada explosion. But before he died he gave me enough clues to locate and speak to the Dark Mother.'

They both almost fall off their chairs. 'You have seen her?' Dr Seter exclaims.

'I have, too,' Seymour says on cue. 'We both spoke to her at the end of the Santa Monica Pier three months ago. She almost killed us both, but in the end decided to let us go.'

'Why would she let you go if you're a danger to her?' Dr Seter asks.

'She obviously doesn't think we are a danger to her,'

I say. 'Or else she thinks we may eventually lead her to the child. That's why she agreed to meet us, to quiz us about the Suzama material.'

'We still need to see your scripture,' Dr Seter says.

'You can't,' I say. 'She destroyed it this afternoon. Furthermore, she might be on the verge of destroying your copy, along with the rest of you.' I pause. 'She was at your lecture last night.'

James's voice is harsh. 'Why didn't you tell us?'

'I didn't know,' I say honestly. 'I only found out today when she called me at home to tell me.'

'Why would she call you?' Dr Seter asks.

'I told you. I think she stays in touch because we – Seymour and I – might possibly lead her to the child. Plus you do not know her the way we do. To you she is just a name. To us she is a witch, who calls to taunt us, to let us know we live in her shadow.'

Dr Seter regards me critically. 'What is her name? Do you know?'

'If I tell you, will you believe me?' I ask.

'Not necessarily,' Dr Seter says. 'But I will at least give more credence to your wild story.'

'Her name is Kalika, Kali Ma. This dark age of Kali Yuga is named after her.'

Clearly Kalika is mentioned in Suzama's scripture. Their suddenly shocked expressions confirm this fact. Yet the information fills me with dismay. Is there no hope for my daughter? I know I am here to solicit aid in killing her but a part of me still longs to discover that I have made a terrible mistake, that all the horrors

Kalika has committed since she drew her first breath are nothing more than misunderstandings. But it is not to be and I know it. Either my daughter dies or we do, and then also the child who can save the whole world. Dr Seter is again having trouble catching his breath.

'Can this be true?' he whispers to himself.

'It is true,' Seymour says. 'I have seen with my own eyes what she can do. She is stronger than two dozen men combined, as fast as lightning. She is already stalking your group. You don't have much time.'

James stares at Seymour. 'How do you know Alisa?'

Seymour shrugs. 'We're old friends.'

James turns to me. 'Neither of you has ever given us a last name. We have no way to check your background. We still don't know if you're with the government or not.'

'The names we have given you are false,' I say. 'So what is the point in giving you a false last name? Surely you can understand our reasons for secrecy. We can talk all night and into the next morning. There is only one way of convincing you that we have found the Dark Mother, and that is to bring you to her. But when you do meet her, you have to be ready to kill her or else to be killed by her. It is that simple. You lose nothing by trusting me enough to check her out. Once again, that is if you have all your forces standing at full readiness.'

Dr Seter scoffs. 'We don't have any forces.'

'You are a poor liar, doctor,' I say. 'The FBI knows about your training exercises and your automatic weapons. They didn't interfere with you because there were agents, like my friend, who knew about the Suzama material and understood what you were preparing for. But those agents are dead now. Kalika killed them. As a result your group is threatened from all sides, politically and spiritually. You might even think I'm a threat, that I've been sent here by the Black Mother to lure you into a trap. Actually, there may be a particle of truth in that. I am not working for her, but if you do choose to confront her you may be wiped out. Seymour is not exaggerating her strength. But at least if you hit first you stand a chance. If you go after her you must hold back nothing. Yet you must first explain to your people what the real nature of the risk is. Tell them that several dozen police and marines couldn't stop her.'

Dr Seter is shaking his head. 'This is all happening too fast. We can't do anything tonight. It's out of the question.'

I don't want to push him, to fry his brain, or even to confuse his mind. I want the decision to be his because I suspect I am not exaggerating when I say many of his people may die. So I assuage my conscience. Yet I cannot let him stall. I feel he is close to agreeing with me. I have told him much that only he would know is true. It doesn't matter to me that I have lied to him a lot as well.

'You knew when the time came there would be no time for hesitation,' I say gently. 'She is down in Los Angeles, right now, in a condo with a wonderful view of the city. We were in her place this afternoon.'

'She told you where she lives?' James asks.

'No. She made a mistake when she called me. That is all I can say. Seymour and I were then able to figure out where she lives.'

'You traced her call?' James persists.

'In a manner of speaking,' I say. 'Dr Seter, this is all real. I know you have been talking about it so long that it has lost some of its reality to you. But you only have to come with me tonight and bring your group, and you will see a five-thousand-year-old prophecy fulfilled before your very eyes.'

He looks at me. 'You are not a normal young woman, Alisa. There is something in your face, in your voice, in your eyes. James mentioned it last night and now I see it.' He pauses. 'How do we know you're not the Dark Mother?'

I smile sadly. 'Some nights I feel as if I am. And even if I were, then that's all the more reason to heed my warning.' Reaching over, I touch his knees. 'Trust the inner senses that Suzama's material has given you. Trust what they are telling you right now.' I pause. 'Your whole life has led up to this moment.'

Dr Seter flashes a faint smile. 'Somehow I can't imagine you are evil.' He turns to James. 'I need to talk to my son, alone, for a few minutes, if you please.'

I stand and point to the entrance. 'We will wait over there. We will give you all the privacy and time you need to decide.'

Of course the moment we leave I stand still and listen to every word they say. It is a short but intense conversation.

James: 'She knew the name of the Dark Mother! No one in our group except us knows that!'

Dr Seter: 'She knows many things I would have thought impossible. But that doesn't mean we can trust her.'

James: 'But you heard her argument. It's the same argument I've been giving you for the last few months. Those incidents we read about were all caused by a single deadly force. Only she has put the pieces together much better than we did. I'm telling you, father, I believe her. I say we throw everything we've got behind her.'

Dr Seter: 'But just last night you were worried she was working for the Dark Mother.'

James: 'She is not behaving like someone who is trying to harm us. Right now she gave us a tonne of information she didn't have to. Information that could be used against the Dark Mother.'

Dr Seter: 'Only if it's true.'

James: 'It is true! Look, she only asks us to trust her so far. We will know within seconds of meeting this person if she is the Dark Mother. But she is right, we must be prepared for a major attack. It is the only way to protect our people.'

Dr Seter: 'But what if she's lying to us? If she's working for the government and is trying to trap our group while it is engaged in illegal activities? Think about it, Jim, we're going to be storming a residence of some kind. If it is a government trap, we'll look like just another evil and confused cult in the eyes of the public.'

James: 'We'll have her with us when we make our attack. If she's lied to us, she'll pay the price.'

Dr Seter: 'That's just talk. You wouldn't hurt her.'

James: 'I don't think I'll have to hurt her. I think our enemy will be so evil our hatred will be turned totally on her.' A pause. 'Let's do it. If we don't, Father, we will regret it for the rest of our lives. That's what my inner feelings tell me.'

Dr Seter is a long time answering. But finally he gives his OK.

9

The attack has yet to begin but already I realize something is very strange. I had initially gone to Dr Seter and James because I knew I was physically and emotionally ill-equipped to kill Kalika. She is too strong for me, and I can't imagine hurting her. All I wanted to do was send in twenty people with guns, close my eyes, and be told it was all over. Your daughter is dead, the world is safe for democracy again. Yet the Suzama Society seems to be much more than twenty people with guns. It should reassure me that they are better prepared than I imagined, yet it does not, and I puzzle over this.

I stand in Suite 3670, in the commercial building across the street from Kalika's condo tower. Olympic Boulevard lies between us and my daughter, but at this time of night – three in the morning – it is rare that a car drives by. Beside me are Dr Seter, Seymour, James, and two sharpshooters with laser-assisted rifles. They have cut away a circular panel in the glass and now are focusing their weapons on Kalika's windows, which are visible, barely – for we are eighteen stories above her. All of Kalika's windows are covered with vertical blinds, however. We have better views of her two balconies and the large pool far below. Of course, we have a clear view of the roof of the tower. It is at this spot that I stare as my doubts continue to grow.

Dr Seter and his son have not assembled a group of spiritual fanatics and trained them how to aim and fire automatic weapons. Instead they have managed to construct the equivalent of a highly trained commando unit. I am staggered by the way they go about surrounding Kalika, who, by the way, is definitely at home. Their attack is much more coordinated than the attack the LAPD and the FBI sprang to capture me and Joel.

There are two units: Alpha Top and Alpha Bottom. The former has somehow managed to make it onto the roof of the building with ropes and pulleys. Alpha Bottom is already on Kalika's floor. The security guards are apparently unconscious, if we are to believe the radio reports that are constantly streaming in. We're all tied together with short wave. Both Alpha Top and Alpha Bottom have ten members each, male and female, all dressed in black. They have night goggles, gas grenades, even grenade launchers. Where they bought all this stuff, I have no idea.

I watch as the last of the Alpha Top team assembles on the roof.

'How do they plan on getting down to Kalika's balcony?' I ask James, pointing at the people on the roof. James is also dressed in black, a radio in his hand. His face shines with excitement. Apparently he likes playing soldier. The whole situation strikes me as odd, and yet I am the one who instigated it – I think.

'The same way they got on the roof,' he says. 'We will lower six of them onto the balconies before we attack, three onto each balcony. We won't attack until everyone is in position. Why?'

'She will hear them on the balcony,' I say.

James peers through a pair of binoculars hung around his neck. 'We have pretty much determined that she is asleep.'

'I wouldn't count on that,' Seymour mutters.

'We must give her a chance to cooperate,' Dr Seter says for perhaps the tenth time. Although the doctor is supposed to be the boss, it is clear to me the attack units are taking orders only from James.

'She'll be given every chance she deserves,' James says. He clicks on his radio. 'Alpha Bottom, this is Control. Are you still holding by the eighteenth floor elevators? Over.'

'Control, this is Alpha Bottom. We are near the elevators. Over.'

'Alpha Bottom, this is Control. Alpha Top will be swinging onto the balconies momentarily. Do not move toward Suite 1821 until you are ordered. Over.'

'Control, this is Alpha Bottom. Understood. Out.'

James studies the top group through his binoculars. Then he clicks his radio back on. 'Alpha Top, this is Control. Any signs that Kalika is in the living room or kitchen area? Over.'

'Control, this is Alpha Top. We have detected no activity in the living room or kitchen area. Over.'

'Alpha Top, are your ropes in place? Over.'

'Control, we are ready to swing down. Over.'

'Alpha Top, this is Control. You may start down. But hold on the balconies until you hear from me. Over.'

'Control, understood. Alpha Top out.'

'You guys seem to know what you're doing,' I say.

James smiles. 'You sound disappointed.'

I give a wan smile. 'I always have a thing for the underdog.' More than a thing. Watching them all converge on Kalika, I feel sick to my stomach. I have to keep telling myself that Kalika is totally unpredictable, that they have to be careful. Dr Seter puts a hand on my arm.

'We have trained for this day for a long time,' he says. 'But we will not shoot first, I promise you that. She will be given every chance to surrender.'

I shake my head. 'She will never surrender.'

In teams of three, dropping off from two points on the roof, the Alpha Top people begin to slide down toward the balconies. They land in seconds; I watch as they unclip the ropes from their belts. Each carries a weapon, has a radio in an ear, and night goggles. The guy in charge of Alpha Top comes back on the line, speaking in hushed whispers.

'Control, we are in position. Over.'

'He shouldn't be talking,' I say. 'She'll hear him. In fact, they should be ready for her to attack. Now. Tell them to get their weapons drawn. She could come at them any second.'

James ignores me. He talks into his radio.

'Alpha Top, this is Control. You will go on my command. Stand ready. Over.'

Separated by a corner of the building, neither group of three can see the other group. This is a major weakness in the plan. They should know to the split second what every one of them is doing. Their radios are not fast enough. James continues to bark instructions.

'Alpha Bottom, this is Control. Move toward Suite 1821. Alpha Top is in position on the balconies. Over.'

'Control, this is Alpha Bottom. Understood. Over.'

The ten people on the Alpha Bottom team will crowd one another as they move along the hallway. I point this out to James and suggest he hold back half of them by the elevators. He brushes aside my comment.

'They know what they're doing,' he says. 'They won't accidentally shoot each other.'

'You don't understand how fast she can move,' I say. 'The more room they have, the more chance they have of getting off a clean shot.'

'I want Alpha Bottom to knock at the door first,' Dr

Seter says. 'She has to be told that she is surrounded and that escape is impossible.'

'She doesn't think in terms of impossibilities,' Seymour mutters. 'I think it will be a mistake to knock.'

James checks with me. 'Do you agree?'

I think of Kalika riddled with bullets while she lies in bed.

'I agree.' I turn to Dr Seter. 'There is no point in talking to her. Honestly.'

Dr Seter trembles. 'But this could be cold-blooded murder.'

'I say we listen to Alisa,' James says. Before anyone can protest he clicks on his radio. 'Alpha Top and Alpha Bottom, this is Control. We will move on the count of five. One . . . two . . . three . . .'

He does not reach five.

There is loud screaming.

We hear it over the radio and through the air.

We look down to see that the balcony farthest from us is empty – of Suzama people, that is. Kalika, alone, is out there, her hair hanging down the back of her white robe. Below her, three individuals in black float down toward the large swimming pool. Float is perhaps too kind a word. They are falling to their deaths, and they know it. The few feet of pool water are not going to absorb their falls. Their horrified screams rend the air and I scream at myself for believing that Kalika would just lie down and die.

The three hit the water, landing on top of each other, crashing through to the bottom. Their limbs and skulls explode on contact. The pool is well lit. Within seconds a red wave expands across the blue water. The screams cease. I turn to James.

'Call off the attack!' I yell. 'Get your people out of there! She may let them go if they pull back now!'

James stares down in horror as blood fills the pool.

'This is incredible,' he mumbles.

I grab him. 'I was wrong! She can't be stopped this way! Tell them to back off!'

He looks at me and frowns. 'No. We have only started to fight.' He touches his two sharpshooters on the shoulders, the two that crouch below us. 'Open fire.'

Their bullets begin to ricochet off the balcony. Kalika moves inside.

'Alpha Top!' James shouts into his radio. 'She is coming.'

No, she has come. Before James can finish speaking, Kalika attacks those on the second balcony. Only my eyes are fast enough to see exactly what she does. The person closest to the balcony door is a woman with long red hair. Kalika grabs her and twists her head all the way around. Catching the dead woman's weapon as it falls, Kalika then shoots the other two in the face. One, a handsome guy with no top skull, falls over the balcony and lands on the sidewalk seventeen floors below. The third one, a short dark guy, simply sits down and dies. Before our sharpshooters can readjust their aim to the nearer balcony, Kalika has retreated inside. And now she has an automatic weapon with her. James struggles to turn his radio back on.

'Alpha Bottom!' he yells. 'You must attack!'

'What has happened to Alpha Top?' the guy wants to know.

'Those on the balcony have been taken out!' James says and forgets all the 'Alpha' this and 'over' that. There is no time for such formalities. 'She is still inside! Get her!'

'Tell them she has a gun!' I say.

'She has a gun!' James yells. 'Alpha Top, you must get down to the balconies! Alpha Bottom is going in!'

The four still on the roof are peering over the edges. They see that the pool is full of bodies and so is one of the balconies. Why, there is even a body down on the sidewalk. They don't want to go anywhere. I wish they would go back the way they came. I know they are in extreme danger just by being on the roof.

'We have to stop!' Dr Seter cries to his son, his face ashen. 'Alisa is right! Don't send any more people.'

The radio is screaming.

Now Alpha Bottom is dying.

They have kicked in her door, violated her space. There are gunshots, sounds of tearing flesh, splattering blood, breaking bones. And over it all I hear Kalika laughing. She is unstoppable and knows it. It is only then I realize that from the very beginning this has been a trap. Seymour was right. Kalika let me hear enough to figure out where she lived. She knew I would try to get help, and since she obviously doesn't like the Suzama group, so much the better that they should come to her to die. I hear one woman begging for mercy and then it sounds as if she is smashed against a wall. James trembles with the radio in his hand.

'Alpha Top!' he shouts. 'Help your partners!'

The four still on the roof look at one another and shake their heads. They would be better off getting down from the roof, yet they must think they are safe up there because they hardly move while the screaming continues. But when it stops, and the firing stops, I finally grab the radio from James's hands.

'Alpha Top,' I say calmly. 'She knows you're up there. Try to go back down the way you came up. Don't wait for her to come to you. Please, listen to me. Swing down to the nineteenth floor and get in the elevator. There's still time.'

But what time there is they squander. A precious minute elapses while they seem to argue among themselves. At the end of that time, Kalika, her white robe now soaked red, peeks over the edge of the roof. They see her, and those left of Alpha Top are too scared even to level their weapons. As Kalika climbs up onto the roof, they slowly back into the corner farthest from her. Even the sharp-shooters at our knees stare in awe. James slaps one on the head.

'Shoot her!' he shouts. 'She's an easy target!'

But my daughter makes nothing easy. As a bullet sparks at her feet, she leaps forward and grabs one of the men and holds him as a shield in front of her. The other three continue to stand immobilized by fear. But now Kalika is looking our way. The sharpshooters cease firing. James throws a tantrum.

'Don't stop!' he screams. 'Kill her!'

'But she's holding Charles,' one protests.

'Oh God, this can't be happening,' Dr Seter moans.

James shoves the guy aside. 'Give me that gun!'

But I stop James. 'Let me,' I say quietly.

He glares at me. 'What do you know about sniper rifles?'

'She knows a lot,' Seymour says.

James continues to glare at me, but finally lets me take the gun.

'Just don't miss,' he says bitterly.

Kneeling behind the stationary rifle, I peer into the telescopic sight. Kalika is standing relatively motionless, but she still has the guy held neatly in front of her. Only her face is visible behind the guy's right shoulder. The laser guide is helpful, even for someone like me who can hit a dime-size object at two miles if I have the right gun. For a moment I am able to plant the red dot precisely in the center of Kalika's forehead. My finger sweats over the trigger. I merely have to pull it and put a bullet in her brain and the night can still be considered a success, at least as far as the world is concerned.

But then I catch sight of her eyes, and I hesitate. She seems to be looking directly at me. Who am I fooling? Of course she knows who tracks her. The fact seems to amuse her because she smiles ever so faintly. Her lips move to form a soundless word, yet I hear it, hear it inside.

'Mother.'

I momentarily lose my concentration. In that time Kalika moves swiftly and with deadly purpose, vanishing from the field of view of my laser scope. Pulling back from the weapon, I watch her throw her human shield off the side of the roof. She tosses her victim straight at the pool – perhaps it amuses her to see the big red splash the screaming people make – and a moment later there is that much more blood to clean out of the filter.

In quick succession she grabs two of the three who are left. These she kills by smashing their skulls together. They are unrecognizable as she lets them fall onto the rooftop, their brains hanging over their collars. Then her attention turns to the final member of the Suzama Society, and I recognize her. Lisa, the accountant from North Dakota, whom I met last night. So great is Lisa's fear that she backs away from my daughter, right off the side of the roof. Kalika does not let her fall, but grabs her at the last instant. James yells at me.

'Why don't you shoot!' he says.

I set the gun down. 'No. I can't kill Lisa.'

'Lisa is as good as dead!' James cries. 'Shoot!'

But Kalika has already disappeared with her prey, a spider crawling back into her web with a kicking insect in tow. The roof is now empty except for two virtually headless bodies.

I stand and look at all of them. 'Stay here. I am going to speak to her.'

Dr Seter grabs my arm. 'You can't go over there, child. It's a bloodbath.'

10 ~~

The moment I am out the door I switch into hyper-mode. Using the stairs instead of waiting for the elevator, I reach the condo in less than one minute. In the distance I hear the cry of a dozen sirens. Yet the police are not really late to respond. Since the beginning of the attack less than seven minutes have elapsed. Kalika was definitely not sleeping.

Standing outside the building is a tide of moaning souls in pyjamas and robes. Somebody should at least turn off the pool lights, I think. The floating bodies create a particularly gruesome sight. A few of the people, all men in their forties, have guns in their hands. They are arguing with one another as I dash inside the building.

I take the stairs to the eighteenth floor. Between the

sixteenth and seventeenth floors I find two brutally slain bodies, their heads literally torn from their bodies.

'Would you be upset if I ripped this bird's head off?'

'Why do you ask these silly questions?'

'To hear your answers.'

The sight of these poor people upsets me greatly, but it makes me pause to ask myself the question: what am I doing? Am I trying to save Lisa in order to bandage my shattered conscience for the other deaths I have caused? Not that Lisa is not worth my effort, but I know she is as James said, as good as dead. And if I die with her who will be left to stop Kalika?

But these questions, like most, are academic.

I hear cries above me. Lisa, in the claws of a jackal.

Picking up an automatic rifle, I continue up the stairs.

Kalika is waiting for me in the centre of her living room. I have to walk over a glut of slashed bodies to get to her. The place is not as neat as it was that afternoon when Seymour and I investigated. There is hardly a square foot of wall or ceiling or floor that is not splattered red. Apparently my daughter let them come as far as they wanted into her home before she welcomed them as only she knows how.

Yet Lisa is still alive. In Kalika's arms.

I level my gun at the two of them.

'It's a coward who hides behind another,' I say to my daughter.

Kalika smiles. Her face, her arms, even her hair are drenched in blood, and she has never looked happier.

Tightening her hold on Lisa, she lifts the young woman a foot off the floor. For her part, Lisa is half in shock, with at least one foot in the grave. Yet she continues to struggle against my daughter, all while making feeble whimpering sounds. The fight in her is instinctive. I believe Kalika has already shattered her mind.

'We did this once before,' she says. 'But you were not carrying a weapon that night.'

'I am not going to put the gun down,' I say.

Kalika chuckles. 'Then I should kill her now?'

'No.' I take a step forward. 'Let her go. Show your mercy.'

'Drop the gun. Show your courage.'

'You will just kill us both.'

'Perhaps,' Kalika agrees.

'You set me up. You wanted me to bring them here. Why?'

'I would think the answer to that question is obvious.'

'The police will be here in minutes,' I say.

'The police do not concern me.' She raises a sharp nail to Lisa's throat. 'I cannot let you shoot me, Mother. I have a mission yet to perform.'

'What is it?'

'To protect the righteous and to destroy the wicked.'

I sneer. 'Tonight is a fine example of that mission of yours.'

'Thank you.' Kalika presses her nail into Lisa's neck. A drop of blood appears and traces a line down the young woman's throat. Lisa, even though in shock, suddenly gasps and struggles harder. But Kalika's hold is stronger than steel. She speaks casually. 'You remember this part, don't you, Mother?'

I begin to panic. I cannot let this girl die. She is almost a stranger to me, true, but she is all that Dr Seter has left. If I can save her, I think, I can save the doctor. I know his heart will give out soon after this night. You will see prophecies fulfilled. Yeah, right. The Satanic Prophecies. How could I make him such promises? Kalika is right about one thing. I lie to suit my needs. It is an old habit of mine.

'You promised me this morning that you would not kill unless it was necessary,' I say.

Kalika digs her nail in a little deeper. The red line on Lisa's throat thickens. Soon the blood will gush. Lisa's eyes are as round as overripe strawberries. Her breathing sounds laboured. Or is that her heart I hear, skipping inside her trembling chest? Lisa is almost gone but still her expression begs for me to save her.

'This is becoming necessary,' Kalika says. 'Put down the gun.'

'I can't.'

'I will open her throat. She will go the way Eric did. You know how much that upset you.'

Now I shake. 'But this young woman is innocent.'

'She came to kill me. Innocence is hardly the word I would apply to her.'

'I brought her here. I am to blame. Please, Kalika, for the love of God, let her go.'

Kalika pauses. 'For the love of God? How can you say

that to me after you have gazed into my eyes? Don't you know I do everything for the love of God?'

With that Kalika scratches her sharp nail all the way across Lisa's throat, opening two of the young woman's major arteries. The blood shoots out as if fired from a hose under tremendous pressure. But I am hardly given a chance to react, to fire through Lisa's body now that it has ceased to be a viable living shield. My daughter is swifter than Eddie Fender was. Lisa gags on pieces of throat as Kalika throws her at me. The blow is enough to knock me over and send my weapon flying. The back of my skull strikes a wall as Lisa slowly slips from me and everything is a blur to me for a moment. There is blood on the back of my own head. I reach up to feel the extent of my injury when I see a figure out of the corner of my eye. It is my daughter holding my gun. She speaks in a kind voice.

'Are you in pain?' she asks.

The room continues to spin. Lisa's body weighs heavily on my lower legs.

'Go to hell,' I mumble.

'I am beyond heaven and hell.' She reaches out and grabs my arm. 'You have friends in the other building. Save me time and tell me what suite they're in.'

Finally my eyes begin to refocus. I stare at her.

'You've got to be kidding,' I say.

She smiles. 'Just thought I would ask. Do you know how to swim?'

'Yes.'

'Do you know how to fly?'

Sounds like a trick question to me.

I don't answer it but it doesn't matter.

Tossing aside the gun, Kalika grabs me by the chest and with one hand drags me outside and onto the balcony where she dealt with the first three members of Alpha Top. Far below the bodies continue to float in the red-stained pool. The police have finally arrived. Numerous black and white units are jammed into the valet parking area, their search beams pointed at us. I would wave but I'm afraid they might shoot me. Kalika sighs in wonder as she sweeps the city night with her dark eyes.

'I told you the view was stunning,' she says.

'I am pleased that my only daughter should be so successful that she is able to afford such a nice place,' I say sweetly.

Kalika leans over and kisses me on the cheek. Her lips are soft and gentle. She speaks in my ear and there is a trace of concern in her voice.

'Can you survive such a fall? Tell me the truth.'

'I honestly don't know.'

She pulls back slightly and strokes my hair. 'Krishna loves you.'

I am having trouble breathing. Her grip is cruel.

'It is good somebody does,' I gasp.

'Did I ever tell you that I love you?'

'No. Not that I can remember.'

'Oh.' A deadly pause. 'I must have forgotten.'

'Kalika—'

I am not given a chance to finish the sentence.

My own daughter throws me over the side of the balcony.

The moon is out, it is true, and it is very bright. But there is no time to allow its gentle rays to pour into the crown of my head and fill my body to float me safely away as it did when the nuclear bomb threatened to kill me. At the moment I could be a mortal. Certainly I fall as fast as one. Kalika has thrown me towards the pool. As the bloody mess rushes towards me, I can only pray that I land in the deep end.

When I hit, my arms and legs are spread as far as they will go. I reason that this will give me more of a chance to break my fall. But I know even before I strike the water that something else will break when I strike the bottom of the pool.

The shock is crushing. There is a flash of red followed by an agony so searing I lose consciousness. But the oblivion is cruel; it does not last. When I awake my face is pressed into the floor of the pool. Indeed I have cracked the plaster, and half the bones in my body. My nose seems to have been obliterated, my face is a pancake of gross tissue. Inside my torn mouth I feel a lump of crumbled teeth. My chest feels as if ribs poke through my lungs and my shirt, pouring more blood into the pool.

Honestly, I don't think I can live through this.

Especially under nine feet of water.

The dead float above me, their expressionless faces inviting me to join them. The water seems to swim with nightmarish creatures. One of my black boots floats by.

My sock, covered in red, is still inside. My spinal cord is possessed by a pain demon. He has brought sharp tools. I throw up in the water and blood and teeth come out and form a ghastly cloud over my head. I start to lose consciousness again, and I know if I do, I will never wake up. Yet my eyes refuse to remain open. They are broken as well. Closing them, I sink into a deeper level of darkness.

Krishna. Let me have one more chance. That is all I ask.

To stop her. To save the child.

My heart keeps beating. The agony keeps throbbing.

Time goes by but pain counts it at a different speed. This time is what is called hard time by all those who have suffered. And hard times bring hard truths. My brains may be leaking from my ears, but I finally understand that Kalika cannot be defeated by guns and bullets. Twenty people, maybe more, had to die to make me understand that.

But I will never understand how she can be so cruel.

'But anyone who sees through the veil of maya cannot fathom the divine will. The veil is stained and the absolute is without flaw. One cannot reveal the other. In the same way, I am your own daughter but you cannot fathom me.'

No matter how many die, I will not understand.

From far away, I feel feverish activity. It comes, I realize, from deep inside me, in my muscles, beneath my veins, and all around my joints. My supernatural body is trying to knit itself back together. Beneath my shirt, I feel my sternum grow back together into one piece. Next there are pops in my legs and ankles. The

102

bones are resetting themselves at a frantic pace. My jaw flexes involuntarily and I feel new teeth pressing up from beneath my mangled gums. Finally I am able to open my eyes, and I give myself a gentle push towards the surface. The beat of my heart has turned to a shriek. If I do not draw in a breath soon, especially with all the repair work going on, my chest will explode.

The night air tastes good. Never better.

On the surface, I am forced to float on my back for a minute before I am strong enough to make my way to the side. There is a crowd gathered, and some of the people in it are cops. I hear screams as I begin to pull myself out of the pool, but a brave cop rushes to my side with a clean blanket. He is fat with a bushy moustache. He carefully wraps the blanket around me.

'You're going to be OK,' he says. 'Just lie here on the deck. Don't try to move. You may have broken bones.'

I wipe at the blood on my face. I know I don't have much time.

'You have friends in the other building.'

'No, I'm fine,' I say. 'Don't worry about me.'

I try to stand but he tries to stop me.

'But you were thrown off that balcony,' he protests. 'It's a miracle you're still alive.'

I finish wiping my face and hair with his blanket and hand it back to him all bloody. 'You're a kind man,' I say. 'But I have to get out of here.'

I move too fast for him to stop me – yet I am far from healed. Even as I dash across Olympic Boulevard, I feel the tissue inside my body struggling to recover. If I meet Kalika in the next minute I will be at a serious disadvantage. Not that it will make much difference. But it is fear that hurries me along, or maybe it is foolish hope. Hope that she might have let some of them survive.

In the office building, the elevator takes me to the thirty-sixth floor. The stairs are too much for me in my condition. When I stagger out of the elevator, the first thing I see is blood. For a moment all hope in me dies. The door to Suite 3670 has been pulverized. Yet there is a sound, soft words, faint moans. I hurry forward and peer inside.

Seymour and Dr Seter huddle in one corner. My old friend appears to be taking care of the doctor, who's having trouble catching his breath. Twenty feet away from them, in the center of the room, the two sharpshooters lie in an ugly heap. It looks as if she kicked each of them so hard in the chest that she ruptured their hearts – an old Sita move. Yet Seymour and Dr Seter appear unharmed. I almost weep I am so relieved.

It is only then I notice that James is missing.

'Where is he?' I demand.

They jump and look over. I am still covered with blood.

Dr Seter gasps. 'We thought you were dead.'

I stride toward them and look down. 'Where is James? Did she take him?'

Seymour stands and shakes his head. 'He went after

you, right after you left. We haven't seen him since.' He hugs me; there are tears on his face. 'Thank God you're alive. We saw her throw you off the balcony. I thought it was all over.'

I comfort him, but also catch his eye. 'That was someone else you saw. Not me.' I turn back to the doctor. 'You have a heart condition. Will you be all right? Should I call for an ambulance?'

'I'll be fine.' He reaches up. 'Just help me up.'

I do so. 'What happened?' I ask.

Seymour gestures weakly. 'The door exploded and she walked in. The guys tried to shoot her, but she didn't give them a chance. Then she pinned Dr Seter to the wall and demanded he tell her where the scripture was.'

Dr Seter looks crushed. 'And I told her everything. I tried to resist but I couldn't.' He stops and he is close to crying. 'Do you think she got James?'

'No.' The voice comes from the door. James steps into the room. He surveys the dead sharpshooters and a shudder goes through his body. 'I am unharmed,' he says.

I step to his side. 'Did you see her leave?'

'Yes. She stole a cop car and drove away in it.'

'Did you see anything else?'

I am asking if he saw me hit the pool and survive.

He stares at me. 'No. I mean, what do you mean? It's a holocaust over there.'

'Nothing. I am sorry about tonight,' I say. 'I know the words sound stupid but I must say them. At least now you can see why she must be stopped.' Placing my hand over his heart, as I had the previous night, I am surprised at how evenly it is beating. He got rattled during Kalika's attack but has quickly regained his cool. I add, 'You have to show me the remainder of your scripture. If it is still there.'

11 ~~~

Kalika was thorough. The Suzama Society has only two members now. The news shocks me. Surely, I say to James as he drives us towards Palm Springs, there have to be some personnel at the centre who weren't involved in the attack.

'No,' he replies. He adds with a bitter laugh, 'We're all true believers. We believed your story, and went after the Dark Mother with everything we had.' The morning sun is bright in his face but James appears close to despair as he thinks about the previous night. 'We don't even have a secretary at the centre now.'

I reach over and rub his shoulders. 'It wasn't your fault. If anyone is to blame, it is I. I knew what she could do.'

'But you did warn us. You warned me. If I had

listened to your suggestions, maybe fewer would have been killed.'

'No. It wouldn't have made any difference. She was determined to kill them all.'

He frowns. 'Why did she spare my father and your friend?'

'That puzzles me,' I say honestly. 'The only thing I can think is that she must believe that either your father or Seymour, working with us, will eventually find the child.'

He is concerned. 'Do you think she's following us now?'

I have been checking to see if we are being shadowed.

'Not at this very moment, no,' I say.

'Do you think my father and your friend will be safe at your house?'

He is not asking about a threat from Kalika. We are all fugitives from the law now, from the government. I have no doubt my description has been relayed to those higher-ups who knew I was at the military base in Nevada. My face has shown up at too many public slaughters lately. There is an excellent chance, I think, that the police or the FBI will be waiting for us at the Suzama Centre in Palm Springs. When the bodies are all identified, they will make the natural link. That's why I have insisted we go to the centre immediately. I have yet to decide if I will kill to see the scripture.

'For the time being,' I say. 'Your father can rest there, and Seymour will take good care of him.' I pause.

'You worry about him, don't you?'

He nods. 'His heart is lousy.'

'Are you adopted?'

My question surprises him. 'Yes. I was adopted late. I was sixteen when my parents were killed in a car accident. At the time Dr Seter and my father were colleagues at Stanford. He started out watching me so I started calling him Dad, at first only as a joke. But now I feel closer to him than I did to my real father. A short time after I moved in with him he found the scripture and then we shared a mission together as well as a house.'

'Where did he find it?'

He hesitates. 'Israel. In Jerusalem.'

'That's not Western Europe.'

'It's better if he's not specific. Where did you find yours? Tell me the truth this time.'

'In Jerusalem.'

He nods. 'And Kalika destroyed it yesterday?'

'She took it. I don't know if she destroyed it.'

'So she lets you live as well.'

'I suppose,' I say, feeling sad. My own daughter tried to kill me. And there had been a time not so long ago when I was willing to risk losing the world to save her. Now I see I have lost my bet, even though I am still angling for another chance to win back what has been lost. I wonder if Krishna heard my prayer while I lay on the bottom of the pool, if he let me live for a reason. I wonder if Paula's child is Krishna.

From the outside the centre appears to be

undisturbed, but once we are in the basement it is clear that someone has been in the vault. Sheets of the scripture lie spread on the table in the centre of the room. James grabs them frantically and studies them. The colour drains from his face.

'She was here,' he says. 'Some papyrus sheets are missing. Others are torn in pieces.'

His conclusion seems logical, yet I can find no trace of her smell in the basement, and that puzzles me.

'Are you sure there are no other members of the Suzama Society alive?' I ask.

'There are just me and my dad,' he says.

I stop him. 'Go upstairs and keep watch. Let me try to read what is here.'

'But less than half of it is here.'

I realize his whole adult life has been built around the document. Giving him a comforting pat on the back, I shoo him away. Finally I am alone with a piece of the puzzle I have never held before. But I have to wonder about what is missing.

The first piece I read deals specifically with the child.

Of all the previous avatars, he who is born at the end of that time's millennium will manifest the greatest divinity to the world. He will have the playfulness of Sri Krishna, the wisdom of Adi Shankara, and the compassion of Jesus of Nazareth. He will be these divine beings, but something more, something that humanity has never seen before.

He will be born in a city associated with lost angels, but it will be dark angels who force him and his mother to flee to the mirror in the sky, where shoes move without feet and the emerald circle is seen in the morning light. There the dark forces will once again converge on him, but a powerful angel will rescue him only to lose him again. Then the place of sanctity will be defiled by red stars, and only the innocent will see the blue light of heaven. Faith is stronger than stone. The rest is a mystery.

The war between the Setians and the Old Ones never ends. I am Suzama of the Old Order. Even as these words are recorded, the mother of an angel burns under Setian stars. Her pain is my pain. I wait for the enemy, for the splinter in the earth element, and for my own death. This splinter will become a crack, and civilization will end as we know it. But all ends are temporary and all life is born from death. I am Suzama and I fear neither this end nor the loss of my own life. For this ancient war is for the purpose of dark angels and blue angels alike. Both are divine in my illumined vision, and all colour is erased in the infinite abyss.

There is another piece of papyrus, torn in two.
It is much thinner than the others.
It speaks of Kalika.

She is the Dark Mother, all consuming and not to be trusted. She brings the light of the red stars, and a wave of red death flows from her fingertips. She is the scourge of the child, not its protector as she claims to be. Her name is Kali Ma, and it is her name that matches the dark age. All who know her will fear her.

'Suzama,' I whisper, shaking. 'You don't know how you curse your old friend.'

But does it matter what she says about my daughter? Wasn't tonight proof enough of my daughter's demonic nature? She laughed as she killed, and no doubt drank the blood of many of those who slumped to their deaths. Suzama can tell me nothing new about my own child.

But what about the holy child? Where is this mirror in the sky, where shoes move without feet and the emerald circle is seen in the morning light? It is difficult to imagine Suzama being any more ambiguous. I almost curse her. The last thing I need now is more riddles, and all the stuff about dark angels and mistaken angels confuses me. Even worse are Suzama's references to the Setians. They were destroyed when Suzama was destroyed, in the great earthquake of ancient Egypt. Why does she go on about the war? That war is over as far as I am concerned.

'I will wait here for you. I will be here when you return.'

But there was no one there when I returned.

Suzama's last prediction to me was wrong.

I call to James and he returns to the basement quickly.

'There are people outside on the street pointing at the centre,' he says. 'I think the police will be here any minute.'

'We will go then. Gather up what is left of the scripture and take it to your father.'

'Aren't you going with me?' he asks.

112

'No. I need some time alone to think. Do you have an extra car?'

He grimaces. 'We have plenty of extra cars now. You can take any one you want. Should I go to your house?'

'Yes. I will join you there shortly. Go out the back way so you won't be stopped.'

He is dying to ask the question.

'Did you find out anything useful?' he asks.

I give a wan smile. 'Only time will tell.'

12 ~~~

On the spot where Paula's child was conceived, on the sandy bluff in Joshua Tree National Monument, I lie in the shade of a tall Joshua tree and stare up at the sky. It strikes me as a small miracle how the sky has not changed in five thousand years. Why, I could be lying on my back in ancient Egypt, beside the Nile, and there would be no difference in the sky.

But it is not easy for me to remember.

Suzama took me in, into her home, her heart. She shared a small shack with her parents. It is ironic that the greatest seer of all time should be born to a blind mother and a blind father. Neither of them ever knew what I looked like, yet they treated me with great kindness. They even tolerated the strange hours I kept. For in those days I needed to drink blood almost every night to quench my thirst. It was still difficult for me to feed myself and keep my victim alive. I lacked the control that was to come with age. Yet many people naturally died in those days during the night, especially the old, and I tried to confine my feeding to them so as to raise fewer suspicions.

When I returned home from one nightly sojourn, I found Suzama awake. At that time I had been in Egypt a month. There was pain in Suzama's large soulful eyes. She sat outside beneath a blanket of stars. I sat beside her.

'What's the matter?' I asked.

She would not look at me. 'I followed you tonight.'

I drew in a sharp breath. 'What did you see?'

'What you do to people.' She had tears. 'Why do you do it?'

I took a while to answer her. 'I have to do it to survive.'

It was true. She of almost perfect clairvoyance could not see what her friend really was. When she had first met me, she had only suspected.

She was horrified. 'Why?'

'Because I am not a human being. I am a vampire.'

Even in those days they had a word for creatures like me. Suzama understood what I meant. Yet she did not flee from me, but instead held my hand.

'Tell me how it happened,' she said.

I told her the entire story of my life, which even though it had just begun, seemed awfully long to me. Suzama heard of Yaksha and Rama and Lalita and

115

Krishna. I told her every word Krishna had said to me, of the vow he had placed me under to make no more vampires, and of the vow he had made Yaksha take to destroy all vampires. Suzama listened as if in a dream. When I was finished she whispered aloud.

'I have seen this Krishna in many visions,' she said.

'Tell me what you see?'

She spoke in a distant voice. 'He has the whole universe in his eyes. The sun we see in the sky is only one of many. All these stars – more than can be counted – shine inside the crown of his head.' She paused. 'You must be a very special kind of monster to receive his grace.'

I was able to relax.

Suzama was telling me she was still my friend.

It was shortly after that night that she began to heal others.

The cures started innocently enough. Suzama was fond of collecting herbs. Even as a child she had had a knack for knowing which ones to prescribe for which illnesses. It was normal for a handful of ailing people to stop by each day for medical advice. Sometimes Suzama would have the sick person stay. She would have the person lie on his or her back and take long, slow deep breaths while she held her left hand above the forehead and her right hand over the heart. Invariably the person felt better afterwards, or at least they said they did.

Then came a crippled man. He had not walked since a massive stone had fallen across his hips five years earlier. He had no feeling from the waist down. At first she prescribed some herbs and was about to send him away when the man begged her to bless him. Reluctantly, as if she knew this act would forever change the course of her life, Suzama put him down on the floor and had him take deep breaths. Her hands shook as she held them over the man, and there was sweat on her face. I couldn't take my eyes off her. A milky white radiance had begun to shine above her head. Even when the man's lower legs began to twitch, I couldn't stop staring at her angelic face. For the uncountable stars were shining through her now.

The man was able to walk home.

After that there was always a line outside Suzama's house. She continued to perform many healings, although only a few matched her healing of the crippled man. For many seriously ill people she was unable to do anything. It is their karma to be ill, she would say. They had the word karma in that part of the world at that time, and they understood its meaning.

More than healing, Suzama preferred to foretell the future and to teach meditation. A series of special meditation techniques had come to her in visions and each of them was related to the worship of the Goddess Isis, the White Goddess, who shone in each soul above the head. Suzama taught mantra and breathing techniques, and sometimes she mixed the two together. I was her first student, as well as her last. While doing the practices she showed me, I began to experience peace of mind. She was my guru as well as my friend, and I always felt deeply indebted to her.

A time came when Suzama's exploits reached the ears of the rulers of the land. The king at that time was named Namok, and his queen was Delar. Namok was forty years older than his wife, and their beliefs, so the rumours said, were contrary to each other. Namok was firmly behind the powerful priest caste at the time, the fabled Setians, who supposedly gained divine insight from the ancient past, as well as from beings in the sky. The Setians worshipped a number of angry-looking deities, all of which were reptilian. I was curious, at the time, why Isis was supposed to be married to Osiris, who was Set's brother. The deities couldn't have been more different. The Setians did not approve of Isis worship, and went out of their way to destroy it. That is why Suzama always conducted her initiations in secret.

But the secret was out as far as Suzama's foretelling abilities were concerned. She was summoned to the Great Pyramid, and as her closest friend, I was allowed to come with her. In fact, Suzama refused to go without me. By this time she knew of my great physical power and felt safer with me by her side.

It seemed that Queen Delar had had a dream the Setian priests and priestesses were unable to decipher, at least to the queen's satisfaction. Delar wanted Suzama to try. Together, we were ushered into the royal meeting room. Its opulence was breathtaking. Never again would Egypt have such wealth, not even in the supposed golden ages of latter years. The very floor we walked on was made of gold.

Both king and queen were present, old and shrewd Namok on his high throne, with his tall and muscular spiritual adviser, Ory, at his right shoulder. Delar sat beside him on her own throne, with her young but hard face. It was Delar who bid us come closer and I couldn't help noticing out of the corner of my eye how Ory watched me. It was as if he had seen me before, or at least had had my features described to him. I wondered if his army of secret police, the dread Setian initiates, who had eyes like snakes, had taken note of my nocturnal ways. Ory wore a special dagger in his silver belt with which, it was reported, he cut out enemies' eyes before eating them. At that time the soul was thought to reside in the eyes.

Delar cleared her royal throat and spoke.

'You are Suzama. Your reputation precedes you. But who is this other person you have brought with you?'

Suzama bowed. 'This is Sita, my queen. She is an Aryan – which is why her skin is fairer than ours. She is my friend and confidante. I ask your permission that she be allowed to remain by my side while I complete your reading.'

Delar was curious about me. 'Are you from India, Sita? I have heard stories of that land.'

I also bowed. 'Yes, my queen. I am far from home, yet I am happy to be a guest in your great land.'

'What brought you to our land?' Ory asked. 'Were you fleeing from danger?'

'No, my lord. It is only a love of adventure that brought me here.'

Ory paused and whispered something in Namok's ear. The king frowned and nodded. But Ory smiled as he asked his next question and I couldn't help noticing how flat his eyes were. His hand never moved far from his dagger.

'It seems improper that a woman of your age should have travelled so far alone,' he said. 'Who were your companions along the road, Sita?'

'Merchants, my lord. They know the road to India well.'

'Then you are also a merchant,' Ory persisted.

'No,' I said. 'I have no special title.'

'But you live in the house of slaves,' Ory said. 'Suzama is a slave. You, too, must be a slave.'

I held his eye and there was strength in my gaze.

'No one owns me, my lord,' I said.

My answer seemed to amuse Ory. He didn't reply but the power in my eyes did not seem to affect him. Perhaps he had goaded me on purpose, I thought.

Delar cleared her throat once more. 'Come closer, Suzama and Sita. I will tell you my dream. If you are able to decipher it, your reward will be great.'

Suzama bowed. 'I will try my queen. But tell me first – did you have this dream at the last full moon?'

Delar was impressed. 'I did indeed. How did you know?'

'I was not sure. But dreams that come at that time are particularly auspicious. Please tell me your dream, my queen.'

'I was standing on a wide field in tall grass with lush

rolling hills all around. It was night, but the sky was bright with more stars than we normally see on the clearest of nights. Many of these stars were deep blue. In the distance was a group of people who were walking into a ship that gave off a brilliant violet light. I was supposed to be on that ship, I knew, but before I could leave I had to talk to a beautifully dressed man. He stood nearby with a gold flute in his hand. He had bewitching dark eyes, was dressed in a blue robe, and had long dark hair. Around his neck was an exquisite jewel – it shone with many coloured lights and hypnotized me. As I stared into it, he asked me, "What is it you wish to know?" And I said, "Tell me the law of life." I don't know why I asked this question, but he said, "This is the eternal law of life." And he pointed his finger at me.'

Delar paused. 'That was the entire dream. It was incredibly vivid. When I woke from it I was filled with great wonder, but also great confusion. It seemed I was given a great secret but I don't understand what it is. Can you help me?'

'A moment please, my queen,' Suzama said. Then she turned to me and spoke in whispers. 'You have had dreams like this?'

My eyes widened. 'Yes. How did you know?'

Suzama merely smiled. 'Who is the man?'

'Lord Krishna. There is no doubt.'

'And why did he point at her?'

'I don't know. Krishna often taught with riddles. He was mischievous.'

'He was careful,' Suzama said to me before turning back to the queen. 'Delar, the answer to your dream is very simple.'

Both the king and the queen sat up in anticipation. Even Priest Ory seemed to lean forward. He was no doubt one of those who had failed to decipher the dream properly.

'The blue stars signify the blue light of divinity,' Suzama said. 'You stood on a spiritual world in the spiritual sky. The man beside you was the Lord himself, come to give you instructions before you were born into this world. You asked the question you did because you wanted to know what law of life you should follow as queen of this land. You wanted to know what was fair, a means by which you could decide how to pass judgment on those you knew you would rule.' Suzama paused. 'He gave you the means when he pointed his finger at you.'

Delar frowned. 'I don't understand.'

'Point your finger at me, my queen,' Suzama said.

The queen did so. Suzama smiled.

'When you point your finger at someone, anyone, it is often a moment of judgment. We point our fingers when we want to scold someone, point out what they have done wrong. But each time we point, we simultaneously point three other fingers back at ourselves.'

The queen looked down at her hand and gasped. 'You are right. But what does that mean?'

'It means you must be very careful in your judgments,' Suzama said. 'Each time you decide fairly about someone, you gain three times the merit. But each time you make a poor judgment, you incur three times the debt. That is the law of life, whether you are a queen or a priest or a slave. When we do something good, it comes back to us threefold. When we harm someone, we harm ourselves three times as much.' Suzama paused. 'The Lord was telling you to be kind and good, my queen.'

Queen Delar was impressed.

King Namok was unsure.

The high priest Ory was annoyed.

The main players in the drama were set.

The dice had been thrown.

It was only a question of how they would land.

And who would be left alive to collect the promised reward.

13 ～

Back in Los Angeles the same day, I do not drive straight to my home in Pacific Palisades, but I do call to see if everyone is safe. Seymour says there is no sign of either the cops or Kalika. It sounds as if he has been enjoying Dr Seter's company, but I don't think joy is a word I could attach to his relationship with James. I promise Seymour I will be home soon.

At five in the evening I am once more in the living room of Mrs Hawkins, in the very house Eric longed to return to before his throat was cut open by my daughter. Hot-tempered Mr Hawkins is fortunately not at home with Mrs Hawkins. As before, she is plump and kindly, always fussing with her hands. Curiously, since I am associated with the kidnapping and death of her son, she does not appear unduly afraid of me. Indeed, she promptly invites me in when I come to the door. But perhaps she believed me the last time I visited, when I told her I did everything I could to save Eric.

'Would you like something to drink?' she asks as she takes a seat across from me.

'No, thank you.' I pause. 'You don't seem surprised to see me again.'

Her face twitches with the painful memory of her dead son. Truly it is not the tragedies that destroy us, but the memories of them. Clearly not a minute goes by when she does not think about Eric.

'I thought I would see you again,' she says.

'Why?'

'You just flew in that night, and then flew back out like a bird. My husband and I have talked about that a lot since you were here.' She flashes a sad smile. 'I think we convinced ourselves you weren't a devil, but an angel.'

'I'm sorry I'm not an angel. I'm sorry I wasn't able to save your son.'

She stops fussing with her hands for a moment. 'You really tried, didn't you?'

'Yes.' I lower my head. 'I tried everything I knew.'

She nods quietly. 'That's what I told my husband. He didn't believe you at first, but maybe he does now.' A pause. 'Are you sure I can't get you something? I just baked some chocolate-chip cookies. Eric used to love them.'

I look up and smile. 'Sure. I would love a cookie.'

She stands. 'I have milk as well. You can't enjoy a cookie without milk.'

'Ain't that the truth.' I have to sit in the pain of the house while she busies herself in the kitchen. Since my rebirth I have noticed I sense the *feelings* of a place much more acutely. The chair where I sit feels as if it has been used to electrocute people. It is Mr Hawkins's seat, I realize. He wanted to keep me from leaving the last time I came to visit. He wanted to call the cops.

Yet I also smell something as I wait for Mrs Hawkins to return.

The foul odor of illness. A human would never detect it, but I do.

Mrs Hawkins bustles in with a plate of cookies and a glass of milk.

'You must have more than one,' she says, setting the plate before me. 'Really, Eric and my husband used to finish a whole plate of these in a single afternoon. But with Eric gone and my – Well, Ted just doesn't seem as hungry as he used to be.'

I pick up a cookie. 'I'll have at least two.'

She sits back down across from me. 'You never told us your name last time, dear. Don't worry, I won't tell it to the police. I would just like to know what to call you.'

'It's Alisa.'

'Where are you from, Alisa?'

'Lots of places.' I sip the milk. It is cold, good. The questions need to be asked but I find myself postponing them.

I'm taking the year off from college, but I'll be in school next year. I just got accepted to SC. I'm going to major in pre-med.

'How do they taste?' she asks.

'Very good.' But I end up putting the cookie down, half eaten. 'Mrs Hawkins, may I ask you a delicate question? It concerns Eric.'

She hesitates. 'What is the question?'

'Your son wanted to be a doctor. He said he wanted to follow in your husband's footsteps. Now I've met your husband, and he seemed like an intense and driven man. That is not a criticism but an observation. Eric was not so driven, yet I imagine some of that intensity must have rubbed off on him.'

'That's true,' she admits carefully.

'You see, this is hard for me. I don't want to walk on your pain, and I apologize if I am. But I was just wondering why, if Eric was so keen to be a doctor, he was taking a year off from college? I mean, I know a break from studying is not so unusual,' I pause, 'but was there a special reason for his extended vacation?'

She stares blankly for a moment. 'Yes.'

'May I know the reason?'

A tear runs down her cheek. 'Eric had cancer. Lymphoma. It had spread through most of his body. It had gone into remission three times but it always came back.' She swallows thickly. 'The doctors said he had less than three months to live.'

'I see.' I am stunned. Eric had told me he wasn't well. Kalika had told me the same thing. Indeed, she had implied that was one of the reasons she killed him. So that he would have a better birth in his next life.

I'm your daughter. You should believe me. I believe you even when I hear you lying to me.

127

Perhaps Kalika had told me the truth.

Mrs Hawkins sobs quietly.

'There were a couple of police officers who came to the door the day Eric died,' I say carefully. 'They were looking for him, but the person I told you about – the one who killed your son – she convinced them to go off with her. And I never saw those men again. I assumed this woman killed them as well. But I never saw an article in the paper about them, and you know what big news any police killing is. I was just wondering, in your conversation with the police about your son, after his body was found, did they make any mention of the fact that they had lost two men?'

Mrs Hawkins wipes at her face. 'No.'

I speak out loud, but mainly to myself. 'It seems they would have, don't you think? If the disappearance was tied up with the same case as your son's death?'

'I would think so. Maybe the police are all right.'

I pick up the cookie again, thinking.

'How did you get on with the policemen?'

'Fine.'

'Are they fine?'

'You don't have to worry about them, Mother.'

'They might be all right,' I say.

Maybe I am worrying about all the wrong things.

14 ~~~

The night I turned myself back into a vampire, I went searching for an ounce of Yaksha's blood to serve as an auroic catalyst. The only place to look, I thought, was the ice-cream truck where Eddie Fender had kept Yaksha's tortured body in cold storage. There I found the blood I needed, frozen beneath a box of Popsicles. But before I scraped it from the floor of the refrigerated compartment, I had a highly unusual conversation with an elderly homeless man with thinning white hair and a grimy face. He was obviously down on his luck. But when I strode up to say hello, he reacted as if he was expecting me.

'You look very nice tonight. But I know you're in a hurry.'

'How do you know I'm in a hurry?'

'I know a few things. You want this truck I suppose.

I've been guarding it for you.'

'How long have you been here?'

'I don't rightly know. I think I've been here since you were last here.'

The ice-cream truck should not have been there. The police should have hauled it away a couple of months earlier. Yet not only was the truck parked where it had been when it held Yaksha, the refrigerator unit was still working, and the homeless man implied he had kept it working for me. That was crucial, because if the blood had melted and rotted, it would have been of no use to me. I wouldn't have been able to turn back into a vampire. I would have possessed no special abilities with which to protect the child.

Now the big question was . . .

Did the homeless man know that?

He obviously knew something.

The bigger question was *how* he knew.

With the sun setting and with no better place to go, I return to the street where I met the man. There, to my utter astonishment, I find him sitting near the spot where the ice-cream truck had been parked. It is gone but the man has not changed. In fact, he is drinking a carton of milk as he was the last time we met. He looks up as I approach and his eyes sparkle in the dull yellow light of the street lamps. He doesn't rise, though. He is an old man and getting up is hard on his knees. I remember I had to help him up the last time. He flashes me a warm smile.

'Why if it isn't you again,' he says. 'I thought you might come back.'

'Have you been waiting for me?' I ask.

'Sure. I don't mind waiting around. Don't have a lot to do these days, you know.'

I crouch by his side. 'What do you do when you're not waiting for me?'

He is shy. 'Oh, I just move around, pick up an odd job here and there, help out where I can.'

I smile. 'Well, you sure helped me last time.'

He is pleased. 'That's good. But you're a bright girl. You know how to help yourself.' He stops. 'Hey, would you like to play a game of cards?'

I raise an eyebrow. 'Poker?'

He brushes his hand. 'No. That's too hard a game for an old fella like me. You have to think too much. How about a game of twenty-one? I'll be the house. I'll play by house rules. I'll hit on every sixteen and give you a tip every now and then if you need it. As long as you promise to tip me if you win in the end. How does that sound? You know how to play twenty-one?'

I sit cross-legged in front of him. 'I am a born gambler. Do you have cards?'

He reaches in his old coat pocket and pulls out a pack. 'Do I have cards? These are fresh from a high roller's blackjack table in Las Vegas. Mind if I shuffle? Those are house rules, you know. Dealer has to shuffle.'

'You shuffle. What are we betting?'

He takes a sip of his milk as he opens the pack. 'It doesn't matter.' Then he laughs and the sound is like music to my ears because it has been so long since I have heard the sound of pure joy. 'An old bum like me – I have nothing to lose!'

I laugh with him. 'What's your name, old bum?'

He pauses and catches my eye. 'Now just one moment. You're the youngster here. You've never told me your name.'

I offer my hand. 'I'm Sita.'

He shakes my hand. 'Mike.'

'Where are you from, Mike?'

He lets go of my hand and shuffles the cards. He is a pro with them; he obviously can shuffle both sides of the deck with as few as five fingers. Yet a trace of sorrow enters his voice. The tone is not painful, more bittersweet.

'Lots of places, Sita,' he says. 'You know how it is when you get as old as I am, one place blurs into another. But I try to keep moving, try to keep my hand in. Where are you from?'

'India.'

He is impressed. 'By golly, that's far away! You must have had plenty of adventures between here and India.'

'Too many adventures, Mike. But are you going to stop talking and start dealing? I'm getting anxious to beat you at what I know is your favourite game.'

He acts offended, although he is still smiling.

'Hold on just one second,' he says. 'We haven't decided what we're wagering. What have you got?'

'Money.'

He nods. 'Money is good. How much you got?'

I reach in my back pocket. 'Three hundred dollars in cash.'

He whistles. 'My sweet lord! You carry your bankroll on you. Now I know that ain't smart, no sir.'

I flip open my wad of twenties. Got them from an ATM machine down the street.

'I don't mind betting this. What are you betting?'

My question seems to catch him off guard. He asks with a trace of suspicion, 'What do you want?'

'Oh. Just a few friendly hints, what you offered. Can you give me some of those? When I win I mean?'

He speaks with mock confidentiality. 'You don't need them when you win, girl. You need them when you win, girl. You need them when you lose.' He begins to deal the cards. 'Sure, I'll help you out. Just don't you get too rough on old Mike.'

I throw a twenty down. 'I'll try to behave myself.'

He deals me a fifteen, bust hand. He is looking strong, showing a ten. He peeks at his hole card and grins. By the rules, I know I should hit. But I hate chasing a strong hand with so little room to maneuver. He waits for me to make a decision, a sly grin on his old lips.

'Going to risk it?' he asks, teasing me.

'Sure.' I scratch the ground between us. 'Hit me.'

I get a seven. Twenty-two. Bust. I'm twenty down.

He deals another hand. I get eleven, and he shows a six, the weakest card he can show. By most house rules I am allowed to double down at this point. But I ask if it is OK to be sure. He nods, pleased to hit me again. I don't know what he'll do if he gets in my debt. I lay another twenty beside my turned-over cards and he deals me a card.

'A nine,' I mutter. 'Twenty. I'm sitting pretty.'

'You are pretty, Sita,' he says as he flips over his cards, showing a five, a total of elevan. He draws and gets a ten, twenty-one, beating me by one again. My forty belongs to him.

'Damn,' I mutter.

I lose the next six hands. Every decision I make is wrong, yet I am playing by the book. The published rules say I should win about half the hands. Yet I don't think he is cheating me, even though he seems to take great pleasure in taking my money. He already has two hundred bucks, two thirds of my bankroll. If I don't win soon I'll have to walk.

On the ninth hand he deals me a natural. Black-jack. He is showing only a seven. I have finally won.

He offers me a twenty. The amount I bet.

'You want it?' he asks, and there is a gleam in his eye.

'You were going to give me a tip,' I say.

'But you won. Fate favoured you, Sita, you didn't have to do anything. When a winning hand is coming around, it's going to come no matter what.' He gathers the cards together. He is down to the bottom of the deck; he has to shuffle again. He comments on the fact, as an aside. 'You know if this was a casino and I had myself a shoe, I could deal as many as six decks without shuffling. What do you think of that?'

I go completely numb.

But it will be dark angels that force him and his mother to flee to the mirror in the sky, where shoes move without feet and the emerald circle is seen in the morning light.

Lake Tahoe, I remember suddenly, was called 'the mirror in the sky' by the original Indians who lived in the area, because they had to hike up the mountain to reach it, and then, it was such a large, clear lake, it looked to them like a perfect mirror reflecting the sky. Also, there is a small but gorgeous cove in the lake called Emerald Bay. Finally, there are casinos nearby that have special shoes for playing twenty-one. As we are playing twenty-one right now, only without one of those shoes that moves without feet.

Kalika had a book on Lake Tahoe.

Mike stares at me. 'Want to play another hand?'

I slowly shake my head. 'It's not necessary, thank you.'

He nods as he reads my expression. 'I guess you'll be on your way now. I'm sorry to see you go.'

I gaze into his bright eyes. 'Are you sorry, Mike?'

He shrugs. 'I know you have a job to do. I don't want to interfere with that none. It's just that I like it when you stop by, you know. It reminds me of when I was young.'

'I'm older than I look. You must know that.'

He gives me a wistful expression. 'Well, I suppose I do. But I have to say you're still a youngster to me.'

I lean forward and hug him, and feel his bony ribs, his dirty clothes, and his love. A powerful feeling sweeps over me, as if I have finally found a member of a family I never knew existed. But the hug can last only so long.

He is right – I have a job to do. Letting go, I climb to my feet. The thought of leaving him is painful. I have to ask the next question even though I know he will not give me a straight answer.

'Will you be here when I return?'

He scratches his head and takes a sip from his milk carton. For a moment he appears slightly bewildered. He quickly counts the money he has won and stuffs it in his coat pocket. Then he coughs and looks up and down and street to see if anyone is listening. Finally he looks at me again.

'I'm sorry, Sita, I don't rightly know. I'm always moving around, like I said, trying to keep my hand in. But I hope I see you again.' He pauses. 'I like your spirit.'

I lean over and kiss his forehead.

'I like your spirit, Mike. Be here for me again. Please?'

He flashes a faint smile. 'I'll see what I can do.'

Suzama to do so. Yet the queen was wise enough not to make it a state order. Suzama refused to teach anyone who was forced into the practice. At the same time the queen instructed a large team of labourers to build a temple to Isis not far from the Great Pyramid, which Suzama refused to enter. The queen wanted an elaborate temple but Suzama persuaded her to construct a modest building, and so Suzama had her own place in which to teach within a year of the king's death. Suzama filled it with plants and flowers and different-coloured crystals brought from all over the continent.

Naturally, during this period, the Setians suffered a great setback as far as their influence was concerned. Yet the queen did not banish them from the land, because Suzama had advised her not to. I questioned my friend about not banishing them. But Suzama felt so strongly about freedom of thought that she even protected what was clearly an evil group. Yet I doubt if even Suzama knew how many assassins Ory sent to dispose of Suzama and me. Of course, none of those assassins ever returned to their leader, even when they came in groups of three and four. I seldom rested in those days and never sat with my back to a door.

But I never drank Setian blood. Just the smell of it filled me with bad feelings. The group was definitely working with subtle powers of some kind, and I began to pay more heed to their rumoured contacts with an ancient reptilian race, which they achieved through a mind-meld process that used identical twins as catalysts.

Even more important, I began to investigate their rumoured liaisons with the direct remains of the same race, which now existed on different worlds circling other suns. I knew the Setians were getting their power from somewhere else, and I wanted to find the root of it. Yet I made little progress.

Even the Setians I killed had great strength in their eyes, a magnetic field they could generate to subdue weaker wills. Naturally, their power did not work on me, but I could see the effect on the people in the city, wherever they were allowed to speak. Suzama should have been welcomed as a great prophet and the masses should have embraced her teachings, yet her following, even when her temple was complete, was relatively small. The Setians were constantly stirring up hate and lies against her.

Fortunately, Suzama did shield the queen from Ory and his cult. Queen Delar wouldn't even meet with Ory once the king died, although I did see Ory from time to time. Even though he was always polite to me, I never failed to hear the hiss of a snake beneath his breath. Why shouldn't I recognize it? In a sense we were cousins. Yaksha, a yashini by nature, had created me. And the yashinis were well known in India as a race of mystical serpents.

Yet Ory never reminded me of Yaksha, who loved Krishna above all things. And my power to influence the wills of others was much different from the power of the Setians. For their power left their victims weak and disoriented. Many never recovered from it and this power became known by the seldom spoken name of *seedling*, because it sowed seeds of consciousness that were not one's own.

I could see that matters would eventually come to a head with the Setians, only the climax came more quickly and with a destructive force greater than I could ever have imagined. Suzama was only nineteen when I received a personal invitation from Ory. He wanted to meet me alone in the desert so that we could discuss our differences and try to put an end to our conflict. This was only six days after I had slain ten of his people who had stolen into the Temple of Isis in the middle of the night. Ory had never sent so many before and I had been lucky to kill them all. Had he sent twice the number both Suzama and I would have died. Actually, I wondered why he had not, which should have served as a warning to me.

I sent back a messenger saying I would be happy to meet him.

He planned to kill me as surely as I planned to kill him.

Before heading to the desert I met with Suzama to tell her my plans. She was in her inner chamber in the temple and in a particularly reflective mood. She was writing when I entered but put aside the papyrus so that I could not see it. Her usual warm greeting was missing. Before I could speak, she wanted to know why I was dressed for the desert.

'You are wrong to think your enemies possess any virtues,' I say. 'I tire of our always having to be on guard.

I am meeting with Ory tonight deep in the desert. He has chosen the spot but I know it well. When the head vanishes, the body falls. It will end tonight.'

But Suzama shook her head. 'This is not my will. You have not asked my permission. Tonight the stars are particularly inauspicious. Cancel the meeting right now.'

I sat beside her. She almost seemed to disappear in the large silk cushions. Dressed in a simple white robe, she wore a blue scarf around her neck. Woven inside it were threads of gold that outlined all the constellations in the sky, even those seen from the bottom of the world. The latter, Suzama said, she had seen in visions. I had no doubt they were correct, even though I would not listen to her when it came to Ory. It was my turn to shake my head.

'I never told you how many of his people I slew last week,' I said.

'How many?'

'Ten.'

She grimaced. 'In here?'

'I was able to deal with most of them outside. But there will be more if I don't destroy Ory now.'

'But you don't know Ory. You don't know what he is.'

'Of course I do. He is a Setian.'

Suzama spoke gravely. 'He is a real Setian. Just as you are no longer human, he is not one of our kind. Those he sent to kill us before were mere students.' She paused. 'I suspect he is not from this world.'

'I don't care,' I say. 'If he comes alone, I can deal

141

with him. And if he doesn't, then I will know and decide what to do. But I know I must face him. It is foolish to wait.'

Suzama was reflective. 'Wisdom is not always logical.'

'Lacking your wisdom, I can only decide based on what I see and know.'

She stroked my leg, which was bare beneath my robe.

'You know, I foresaw this conversation,' she said. 'Nothing I say to you right now will change your mind. That is because of who you are and because of the stars above. They pretend to be your stars but they're not.' She paused and spoke as if she were far away. 'They are arranged as they were the night you were transformed into a vampire.'

I am shocked. 'Is this true?'

She nods solemnly. 'The serpent walked the forest. The lizard crawls in the sand. It is the same difference.' She squeezed my leg and her eyes were damp. 'Tonight is a time of transformation for you. Do you understand what I'm saying?'

'Yes. Death is the biggest transformation. Ory might kill me.'

'Yes. It is possible.'

'You don't know for sure?'

She was a long time answering.

'No. The Divine Mother does not show me.' She shook herself and came back to Earth, for a moment. She kissed the side of my face. 'Words are useless tonight, even written words. Go then, and go with light.

THE LAST VAMPIRE 5: EVIL THIRST

I will wait here for you. I will be here when you return.'

I hug her. 'I owe you a great deal. Tonight, perhaps I can repay you.'

There was a place twenty miles from the city, deep in the desert, called the Bowl of Flies. In the late spring the flies would be so thick there during the day that it would be hard to breathe without inhaling them. Yet at night they would all but vanish, and there was no reason to explain why they came at all. There was nothing for the flies to eat, unless a small animal chanced to die there. But then again, an unusual number of animals did collapse in that spot. Even a bird could seize up in midflight and fall dead into the place.

Ory wanted to meet me in the bowl.

I arrived early to see if he had assassins hidden. The area appeared empty for far around. There was no moon but I didn't need it. My eyes were not drawn to the sky as they usually were when the stars were so bright. Suzama's words continued to haunt me. She had ended our goodbye almost in midsentence. *Words are useless now.*

Ory was suddenly there, sitting on a camel.

It was strange how I hadn't heard him approach.

He got down off his animal and slowly moved towards me. I had also come on a camel but had sent my beast off. For me to run twenty miles across the desert at night was nothing. On the way home I hoped to be carrying Ory's head. Like me, he wore a long naked sword in his belt, along with his sharp dagger.

Listening closely, I could still detect no others, and I thought him a fool to meet me under such circumstances. Yet he smiled as he approached, his huge bald head shiny even in the faint starlight. It smelled as if he had oiled his skull before coming, a disgusting ointment smell.

'Sita,' he said. 'I thought maybe you would not come.'

I mocked him. 'It is not often I am granted an exclusive audience with such a renowned spiritual figure.'

'Do you know whence our spiritual power comes?'

'An unhappy place. A place without love or compassion. I do not know the name of this place, but I do know I never want to go there.'

He stood close, yet his hands stayed clear of his sword. He gestured to the sky. 'This world is not the only one. There are many kingdoms for us to rule, and I can gain you safe passage to these other places, if you will join me. I have watched you closely these last two years, Sita, and I know you are one of us. You have power, you take what you wish. You kill as a matter of course to satisfy your hunger, to satisfy your lust for life. You move without the burden of conscience. Yet you hide behind the dress of that slave fortune teller. This I do not understand.'

'I hide behind no one. Suzama is much more than a seer of the future. She sees into the hearts of men and women. She brings peace where there is pain, healing where there is sickness. The Setians do none of these things. They are interested in power for power's sake. Nothing could be more boring to me, or more

144

offensive. You think we are kin only because I am strong. But that is the only thing we have in common, and before this night is over, even that will not be true. Because you will be buried in the sand, and I will be laughing in the city as I free it of the last of your kind.'

He was amused at that. 'Does your blessed Suzama permit such killings?'

'I will tell Suzama about it after I am done.'

'And you think you could destroy all Setians so easily?'

I shrugged. 'I have had no trouble in the past.'

He came close and his smile vanished. 'You are a fool. I sent mere apprentices to test your strength. In all the time you have been in the city, you have met fewer than a handful of our secret order. And you didn't even know them when you met them. We seldom come out from the depths of the Great Pyramid. Only I, Ory, the leader regularly attends to the things of this world. But I will not share this world with another, neither you nor Suzama. It is your choice. You join us now, and swear a sacred oath to me, or you will not leave this place alive.'

I laughed. 'You keep telling me what I don't know. I tell you that you don't know what I am.' I drew my sword. 'The blood that runs in my veins is not human, but I have the strength of many humans. Draw your sword and fight me, Ory. Die like a soldier rather than a coward and fake priest who puts silly spells on unsuspecting souls.'

But he did not draw his sword. He lifted his arms upward.

A strange red light shimmered in his eyes.

His voice, as he spoke, boomed like thunder.

'Behold the night of Set, the will of those who came before humanity. It lives inside the stars that shine with the light of blood. Look up and see what force you think to defy.'

Such was the strength in his voice, that I did glance up for a moment. To my utter astonishment the night sky had changed. Above me were fresh constellations laid over the old ones. They shone with brilliant red stars that seemed to pulse like stellar hearts feeding the burning blood of one huge ravenous cosmic being. Just the sight of them filled me with nausea. How had he managed to change the heavens? He must be a powerful sorcerer, I thought.

I drew my sword and moved towards him to cut off his head.

But there was flash of green light.

The metal of my sword flowed like liquid onto the sand.

My hand burned, the flesh literally black. The pain was so excruciating that I was forced to my knees. Ory towered over me, and behind his large skull the red stars seemed to grow even brighter. It was as if a bunch of them had clustered together and begun to move towards us. Through the mist of my agony I saw them form a circle and begin to spin. The very air seemed to catch fire around them. Ory gloated over me.

'We Setians control the elements,' he said. 'That was fire, in case you didn't know. Now I will show you the earth element.'

146

He laid his big foot on my chest and kicked hard. He was many times stronger than I, I realized too late. Crashing down hard on my back, my arms spread out to my sides as if I were about to be crucified. No doubt that was the effect he was searching for. Before I could bring them back up and defend myself, the red stars over his head seemed to throb again and I heard the sand crack on both sides. For a moment it seemed alive, the very ground, liquid mud shot through with veins of brains, and I watched in horror as it reached out like a thick first and grabbed my lower arms and covered my hands. Then the sand turned to stone and I could not move. All this seemed to happen in a moment. Ory withdrew his dagger and knelt beside me and held the tip close to my eyes.

'Now you have seen a demonstration of real power,' he said.

I spat in his face. 'I am not impressed.'

He wiped away the spit and played the tip of the dagger over my eyelids. 'You are beautiful, Sita. You could have been mine. But I see now it would have been impossible to dominate you. Above all else a Setian must control those who are beneath him.'

'Kill me and be done with it. I am tired of talking to you.'

He smiled softly. 'You will not die easily. I know how quickly your wounds can heal, but I also know that a deep wound cannot heal around a dagger such as this, which is poisoned, and which will fit nicely somewhere in your barren womb.'

He stabbed me then, low down in my abdomen, and the blade burned like ice frozen from the tears of a thousand previous victims. I knew then that the stories about him and his dagger were true. He had cut out many eyes and eaten them in front of his victims. But he wouldn't blind me now because he wanted me to see the sun when it rose, and the millions of flies that would cover my body. His poison was subtle, not designed to immediately kill, but to draw out my agony.

I noticed that the red stars were no longer in the sky.

Ory stood and climbed back onto his camel.

'The earth can move as easily in the city as it can in this place,' he said. 'When the sun is high in the sky, the Temple of Isis will be buried along with your precious Suzama. You may hear the destruction even from here. Just know that the flies that feed here are always hungry, and that it will not be long before you join her.'

'Ory!' I called as he rode off.

He paused. 'Yes Sita?'

'I will see you again someday. It is not over.'

'For you it is.' He laughed as he rode away.

The sun rose and the flies came. Slowly my wound bled and steadily my pain increased. It seemed as if the desert wind were fire and the sky rained darts. The sound of the many flies sucking on my blood was enough to drive me mad. The filthy insects polluted my soul as much as my wound. All I had to look forward to was the midday sun, when my friend would die. I had a feeling I would hear something.

The day wore on. Breathing became a nightmare. Existence itself was the greatest torture. How I prayed to die then, for the first time ever. How I cursed Krishna. Where was his fabled grace now? I had not disobeyed him. Only he had set me up before an unstoppable foe. There was no hope for the world, I realized. The Setians were worse than a million vampires. And they were spreading across the stars.

The sun reached its high point. It was a red sun.

The interior of my skull began to boil and I heard myself scream.

Then the noise came, waves of rolling thunder. The ground began to shake, then to dance, tearing apart at the seams. The frozen sand that bound my arms and legs cracked, and I would have been able to stand if the entire desert had not suddenly been transformed into a torrential ocean. What had Ory set in motion? The elements had gone insane. The earth believed it was water. Beyond the Bowl of Flies I heard sand dunes pitch and break like waves upon a shore.

Then it stopped and all was silent.

Pulling out the dagger, I brushed off the flies and crawled out of the bowl. When I reached the upper rim, I stared at a desert I did not recognize.

It was entirely flat.

Slowly, for me, my wound healed.

Somehow I managed to stagger back to the city. Ory's poison was still in my veins but maybe it had lost some of its potency. When the city finally came into view, I saw that Ory's day had passed, as had Suzama's.

Either Ory had lost control of his precious earth element or else Suzama had seized control of it at the last moment and stuffed it down his throat. The worship of Isis and Set was over for that time.

A gash in the earth as thick as the Great Pyramid had opened up and swallowed the bulk of the city. The pyramid and all the other temples were gone. Those buildings that had not fallen into the chasm were nevertheless flattened. A handful of survivors stumbled around in the midst of this destruction but few looked as if they still possessed their wits.

I searched for Suzama but never found her.

Not long afterward I left Egypt.

16 ~~~

We cannot get a flight to Lake Tahoe or even into Reno. San Francisco is our next best choice. The four of us, Seymour, James, Dr Seter, and I, fly to San Francisco and rent a car in the Bay Area. Airport security has not allowed us to take weapons with us, so along the way, close to ten o'clock, I have the others wait while I break into a gun shop and steal two shotguns and several rounds of ammunition. James seems impressed when I get back to the car. He sits up front with me while Seymour talks to Dr Seter in the backseat. The doctor is not looking good, and I wonder if he suffered a mild heart attack the previous night.

'How did you get into the store?' James asks as we race back onto the freeway and head east at high speed.

'I picked the lock,' I say, doing the driving.

'Did an alarm go off?' James asks.

'Not one that I could hear.' I glance over my shoulder. 'Do you need to use the restroom, Dr Seter? There's a gas station a couple of miles ahead.'

His face is ghastly white but he shakes his head. 'We don't have time. We have to get there before she does.' He pauses. 'I'm still furious at myself that I didn't allow you to see all of the scripture the first night. How were you able to decipher the clues as to the child's location so quickly?'

'I had a little help,' I say.

'From whom?' James asks.

'You wouldn't believe me if I told you.'

'I think everyone in this car is ready to believe anything,' Seymour mutters.

'Ain't that the truth,' Dr Seter says.

Yet I hesitate to talk about Mike. 'A little bird helped me.'

James gently persists. 'Does this bird have a name?'

I give him a look. 'Not that I can remember.'

We reach the mountains surrounding Lake Tahoe and I plow up the winding road that leads to the lake. The others sit, clutching the ceiling grips; I have rented a Lexus sports coupe and I push the car to its limit. Dr Seter looks as if he will vomit over the backseat but he doesn't complain. There's too much at stake.

As we come over the rim of the mountain and see the lake, I smell Kalika. I am surprised at my own surprise because I should have expected her to be here, but in reality I didn't. Yet I still don't think she has deciphered Suzama's code before me. On the contrary, I think she is following us, using some invisible psychic tracking. I believe she still waits to see what moves we'll make next. And this is a paradox for me because I realize I might endanger the child most by trying to find it to protect it. Certainly there must have been a reason why my daughter has left so many of us alive. She didn't know where I was when I was at the hospital with the child. Yet she knew where I was when I was living in Pacific Palisades with Seymour. I have to wonder if the child has a mystical shield around him that Kalika can't pierce but maybe I can.

It may not matter.

If I can smell her, she can see us.

But I cannot have come this far just to turn away from the child. I cannot trust in my theories. I only know that if I can find Paula and her baby I can take them to some safe place. That is logical; it is something I can envision without employing the wisdom or intuition of Suzama. Starting downhill, I floor the accelerator and turn towards Emerald Bay.

We reach it twenty minutes later.

The spot is one of the most enchanting in all of nature. The bay is maybe two hundred yards across, sheltered on three sides by majestic cliffs with tall pines hugging them. The isthmus is narrow, giving the bay excellent shelter from the lake itself, which can get rough in stormy weather. There is a tiny island in the centre of the water, a place for children to play and adults to relax. Even at midnight, beneath the brilliant moon, the circular bay is magical. But tonight it is silver, not emerald. Silver like the dagger Ory stabbed in me.

For some reason, I have to remind myself that that was long ago.

My abdomen cramps and I brush away a fly that has entered the car.

The odour of Kalika overpowers my other senses. Truly, since being touched by Yaksha's blood, my sense of smell has become my most potent weapon. Rolling down my window all the way, I use my nose like a needle on a compass, and it doesn't fail me. It points in only one direction, towards a small wooden house set on redwood stilts above an abandoned stone church at the floor of the cliff, not far above the water. The place is almost hidden in the trees, but I see it.

I drive faster.

I stop some distance from the house. The road we're on circles all of Lake Tahoe but at this place it is three hundred yards up the side of the mountain. Grabbing a shotgun and ignoring the others, I slip six shells into it. The remainder of the ammunition is in the box that I stuff into my pocket. Popping open the driver's door, I am almost outside when James grabs my arm.

'Where are you going?' he demands.

'Some things you can't help me with,' I say.

'Alisa,' Seymour says. The others only know me by that name.

'It has to be this way.' I shake off James. 'Stay and take care of one another. She may come this way yet.'

I don't give them a chance to respond. Jumping out of the car, I run around the bend, and the moment I am out of sight I switch into hypermode. The tangled trees and uneven boulders don't even slow me. I reach the house in thirty seconds.

The front door has already been kicked in.

Kalika was watching which way my nose turned.

Inside I find Paula staring out a window that overlooks Emerald Bay. There is a small boat on the cold water, with an outboard motor softly churning through the night, heading away from us. Grabbing Paula from behind, I turn her around.

'Did she take the child?' I demand.

Pretty dark-haired Paula is the colour of dirty snow.

'Yes,' she says with a dry voice.

'Stay here.' I pump my shotgun. 'I will get him back.'

The next moment finds me outside, running along the edge of the bay. In places this is difficult because the sides are sheer stone. When I come to such a spot I jump higher for any inch of ledge that will support my feet and keep running. Kalika's outboard motor is not very strong. I reach the isthmus seconds before her boat does. Dressed in a long white coat, the baby wrapped in a white blanket on her knees, she looks up at me as I raise my shotgun and take aim at her bow. She is only fifty yards away. Her eyes shimmer with the glow of the moon and she doesn't seem to be surprised. The baby talks softly to her, infant nonsense. He is not afraid, but fear is almost all I know as I sight along the barrel and squeeze the trigger.

The blast of the shotgun echoes across the bay.

I have blown a hole in the front of the boat.

Water gushes in. Kalika grabs the handle of the outboard and turns the boat around. For a moment her back is to me, an easy shot. Yet I don't take it. I tell myself there is a chance I might hit the child. At first Kalika seems to be headed back towards the beach below Paula's house, but then it is clear the miniature island in the centre of the bay is her goal. Perhaps the water is gushing in too fast. Kalika picks up the child and hugs him to her chest even before the boat reaches the island. Then she is up and out of the sinking craft, scampering up the dirt path that leads to a small abandoned house at the top of the island. Sliding the shotgun under my black leather coat, I drive off the low cliff and into the water.

The lake temperature is bracing, even for me. But vampires never like the cold, although we can tolerate it far better than human beings can. My stroke is hampered by my clothes and gun, but I reach the island in less than a minute. Shivering on the beach in the rays of the moon, I remove the shotgun and pump another round into the chamber. There is a good chance it will still fire. If it doesn't then this will be the last moonlit night of my life.

I find Kalika sitting on a bench in the stone house at the top of the island. It is not properly a house, more an open collection of old walls. Last time I was here a guide told me people came here for tea during the Second World War. Kalika sits with the baby on her lap, playing with him, oblivious of me and my shotgun. I feel I have to say something. Of course I am not fooled. I keep my weapon held ready.

Yet maybe I am the biggest fool of all.

'It is over,' I say. 'Set the child down.'

Kalika doesn't even look up. 'The floor is cold. He might catch cold.'

I shake my gun. 'I am serious.'

'That is your problem.'

'Kalika—'

'Do you know what name Paula gave the child?' she interrupts.

'No. I didn't stop to ask her.'

'I think she named him John. That's what I've been calling him.' Finally she looks at me. 'But you know Mike, don't you?'

I am bewildered. 'Yes. Have you spoken to him?'

'No. But I know him. He's a bum.' She lifts the child to her breast. Kalika has a voluptuous figure; she could probably bear many healthy children. God knows what they would be like. She strokes the baby's soft skull. 'I think we have company.'

'What are you talking about?'

'Your friend is coming.'

'Good,' I say, although I don't hear anyone approaching. 'More reason for you to surrender the child.' I grow impatient. 'Put him down!'

'No.'

'I will shoot.'

'No, you won't.'

'You murdered two dozen innocent people. You ripped their hearts and heads off right in front of my eyes and you think I can still care for you? Well, you're wrong.' I step closer and aim the shotgun at her face. 'You are not immortal. If I fire and your brains splatter the wall behind you, then you will die.'

She stares at me. We are out of the moonlight. There should be no light in her dark eyes at all. Nevertheless they shine with a peculiar white glow. I had thought it was red the last time I saw them during our confrontation on the pier. But maybe the colour is not hers but mine. Maybe she is just a mirror for me, Kali Ma, the eternal abyss, who destroys time itself. My mother myself. I cannot look at her with the child and not think of when she was a baby.

'The body takes birth and dies,' she says. 'The eternal self is unmoved.'

I shake my shotgun angrily. 'You will move for me, goddamn you!'

Kalika smiles. She wants to say something.

But suddenly there is a blade at my throat.

'I will take that shotgun,' James says softly in my ear.

I am surprised but not terribly alarmed.

'James,' I say patiently, 'I am not going to shoot the child.'

He presses the blade tighter and forces my head back.

'I know that, Sita,' he says calmly. 'I still want the gun.'

I swallow. Now I am concerned.

'How do you know my name?' I ask.

He grips the shotgun and carefully lifts it from my hands.

'We have met before,' he says. 'You just don't remember me.'

'She remembers,' Kalika says, standing now, her expression unfathomable.

James points the shotgun at her while he keeps the blade at my throat. Out of the corner of my eye I get a glimpse of it. A dagger of some kind, ancient design, cold metal. James is calm and cool. He gestures with the tip of the shotgun.

'You will set the child down on the bench beside you,' he says to my daughter. 'If you don't I will shoot, and you know I won't miss. Either of you.'

Kalika does not react.

James scrapes me lightly with the knife and my throat bleeds.

'I will kill your mother,' he says. 'You will have to watch her die.'

A shadow crosses Kalika's face. 'No,' she says.

James smiles. 'You know me. You know I do not bluff.'

Kalika nods slightly. Really, it is as if she knows him well.

'All right,' she says in a soft, perhaps beaten, voice.

'Do it!' James orders.

Kalika turns to set the child down. The baby is almost out of her hands when I see her change her mind. Maybe James sees the same thing, I don't know. But he is ready for her when she suddenly grabs the baby and bolts. Kalika moves extraordinarily fast but James is no slouch when it comes to reflexes.

He shoots her in the lower back.

Kalika staggers but manages to hold on to the child. Keeping his blade tight to my throat, he pumps the shotgun again and takes aim. It is then I ram an elbow into his side. He seems ready for that as well, because even though I have hurt him, he manages to draw the blade all the way across my throat. And he doesn't just nick me. Suddenly my life's blood is pouring over my chest and James has got Kalika in his sights again and there is absolutely nothing I can do to stop him.

James shoots Kalika in the back, behind the heart.

Kalika is covered in blood. She tries to turn, perhaps to attack, but seeing James pumping again, she puts her back to him once more. He fires a third time, hitting her right shoulder. Kalika slumps to the floor, her right arm useless now. Still she manages to hold on to the child, to shelter him from the blasts that ravage her body. As I collapse to the floor, James pumps again and points the shotgun at Kalika's head, actually touching her left temple with the black barrel. He still has the dagger in his right hand and I finally recognize it.

Ory's knife. I feel his poison once more in my system.

I even recognize Ory's voice when James speaks next. Funny how I didn't before. Too bad, huh.

'I just want the child,' James says to my daughter.

She stares up at him. 'Your kind never wants just one thing.'

He pulls the trigger back dangerously far.

'You missed me at the condo,' he says. 'That was your chance. But you will have no more chances if you do not do what I say. Nor will the child.'

Kalika stares up at him a moment.

Then she hands him the baby with her left arm.

He takes the infant in his knife arm.

He turns to walk away.

Kalika tries to get up.

'No!' I gasp, choking on my own blood.

James pivots and shoots her directly in the heart. Stunned, she staggers back. He pumps again and shoots her in the exact same spot. Her chest cavity literally explodes. Her white coat and white dress are a mess of red tissue and torn threads. Reaching out a feeble left arm, trying to give it one last desperate try, she suddenly closes her eyes and falls face first on the floor. James stares down at her for a moment and then drops the shotgun and kneels beside me. The infant's face is only inches from my own but I am unable to reach out and touch him. The baby seems worried, but James looks as if he is having a good time.

'What did you tell me?' he asks. '"I will see you again someday. It is not over."' He pauses. 'Yeah, I think that was it. Well, at least you were half right.'

I drown in red blood. My voice bubbles out.

'How?'

'How am I here again in a different body? That is a Setian secret, isn't it? But to tell you the truth I never left. Oh, I have transferred many times, into many forms, but that is a small trick for beings such as ourselves.' He glances at motionless Kalika. 'It is a pity your daughter had to destroy my entire crop of new apprentices. But there will be more from where they came.'

'What?' I whisper.

He chuckles. 'What am I going to do with the child now that you have led me to him? Honestly, you don't want to know. Better you go to your grave with no horrific image in your pretty head.' He raises the dagger. 'Where do you want me to put in the poison? It is a new and improved brand. It is guaranteed to kill even the strongest of vampires. And slowly.'

'Go to hell,' I gasp.

'Sita, I just came from there.'

He stabs me in midback and leaves the blade in.

I am too weak to pull it out. To find it, even.

James stands and walks away with the child.

Finally, I hear the infant begin to cry.

17 ~

Red, searing pain and black despair. These two colours, these two forms of torture, are all I know for the next few minutes. It is not as if I lose sight of the room, it is just that I see it from another angle. A place of pain and judgment where my soul floats above the boiling cauldron I am sure is waiting for me on the other side. To realize I have been working all along for the enemy, that I was in fact their greatest ally, is too much for me. Death, if it would just involve oblivion, would be more than welcome. But I know there must be a special hell prepared for the one who sold the messiah to the jackal.

From far away I feel something moist and warm touch my lips.

It tastes like blood, very sweet blood, but it is such a

potent elixir that I swear I have never encountered it before. Before my mind knows it, my body is hungrily licking the substance. The flow of blood that has been steadily dripping from my throat finally begins to slow. At first I think it is because my body is running out of blood, but then I realize I am healing, which should be impossible with a severed neck, a knife in my back, and Setian poison pumping in my veins. Yet after a time my vision clears and I am able to see normally.

My daughter lies beside me.

She is feeding me her own blood with her cupped palm.

For a moment I think that means she is recovering. But then I see that her horrible wounds have not healed at all. My eyes register my sorrow but she smiles even now.

'There is only enough life left for you,' she says.

I push her hand away. 'You mustn't. You are the only hope.'

'You are.' She forces more of her blood down my throat and then rolls me on my side. There is a sharp pain in my back as she pulls out Ory's dagger. I still feel the poison in my system, however, crawling through my veins and feeding on my internal organs. Kalika opens the vein on her wrist and forces me to feed, and it is as if the current of her life energy overwhelms the poison, and I feel it die inside me. A peaceful warmth steals over my physical form. Already I think the wound in my throat has closed. Yet inside I am still in torment. Even as I sit up Kalika seems to lose strength and lies back down. The massive wound to her chest is still open and I cringe because I worry I may actually see her heart beating, or slowing down. I don't know, of course. I do try to open my vein to drip my blood over her wound, but she stops me.

'It's too late,' she says.

This death I cannot bear.

'No,' I moan.

'You see I did not want to harm the child. I just wanted to protect him from the Setians.'

'That's why you came into this world?'

'Yes.' She raises her left hand and touches my hair. 'And to be your daughter.'

The tears on my face are so red. They will stain my skin, I think, and I will carry the burden of this loss the rest of my days, out where people can see it. I want to bury my face in her chest but I am afraid I will hurt her more. So I take the hand she touches me with and I kiss it.

'I should have listened to you,' I say.

'Yes.'

'You never hurt the police, did you?'

'No.'

'And you knew Eric had a fatal illness?'

'Yes. His suffering would have been worse if I had not killed him.'

My voice is choked. 'You should have told me.'

This amuses her. 'You hear what you wish. You are more human than you know. But that is your greatest strength as well. Krishna loves all humanity as his children.'

'Who is the child, Kalika? Is he Krishna? Is he Christ?'

Her voice is weak, her gaze far away. 'He is like me, the essence of all things. A name, a title, does not describe him. Divisions are for men. God knows only one being.'

'Does the child need my help to survive?'

She is a long time answering. Her eyes are focused on the ceiling.

'You will help him. That is why you were born.'

Sobs rack my body. 'All this time you never lied to me.'

That makes her look at me. 'Once I did. When I told you I would not let you stand in my way to the child.' A spasm shakes her body and I hear her heart skip as she begins to die. 'I could never hurt you, Sita.'

'How do I stop Ory?'

'Your age-old weapons, strength and cunning, will not do it.'

'But what will?'

'Faith is stronger than stone,' she whispers.

'The scripture.' I am confused. 'But it spoke against you.'

That makes her smile. 'Parts Suzama wrote. Parts Ory wrote to make it look like Suzama's writing.'

'The papyrus about you was of a different texture.'

'Yes. You cannot believe everything you read, even when it is supposed to be scripture.' A convulsion suddenly grips her body and her back arches off the floor. My tears are a river. Five thousand years of life and death have not prepared me for this. To see my own daughter die, all because of me – how cruel the irony is. Yet Kalika, with her failing strength, pulls my hand down and kisses my fingers. 'Words cannot inspire faith. Only love can destroy the maya.'

'Is this just an illusion to you? Even your own death?'

She squeezes my hand and her eyes are bright.

'You are no illusion. I really am your daughter.' A sigh escapes her lips and her eyes close. Inside her chest I hear her heart stop, but there is air left in her lungs, and she says in that special soft voice of hers, 'I love you, Mother.'

Those are her last words.

She is gone, back to the abyss from which she came.

Another death, another farewell, waits for me on the shore, on the beach beneath Paula's house. There I find Dr Seter slumped against a stone wall, his skin the blue colour of a failing cardiac patient's. Seymour and Paula are nowhere to be seen. Dr Seter has had a major heart attack and I do not have to stretch my imagination to figure out how he got it. James returned with the child and revealed that he was not a nice and kind son, after all. As I kneel beside the doctor, he opens his eyes and gasps for air.

'You're bleeding,' he says.

I am soaked with blood but I am no longer bleeding.

'I am all right.' I put a hand on his chest and feel his erratic pulse. 'Can I get you a doctor?' I know that will not help him, and am relieved when he shakes his head.

'I am finished,' he says, and his face is so sad. 'I never knew.'

'I didn't either.'

He is bitter. 'Suzama lied to us both.'

'No. Most of the scripture was true. James only created the part that dealt with Kalika.' I pause. 'She was my daughter.'

He is amazed. 'Where is she now?'

'On the island. She's dead.' I sigh. 'We were fools.'

He weeps for my pain. 'I was the fool. It was my arrogance that made me believe God was giving me visions. That I understood the mind of God.' He coughs. 'James put those dreams in my mind. He led me to the scripture.'

I nod. 'He led you to where he buried it.'

'But why would he do these things? How could he do them?'

'He was never your son. He only came into your life to use you. He possesses the body of the young man we see. He is neither young nor is he human. Please do not blame yourself, Dr Seter. I fought with this creature long ago and I did not recognize him. If anyone is to blame it is I.'

He stares up at me. 'Who are you, Alisa?'

'I am your friend.' I hug him. 'And I will get the child back.'

My words seem to comfort him. He dies a minute later but there is peace written on his face. He was a good man, I know.

Paula stands behind me.

'Sita,' she says gently.

I turn and look at her. Around her neck she wears a blue scarf with gold threads running through it. These threads make a wonderful design, but I am in too much of hurry to pay it much heed. Letting go of Dr Seter, I stand and step to her side.

'I know where the enemy is taking your child,' I say.

She nods. She believes me, she always has. Such faith.

'Your friend,' she says.

I grab her arms. 'Seymour!'

She nods her head to the side. 'He is out front. He has been shot.'

'Is he dead?' I ask.

She hesitates. 'He is close.'

I gaze at the small island in the centre of Emerald Bay. I had swum back ashore. It had not been easy to leave my daughter's body.

'Find a boat,' I say to Paula. 'That was my daughter who took your child, but she was only trying to protect him. Her body is on the island, in the house. Please bring her back here and wrap her in a blanket until I return.' I turn away. 'I will take care of Seymour.'

She stops me. 'I will help you with your friend first.'

I shake my head. 'No, Paula. I have to be alone with him to help him.'

There are tears in her eyes. 'Your daughter gave her life to save John?'

'Yes. She gave more than any of us knew.'

Seymour lies on his side in a pool of blood fifty yards up the hill from Paula's house, wedged cruelly between two large rocks. James had shot him in the stomach. One close-range blast was enough. He is unconscious and slipping away fast. The child is gone, and this time I do not have the mystery and magic of the universe in a convenient vial in my pocket. The only way I can save him is to grant his oldest wish. That I will do for him because I love him, and I know Krishna will forgive me. Indeed, if I can only find the child again, and give him a chance to grow old enough to understand me, then I can ask him to take away my vow. Leaning over, I open a vein and whisper in Seymour's ear.

'Now, old buddy, just because you're going to be a vampire doesn't mean you automatically get to sleep with me. We'll have to date first.'

I give him my blood. It is all I have to give.

18 ⤳

The next evening, at sunset, I arrive at the bluff in the desert where the child was conceived. The tall Joshua trees stand around me like guards that would offer me help if they could. But there is no one to help me. Even my own strength and cunning cannot aid me if I am to believe my daughter and Suzama.

I have brought the dagger James stuck into me.

It is my only weapon, pitiful as it is.

Faith is stronger than stone.

James will not simply murder the child. The divine blood is as important to a demon as it is to a saint. Only the two do not make the same use of it. I know he will have to bring the child to this spot. He did not locate the Suzama Centre in Palm Springs, so close to this place, by coincidence. Plus my old friend has said as much.

Then the place of sanctity will be defiled by red stars, and only the innocent will see the blue light of heaven.

Am I the innocent? At the moment I feel far from it. I know Kalika told me that my thoughts blinded me but I still cannot stop thinking how she let James get so close to the child when she clearly knew what he was and where he was. Of course it could be argued that I stopped her from fleeing, yet in the last minutes of her mysterious life she was content to quit running and sit and play with the child to let what was to be be. James clearly used me to defeat Kalika; he could not have done it alone. Yet Kalika let herself be defeated. Was it because she wished to fulfill the ancient prophecy?

There the dark forces will once again converge on him, but a powerful angel of mistaken colour will rescue him only to lose him again.

No one mistook Kalika more than her own mother.

But what am I to do now?

The rest is a mystery.

For once, I wish Suzama had hinted a little more.

What am I to have faith in? I do not miss the fact that Suzama placed faith and stone together in the same sentence, since it was Ory's control of the earth element that allowed him to defeat me the last time. All right, I have faith in the child. He seems like a cute little guy with incredible vibes and a darling smile. I love him, I really do, and I only got to hold him for a short time. But what am I supposed to do with this faith? It seems I should be able to use it somehow.

The sun slowly sets. The stars come out.

The moon has yet to rise.

I stare at the stars and pray for them to help me.

Then I realize something quite extraordinary.

The last time I went to see Suzama, she was wearing a blue scarf that had gold threads woven in it depicting the constellations in the sky, both the northern and the southern sky. Last night Paula was wearing a blue scarf as well, also woven with a pattern in gold thread. In fact, the more I think about it, the more convinced I am that the scarves are identical.

I am hardly given a chance to wonder how that could be possible.

Because something strange starts to happen.

The more I visualize those hauntingly beautiful star patterns in Suzama's scarf the brighter the stars above me grow. And what is even stranger is that this experience has already been described to me by Paula.

'The sky was filled with a million stars. They were so bright! I could have been in outer space . . . It was almost as if I had been transported to another world, inside a huge star cluster, and was looking up at its nighttime sky.'

The stars grow so bright I can feel their energy on the top of my head, streaming down into my whole body. One star in particular, a bright blue one straight overhead, seems to soar in brilliance as I look up and concentrate on it. It grows in size. It could be a blue saucer racing toward the earth. A high-pitched sound starts to vibrate through the area. Paula's words are still in my mind.

'The rays of the star pierced my eyelids. The sound pierced

my ears. I wanted to scream. Maybe I was screaming. But I don't think I was in actual physical pain. It was more as if I was being transformed.'

I think I am screaming too. This is how it felt when the moon would pour into the top of my head and turn me into a nice friendly ghost that could float off on the desert wind. But this vibration is thousands of times more intense. It feels as if the starlight is irradiating the nerve fibres in my spinal cord, changing them into magnetic circuits on a cosmic grid, a stellar system of communication and propulsion that has been there since the beginning of time, even though no one imagined it existed. I only have to want to plug into it to be able to use it. At the same time, I don't know if I am in physical distress. Blissful terror is a better expression for it; the entire experience is destroying everything that I thought is me, and yet there is relief in the destruction as well. But just when I think I will either explode or turn into a galactic android, it stops.

Unlike Paula I do not black out.

I am suddenly floating high above the desert.

In a glistening blue body.

It is very nice. This body, this state of being, carries none of the burdens of the physical realm. I am quite content just to float around with the stars. I can still see the desert far below, the rolling hills of sand, the edges of the shadows of the tall Joshuas shimmering under the intoxicating rays of the galaxy's stars. I realize then how crucial a role the stars play in our lives, their constant subtle influence bubbles on the edges of energy fields we are unaware we possess. Yet I do not think about it too much because I cannot be bothered thinking.

After some time I become aware that there is a highly dense bundle of red energy descending from above. Just the sight of it fills me with revulsion and I want to get out of its way. It is the opposite of what I am; it is neither love nor bliss. I desire to avoid it at all costs and I know that I merely have to will myself to be gone.

It is only then that I fully remember who I am.

The transformation had caused me momentary amnesia.

I remember why I have come to the desert. The child.

Far below me, I see James holding the baby. He is encapsulated in the same red light, but the baby glows in his arms like a tiny blue star. My awareness goes up and down, back and forth between them. As the red energy bundle comes closer I see that it is taking on substance, gaining the vague shape of a flying saucer. It seems as if from an unseen realm I am presented with a choice. I can try to enter this ship, in my blue body, and stop what is being planned by the Setians, or I can simply float away and be happy. Yet if I choose the former course, there is danger. I can become trapped, I sense. My very soul can be chained in a place of demons.

Because if I go into the ship I will have to go into a demon.

The choice, the universe seems to say, is mine.

I think of Kalika then, of her great sacrifice.

This thought makes the choice for me.

I float into the ship.

It is a vessel of serpents. There are six of them, big ugly brutes with long tails and scaly hides, thick snouts and cold, dead eyes, all sitting around a square viewing port and each manipulating controls of some kind. But one is clearly in charge. Besides being the largest, he has the most highly charged energy field. He is like a swollen red sun from the wrong side of the galaxy. And I know he is the one I have to attack.

In a moment I am inside his body.

His mind. What a pit it is.

This is a true Setian, a genuine demon. His lusts and passions seem to spin in a vortex, yet he is highly intelligent and has worked long and hard to attain the rank he now holds. He is being sent by his superiors on this important mission to bring back the human avatar, the crowning jewel of all prizes. If he is successful, he will be given an opportunity to consume the energy of the child with his masters. His name is Croka and he lives off the emotions of hate and fear. They are food to him as humans are food to him. He can consume the holy child and be strengthened by him. On his home world, I see that black ceremonies will be performed to prepare the feast.

But Croka is not yet aware that I am in his mind.

The ship lands in the desert and the six Setians climb out into the night air. Still inside Croka I move with them. Yet I know this ship, these creatures even, are not really physical. The average human, if he or she were to pass this spot, would see nothing, yet he or she would most certainly feel a great dread. Simply to be inside Croka's mind is a torture as great as any that I have ever known. It is as bad as seeing my own daughter die. Yet I am now determined that her death will not be in vain.

James can see the Setians. He bows as they sit in a semicircle around him. He stands respectfully, the child in his hands. Little John gazes at them in wonder, the red light cracking and sparking around his blue aura. Clearly the baby can see them, yet he does not cry out. The reptilian Setians are large; even though they are sitting, their ugly heads rise above James's. The one farthest from Croka bids James bring the child closer. It seems the monster wants to gloat over it, paw it even, and this to me is unbearable. Yet I know the creature will not really harm it. The feast is planned for later, on the Setian hell planet.

James brings the child to each beast, and each one pokes at it a bit. The child does not cry out and this seems to annoy both the visitors and James. Finally it is brought to Croka, but before he can touch it my eyes fasten on the child's eyes, and so, in effect, the Setian commander's eyes are also focused, against his will actually, on the same spot, on the profound gaze of the infant. It is only then that Croka becomes aware that I am sitting deep within his mind, and I understand that this is the moment of greatest danger. For Croka, like most advanced Setians, is a master of *seedling*, the manipulation of will, and I feel his furious will suddenly rise up against mine.

He reaches for me too late, because I already have the *kavach* of the child's gaze, the armor or protection of the avatar, and seedling loses all power in the presence of a saint. Like Ory of old, Croka carries a dagger in his silver belt, and I reach for it with Croka's own arm. Before the Setian can stop me, before James even knows what I am up to, I stab the blade in James's left eye.

Then all at once I am back in my vampiric body.

Back in the desert with only James and the child standing before me. The saucer and the Setians appear to be gone. But James is in pain, and I realize that I have already stabbed his *own* knife into his eye. Well, I think, this time I must have come out of nowhere on him. Quickly, before he can recover, I withdraw the knife and poke it in his other eye, effectively blinding him. He howls in pain and the blood that pours from his wounds is black and foul smelling.

He drops the child and puts his hands over his torn eyes.

I catch the child before he hits the ground and set him down gently.

Then I turn back to James.

'Jimmy,' I say sweetly, 'where do you want me to put the poison? It is a new and improved brand. Guaranteed to kill even a slimy lizard like you.'

He swings at me with his right arm and misses, spinning helplessly in front of me, and I stab the knife in his spine behind his heart, just where he shot my daughter. Screaming in agony, he falls to his knees and bows his head. His flaying hands desperately strain to pull out the knife but I know just how powerful the poison is, soaked deep in the folds of the blade itself. He is already doomed.

'Sita,' he gasps. 'You don't understand what this moment means to this part of the galaxy. You can't interfere.'

I laugh. 'Are you talking about your lizard friends? They are probably still here right now. I'm sure they are, but they don't have a physical body like mine. They have to work through scummy agents like you. And right now their poor agent can't even see well enough to tie his own shoes. Oh my.'

His face is a mass of black blood. Yet it is as if he is weeping.

'You can't do this,' he says. 'This night was planned for ages.'

I kick him and he cries out again.

'Yeah?' I say. 'Who planned tonight for ages? Not Suzama. Not me. I just wish there were a swarm of flies here and I had the luxury of killing you slowly. But I have other things to do right now.' I grab him by his mane of messy hair and pull his head back, exposing his throat. 'This, I am going to enjoy.'

'Wait!' he cries. 'I have not completed my mission! I will not be allowed to transfer to another body!'

I pull out the dagger impaled in his spine.

'James,' I say. 'I honestly don't care.'

'Stop!' he screams. 'I don't want to die!'

Ah, there is a divine sweetness to total revenge.

God might not agree but I would argue the point.

'Then you should never have been born,' I say.

His blood, when I open his neck, flows like black ink.

There is a loud hiss in my ear. The wind tugs at my hair.

A flash of red light momentarily blurs the stars.

The Setians have left, and in a hurry.

I let go of James and he falls dead on the sand.

Drawing in a deep breath of fresh air, I laugh out loud.

The child laughs with me as I carry him back to the road.

I think he likes me. Really, he is so cute.

book six

CREATURES
OF
FOREVER

And for Jambi, wherever she may be

1 〜

I am a very powerful vampire. In the recent past several encounters have served to increase my abilities. My creator, Yaksha, allowed me to drink his blood before he perished. Yaksha, who originally made me a vampire five thousand years ago, was much stronger than I was. His final transfusion of blood heightened my strength as well as my senses, both my physical senses and supernatural ones. After that my blood was mingled, through the secret of ancient alchemy, with that of the divine child. I am not exactly sure what this child's blood did for me because I am still not sure what this child can do. Yet it did make me feel stronger, definitely more invincible. Finally, before she died, my own daughter Kalika gave me her blood in order to save me. And this last infusion has done amazing things for me.

Really, I feel I have become my daughter, the irreproachable Kali avatar, and am capable of anything. The feeling is both reassuring and disturbing. With all this increase in power, I have to wonder if I have grown any wiser.

I am still up to my old tricks.

Killing for kicks, and for love.

In a sense, since vampires are considered dead by living beings, I killed my friend, Seymour Dorsten, by making him a vampire. But I only did this to prevent his certain death. I have to wonder if Lord Krishna will forgive me this – the third exception to my vow to him. I question if I am still protected by his divine grace. Actually, I wonder if Krishna has allowed me to become so powerful because he no longer intends to look after me. It would be just like him, to bestow a boon and a curse in the same act. God has a wicked sense of humour. I once met Krishna and still think about him.

At present I sit in a bar in Santa Monica with Seymour on the stool beside me. We are drinking Cokes and chatting with a young lady, but Seymour is thinking of blood and sex. I know his thoughts because, since drinking my daughter's blood, my mental radar has become incredibly sensitive. Before I could only sense emotions, now I get all the particulars. And I know that while Seymour flirts with the young lady, the guy at the end of the bar, with the swan tattoo on his left wrist and the shine on his black wing tips, is thinking of murder.

I have been watching this guy since I sat down, quietly reading his mind. He has killed twice in the last month and tonight he wants to make it number three. He prefers helpless young females, who silently scream as he slowly strangles them. But even though I try to catch his eye – smiling, winking – I am not successful and that puzzles me. I mean, I am cute and helpless looking, with my long blond hair and clear blue eyes, my tight blue jeans and my expensive black leather coat. But I intend to kill this guy, oh yes, before the night is through. He will die as slowly as his victims, and I will not feel a twinge of guilt.

'So what do you do when you're not partying?' the girl asks Seymour. She is pretty in a lazy sort of way, with short red hair that has been cut to mimic that of a popular magazine model, and nervous glossy lips that need to be moving, either talking or drinking. She is currently drunk but I do not judge her. Her name is Heidi and I know to Seymour she is the second cutest thing in the world. Since becoming a vampire, he has conquered his virginity and then some. But I haven't slept with him, and I suppose that is why I'm still a goddess in his eyes. Seymour leans close to Heidi and smiles sweetly.

'I'm a vampire,' he says. 'Every night is a party to me.'

Heidi clasps her hands together and laughs heartily. 'I love vampires,' she says. 'Is your sister one as well?'

'No,' I interrupt. 'I have a day job.'

'She works undercover for the LAPD,' Seymour

continues. 'She's really good, too. Last week she caught this thief in the act and blew off the back of his head.'

Heidi frowns, her lower lips twitching. 'Do you carry a gun?' she asks me.

I sip my Coke. 'No. My hands are lethal weapons.' I know Seymour intends to sleep with this girl, and I don't mind. But I don't want him to use his eyes to manipulate her into bed. This is a warning I have repeatedly given him, that his vampiric will cannot be used to dominate human will in order to gain sex. To me, that is just another form of rape, and so far Seymour has obeyed my rule. Also, I have forbidden him to drink from his conquests. He lacks the skill and control to stop feeding before he kills a person. For that reason, when he has to drink blood, he does so with me beside him. But unlike Ray, Seymour is not squeamish about blood. He loves being a vampire so much so that he should have been born one.

'Do you know karate?' Heidi asks me.

'She is a walking Kung Fu machine,' Seymour gushes.

I stand and cast Seymour a hard look. 'I am going to go talk to this guy at the end of the bar. I'll meet up with you later. OK?'

Seymour understands that I intend to kill this guy. He is not squeamish about blood, but death still disturbs him. We have never actually killed any of his meals. He pales slightly and lifts his glass.

'Let me know what you're up to,' he says.

'Good luck,' Heidi exclaims as I step past.

'Thank you,' I say.

The guy at the bar notices my approach and makes room for me. Sliding onto the chair beside him, I bat my long lashes and smile innocently. I am sweet, the type I hope he enjoys.

'Hello,' I say.

'Good evening,' he replies. He is terribly good looking, and young, twenty-two at most, with a Rolex on his wrist to cover his tattoo and a seductive smirk on his adorable face. His hair is longish, brown and curly. 'What's your name?' he asks.

'Alisa,' I say, not being too secretive because I know he won't live long enough to repeat it. 'You?'

'Dan. What're you drinking?'

'Coke. I'm on a diet.'

He snorts. 'What kind of diet is that?'

I laugh softly. 'An all-sugar diet. Do you come here often?'

He sips his scotch. 'No. To tell you the truth, this place bugs me.'

I'm already tired of making conversation. I just want to kill him and be done with it. Since inheriting Kalika's psychic abilities, I have gone out of my way to kill a few bad apples. Of course, I have no intention of making it my life's work.

'Do you want to leave?' I ask.

He acts surprised. 'Who are you?' he asks, with an edge to his voice.

I catch his eyes. I have a very strong stare. Just by looking at metal, I can make it turn to liquid. I pitch my voice so there is no way he can refuse my invitation.

'Just a girl. You're looking for a girl, aren't you?'

He finishes his drink and stands. 'Let's go,' he barks.

Out on the street, he walks fast towards a car he never seems to find. I have to adopt a brisk pace to keep up with him. People move past us in the dark, the nameless faces of a humanity I have known forever. The summer air is warm.

'I have a car if you can't find yours,' I finally offer.

He shrugs. 'I just thought we'd take a walk first, get to know each other.'

'Fine. What do you do for a living?'

'I'm a plumber. What do you do?'

'I'm an artist.'

He is amused. 'Oh, yeah? Do you paint?'

'I sculpt. Statues.'

He gives a wolfish grin. 'Nudes?'

'Sometimes.' It's so nice to get to know each other.

Yet there's something wrong, more than the obvious. He's not at ease with me, and his discomfort goes beyond his thoughts of wanting to murder me. He fantasizes how my bright blue eyes will dim as my brain dies beneath his grip. Yet I am more than just another victim to him.

He is afraid of me.

Someone has told him something about me.

But who that someone is, I don't know. My concentration is divided between Seymour and my situation. Yet I don't know why I should worry about Seymour. Certainly Heidi is not going to harm him. I scanned the girl's mind for a few seconds when I met her and there was nothing in there but thoughts of drink and sex. No, I tell myself, Dan is all that matters. I wonder where he's leading me, who we'll meet on the other end. He makes a sharp left into a dark alleyway. Naturally, to my eyes, everything in the alley is perfectly clear.

'Where are we going?' I ask.

'My place,' he says.

'Can you walk to your place from here?'

'Yeah.' He pauses and studies me out of the corner of his eye. Although he's striving to act cool, his breathing is rapid, his heart pounds. He definitely knows I am more than I seem, more dangerous than a cop with a gun. But he doesn't know I'm a vampire. There are no images in his mind of my drinking his blood. But the farther we walk, the more difficult his thoughts are to penetrate – another mystery. Yet I know he is worried what will happen with me in connection with another, how our meeting will go. This *other*, I sense, is also dangerous, in the same way he thinks I am.

The other is close. Waiting.

Are we going to meet another vampire?

There should be no other vampires, other than Seymour and myself.

I smile. 'Do you live alone?'

'Yeah,' he says, and his hands brush against his coat pocket. I realize he has a weapon there, and wonder why I didn't spot it before. The gun must be unusually small, I think. But when I sniff with my nose, I detect not even a trace of lead or gunpowder in the air, and I can smell a bullet from a quarter of a mile away. My questions pile one on top of the other, but I am far from ready to walk away from the encounter. There is a puzzle here – I must solve it.

'I live with my brother,' I say.

'The guy back at the bar?'

'Yeah.'

'He doesn't look like your brother.' There is a bite to his remark. For some reason, Seymour is still very much on this guy's mind. Why?

'We had different fathers,' I say, and my own hand brushes against the knife I wear in my belt beneath my black leather coat. Nowadays, I can kill a man at better than a mile with my trusty blade. Even good old Eddie Fender, a psychopath if ever there was one, would be useless against my new and improved reflexes.

Dan snorts. 'I never knew my father.'

That is one truth in a string of lies.

There is a warehouse at the end of the block, a shabby affair built to house dirty equipment and sweaty workers. Using a key, he opens the door and we go inside. The warehouse is chock full of shelves of metal gear, the nuts and bolts of larger pieces of machinery. There is a pronounced smell of diesel fuel. The yellow lights, coated in grime, are few and far away. The shadows seem to shift as Dan turns towards me. If he reaches for his weapon, I will put a foot in his heart. Already, I think, I should kill him. Yet I want to know why he has brought me to this place, who the other is. Even thought I reach out with my mind, I sense no one else in the building. He studies me in the poor light.

'Are you really an artist?' he asks. His curiosity is genuine, as is his continuing fear. He wants the other to arrive soon, so he can return to the streets.

'No,' I say. 'I lied.'

My remark unsettles him. He thinks about his weapon – the small something in his coat pocket. He shifts uneasily.

'What are you then?' he asks.

'A vampire,' I say.

He smiles, a lopsided affair. 'No shit.'

'Yeah. It's true.' Still staring at him, I begin to move around him. He feels my eyes – I let the fire enter them, sparks of pressure. Sweat appears on his forehead and I continue. 'I am a five-thousand-year-old vampire. And you are a murderer.'

His upper lip twists. 'What are you talking about?'

'You, Dan, your private occupation. Because I'm a vampire, I can read your mind. I know about the two girls you killed, how you strangled them and then ate a big red steak afterwards. Killing makes you hungry – that's one of the reasons you do it. That's opposite of me. I kill to satisfy my hunger.' I reach out and finger the sleeve of his shirt. 'I'm thinking of killing you.'

He brushes my hand away. Yet he doesn't go for his gun. Someone has warned him that could be fatal. 'You're insane,' he says angrily.

I laugh softly. 'You don't mean that, Dan. Someone told you I was different so you're not completely surprised by what I say. I want to know about that someone. If you tell me now, tell me everything you know, I might let you live.' Once more I reach out. This time I touch his left ear, but before he can swat my hand away, I pinch it. Rather hard, I think. He is in pain. 'Talk,' I say softly.

'Stop,' he pleads, as I force him to bend over.

'Just a slight tug of my hand,' I say, 'and your ear will separate from your head. I am very strong. So talk to me, while you still can. Who is to meet me here?'

'I don't know.' He squeals as I twist his ear. 'I don't know!'

'Tell me what you do know.'

He gasps for air. 'She is just someone I know. She came to me after I killed the first girl. She said I could work for her. She gave me money. Please, you're hurting me. Let me go!'

I shake him hard. 'What is so special about her? Why didn't you just kill her and take her money?'

Red appears on the left side of his head. His ear is coming loose. He tries to straighten up and I force him back down.

'Her eyes,' he cries. 'She has strange eyes.'

I pause, and then let him go. He is bleeding badly now.

'What is strange about her eyes?' I ask quietly.

He holds his hand to his ear, panting. 'They're like yours,' he says bitterly.

'Is she a vampire?' I ask.

He shakes his aching head. 'I don't know what she

is.' He takes his hand away; it is soaked in blood. 'Oh God.'

I frown. 'Does she have exceptional strength?'

The blood continues to drip from his ear onto his blue shirt. 'I don't know. She never hurt me like you just did.'

'When is she coming here?' I demand.

'She should be here now.'

There is a sound off to my right, deeper in the warehouse. As I whirl to confront it, I also reach into Dan's coat pocket and remove his weapon. It is not something I can use to protect myself, not without study. It is a small rectangle of metal, with buttons on the side. Really, it looks like some sci-fi creation to defeat alien monsters.

Two figures move in the shadows beyond the towers of drawers. One is Heidi, the other Seymour. Heidi has one of these funny little boxes in her right hand, pressed to Seymour's neck. She stands behind him, using him as a shield. She is no longer drunk. When she speaks, her voice resonates with power and authority.

'Throw down the matrix or I will kill your friend,' she says. 'Do so now.'

The matrix will take me several minutes to master and is of no use to me right then so I throw it down. Heidi takes a step closer, bringing Seymour with her. It is clear, from her body language, that she is stronger than my vampiric friend. The big question is, am I stronger and quicker than she is? Seymour stands relatively still, knowing the danger is real. Heidi's expression is harder to decipher. There is an emptiness to it, an almost total lack of humanity. I wonder at the transformation in her, and realize that Seymour and I have been set up. Dan fidgets on my left, anxious to be gone. His left ear continues to bleed freely. He speaks to Heidi.

'I have done everything you asked,' he says.

She nods. 'You may leave.'

Dan turns towards the door we entered.

'Wait,' I say in a simple yet powerful tone.

Dan pauses in midstride and glances over at me, sweating, bleeding, shaking. But my attention is on Heidi, or on the creature inside her. Right then she reminds me of James Seter, Ory of ancient Egypt, the Setian that possessed Dr Seter's adopted son. Yet there is something different about her as well.

'I don't want Dan to leave,' I add softly, planting the idea deep inside Dan's mind, so he has no choice but to stay. But I am not the only one in the room with subtle powers.

'Leave now,' Heidi tells Dan.

His paralysis breaks. He takes another step toward the door.

I reach out and grab him, and now Dan is my shield. My fingers are around his neck and I push him toward Heidi and Seymour.

'Release Seymour or I will kill him,' I say.

In response Heidi levels her matrix in our direction and pushes a button on the side of the black box.

There is a flash of red light, and I let go of Dan and dive to the side, behind a tower of drawers. The weird light hits Dan and he is vapourized. Just like that, on a gust of burning air, he vanishes on the tail of a piercing scream.

Wow, I think. Heidi has a ray gun.

In a flash, I move through the building, using the equipment and machinery as camouflage. Heidi seems able to follow my movements, but not well. I estimate her powers to be equal to mine before Yaksha, the child, and Kalika restyled my nervous system. Yet her psychic control must be greater. In the bar she knew who I was, but I knew nothing about her.

I end up in a dark corner, up high, behind a bunch of boxes. For the moment, Heidi seems to have lost me. But I know if I speak to her, she will find me. Yet I am capable of projecting my voice, making it bounce off inanimate objects. Perhaps I can fool her yet. I do want to talk to her. She continues to keep Seymour close.

Heidi finally stops searching for me.

'We do not wish to destroy you,' she calls out.

'Could have fooled me,' I reply.

'We wish to meet with you, make you an offer,' she says. 'Come out where we can speak. You know this to be true. We could have killed you in the bar if your death was all we wished.'

'I will come out only after you have explained who you are,' I say. 'And don't threaten Seymour. He is all you have to bargain with, and I think we both know it.'

'We are of an ancient tradition,' she says. 'Our line is mingled with yours, and with that of others. We hold all powers. This world moves toward a period of transition. The harvest must be increased. We are here as caretakers, as well as masters. If you join us in our efforts, your reward will be great.'

'Could you be a little more specific?' I say.

'No. You agree to join us or not. The choice is simple.'

'And if I refuse?'

'You will be destroyed. You are fast and strong, but you cannot survive against our weapons.'

'But I must have something you don't have,' I say. 'Or else you would not be interested in my assistance. What is this thing?'

'That is not to be discussed at this time.'

'But I want to discuss it.'

Seymour cries out in pain.

'This one is dear to you,' Heidi says. 'And you are wrong. We have more to bargain with than his physical shell. At the moment I am twisting off his arm. If you do not come out of hiding, he will be destroyed.'

I hear no bluff in her voice.

'Very well,' I say. 'But if I show myself, you must give me your word that neither Seymour or myself will be destroyed.'

'I give you my word,' she says flatly.

I wish I still had the matrix with me, even if I don't know how to use it. But it is still in her sight lines: I cannot get to it. All I have is my knife. Just before I step into the light, I position it on a shelf near the circular area where Heidi holds Seymour captive. I point the tip of the blade toward them, then I appear around a tower of shelves. Heidi is not surprised. She continues to press the matrix into Seymour's neck.

'Release him now,' I say.

'Not yet,' she says. 'Not until you join us.'

'Don't be foolish,' I say. 'I cannot join a group I know nothing about. Where are your people from?'

'Here, and elsewhere.'

'Are you from another world?'

'Yes and no.'

'Are you human?'

'Partly.'

'How many are in your group?'

'The number cannot be measured by human or vampire standards.'

'So you know I am a vampire. Who told you?'

'You did.'

'No. When?'

'Long ago.' Heidi shakes Seymour and I hear the bones in his spine crack. 'Enough of these questions. You join us now or you will be destroyed.'

'What do I have to do to join you?' I ask.

'You must swear an oath, and offer us a large portion of your blood.'

'What do I get in return?'

'I have told you. Power.'

'Power to do what?'

She sharpens her tone. 'Enough! What is your decision?'

Since she has a weapon at my friend's throat, I feel I have no choice. 'I will join you,' I say. 'On the condition you release Seymour.'

'Agreed.' She pushes Seymour forwards so that he stands midway between us.

'Seymour,' I say quickly. 'Leave this place.'

He has been hurt and frightened, but he is no coward.

'Will you be all right?' he asks. He does not want to leave.

'Yes,' I say firmly. 'You cannot help me by remaining. Leave.'

He turns toward the door.

'No,' Heidi says. Seymour stops – there is strength in her tone. 'He is not to leave. He is to be your sacrifice.'

'We have an agreement,' I say bitterly. 'He is to be let go.'

'No,' Heidi repeats, and there is cold evil in her voice. 'I agreed only to release him. I have done so. But to join us you must sacrifice him. It is part of your initiation.'

My tone is scornful. 'Is this the way of your people? You splice words so thinly they become lies.'

Heidi points the matrix at Seymour's back. 'Your choice remains the same. You have five seconds to make it.'

I imagine she is good at keeping time. Seymour's face is ashen. He believes, either way, that he is a goner. But I have not lived five thousand years to be so easily tricked. Clearly this creature knows a great deal about me, but not everything. Since the recent infusion of Kalika's blood into my system, I have the ability to move things with my mind, as well as read minds. I have no doubt my daughter could effortlessly affect objects from immense distances. This psychokinesis, however, requires great concentration on my part and I have never used it under adverse conditions. Up at Lake Tahoe, where my friend Paula lives with the divine child, I have only practiced pushing rocks and sticks from place to place.

But now I must move a knife.

Push it through Heidi's throat.

The blade is above and behind her. I can see it; she cannot. Yet I am afraid to focus completely on it, afraid Heidi will guess what I am up to. Instead I must continue to stare at Heidi, while I think of the knife, only of the knife. Rising up on its own, flying through the air, digging deep into her soft flesh, slicing open her veins, ripping to pieces her nerves. Yes, I tell myself, the knife will fly. It can fly. The very magnetism of my mind commands it to do so now. At this very moment.

'You have two seconds,' Heidi says.

'You have only one,' I whisper as I feel my thoughts snatch hold of the cold alloy, a special blend of metals, far more powerful than steel, an edge far sharper than that of a razor. For me, it is almost as if I hold the blade in my fingers. There is pleasure for me in this killing. But for her, there is only surprise.

The blade swishes through the air.

Heidi hears it, turns, but too late.

The knife sinks into the side of her neck and suddenly her blood is pouring onto the dirty floor. Yet I do not take this to mean my victory is complete. Heidi's will is strong; she will not die easily. Even as her left hand rises up to remove the blade, her right hand brings up the matrix and aims it at both Seymour and me. We are standing in a straight line in front of her. I anticipate this move, and already am flying towards my friend. I hit him in the knees just as a flash of red light stabs the air where he was standing. Together Seymour and I roll on the floor. But I am quickly up and kick the matrix from Heidi's hand before she can get off another shot. My knife in her neck has slowed her down some, but she almost has it out, and perhaps she is capable of healing even fatal wounds, as I can. But I will not give her the chance. Before she can totally remove the knife, I reach out and grab her head and twist it all the way around, breaking every bone in her neck. She sags lifeless in my arms, dead, but still I am not finished with her. Ripping off her head, I throw it into the far corner. Now there is no way she can recover.

'Nice,' Seymour says behind me.

'Get those two weapons,' I say as I drop to my knees and examine Heidi's headless corpse. 'We are leaving here in a few seconds. Her partners must be nearby.'

'Understood.'

While Seymour goes off to collect the two ray guns, I rifle through Heidi's clothes, coming up with a wallet and a passport. These I will study later. Feeling her from neck to foot, I find nothing else on her person. Seymour is quick on his feet. Already he stands behind me with the matrixes in his hand.

'Who was she?' he asks.

'I haven't the slightest idea.' I stand. 'Let's get out of here.'

2

The following morning I sit beside Paula Ramirez on the edge of Emerald Bay in the area of Lake Tahoe. The sun is brilliant in a clear cerulean sky. Inside Paula's house, Seymour sleeps, a young vampire still allergic to the sun. Now the sun doesn't affect me in the slightest, and again I must credit this to my daughter's blood. Even the burning Surya, the sun god, could not intimidate the Dark Mother, Kali. Kalika's ashes rest in a vase that sits beside me in the sand. I have brought the vase with me from the house. I don't know why. Except I still miss her so, my beautiful, mysterious daughter, killed by a Setian.

Paula holds her three-month-old son, John, and listens as I describe what happened in Los Angeles. I have driven all night to reach Paula. The infant kicks his

bare feet in the cold water. He looks and sounds happy.
I am happy just to see him. He always has that effect on
me. It was this child's blood that brought Seymour back
from the dead. Yet I did not take John's blood – once I
had saved him from the Setians – to save my daughter. I
knew it was not what she wanted. But I ask myself over
and over how I could not have wanted it.

Unfathomable Kalika, Kali Ma, where are you now?

I finish my tale and Paula sits quietly staring at me
with her warm eyes.

'She said she saw you before,' she finally says. 'Do
you think she was lying?'

'It was impossible for me to tell if she was telling the
truth or not,' I explain. 'She seemed to operate under a
psychic shield. It was very strong – even I could not
penetrate it. Certainly I could not bend her will to mine.'

'But there wouldn't be any reason for her to lie
about such a detail.'

'Perhaps. But still, I don't remember her.'

Paula stares out over the sparkling water at the small
island in the centre of the bay where Kalika met her
end. 'You know I have begun to remember many
things, Sita,' she says softly.

I nod. I've suspected for a while that certain
memories were returning to her, but I have waited until
she felt ready to talk about them.

'Suzama?' I say.

'Yes. I remember Suzama.'

I suspected this, but still the statement is stunning to
me. Paula remembers Suzama, my mentor from my

time in ancient Egypt, because she is the reincarnation of Suzama. It is the only logical explanation, and I ask her to confirm the truth for me. Paula shakes her head.

'We may be the same from life to life,' she says. 'But we are also different. Do not expect Suzama to answer when you speak to me. Her time was long ago.'

I probe deep into Paula's brown eyes and feel a rush of joy, and of sorrow. 'But she is in you,' I protest. 'A part of me must have known that from the beginning. When I met you at the bookstore, I knew I could not leave you. You are Suzama, the great oracle. Can't you just admit it?'

She is flattered by my praise, and yet unmoved as well. 'Perhaps I can't because I'm not able to see what happens next.' She pauses. 'Yet I knew, when you were down in Los Angeles, that you would confront something very old.'

I lower my voice. 'Then you know who she was?'

She shakes her head. 'I have a feel for her, that is all.' Reaching down, she touches the clear water, then feels John's feet to see if they are getting cold. She adds in a serious voice. 'Interesting how she mentioned the harvest.'

'Yes. I didn't understand that. What harvest was she talking about?'

Paula is thoughtful, her eyes focused far away, as Suzama often was.

'There is a time coming soon,' she says, 'when everything will change. I have seen this in what people call visions, but which aren't visions at all. People will either move forward or else repeat what they have already done.

I have to think about this.

Suzama never made casual prophecies.

'What will people move forward to?' I ask.

'An entirely different type of life. One we cannot even imagine as we sit here. Those who do go forward will live in light and bliss.'

'But Heidi was wicked. Why would she want to increase such a harvest?'

Paula wipes the water off John's feet and warms them in her lap. 'There are two kinds of harvests,' she says. 'There are two kinds of people. Those who serve others and those who serve themselves. You know this – it is nothing new. Of course, no one is one hundred percent one way or the other. No one is a perfect sinner or a perfect saint. But where there is a dominance of self-interest, a negative harvest will come about for that person. Where there is a dominance of love, a positive harvest will happen.'

'You know these things for fact?'

'Yes.'

'Suzama . . .' I begin.

She smiles. 'Paula. Please?'

'Paula. When will the harvest occur?'

'The date is not set. But some time in the next twenty-five years the change will occur.'

'Will everyone be harvested?'

'Not at all.'

'What is the criteria?'

'I knew you would ask that. The criteria, I believe, is the same for both sides, positive and negative. Yet it has nothing to do with religious persuasion, higher learning, physical health or beauty, relative importance in society. None of these qualities will matter.'

'Then what will the criteria be?' I repeat.

'It is difficult to describe.'

I am frustrated. 'Try.'

Paula laughs, and so does her child. John is for the most part a happy baby, but he can cry in the middle of the night with the best of them. Many times I have changed his diapers to allow Paula to sleep. Since drinking my daughter's blood, I seldom need to rest.

'Life is the criteria,' she says finally. 'Who is alive, who is not. Remember, those who are negative can be more full of life than the most positive of people.' She punches me in the arm. 'Take you for example.'

I am her naive student, from long ago, and her remark wounds. It strikes me then how much our relationship has changed since we met. Then I was the sole knower of profound secrets. Now I truly feel I am her student and study at her knee. Mystery surrounds her like a halo. I love her so much, but she scares me.

'Am I only fit for the negative side?' I ask quietly.

She laughs more. 'Silly vampire. No, don't be ridiculous. Who more than you is ready to give her life for others?'

I gesture helplessly. 'But I have killed so many over the years.'

She is compassionate. 'It doesn't matter, Sita. Really, I know this for a fact.'

I have to smile. 'I suppose you would since you have such a special child.'

'You understand what I am saying. The issue of harvest is separate from the type of harvest. Whether a person will go forward is dependent on his or her life vibration. Whether he or she will enter a positive realm or a negative one depends on the quality of his or her heart.'

'Tell me more about this next realm?'

'I cannot.'

'But you see it?'

'Yes. But words do not describe it. The next dimension is even beyond the realms souls encounter when they die.' She pauses to run her hand through John's silky brown hair. How will the world react, I wonder, to a brown messiah? Of course, no race would satisfy everyone. Paula adds, 'The coming harvest will affect heaven and earth.'

'Is that why John was born? To increase the positive harvest?'

'Yes. But . . .' She does not finish.

'What?'

Paula frowns and then sighs. 'Something is wrong. The plan is off.'

'What are you talking about? What plan?'

'God's plan.'

'He makes plans? Are you sure about that? I always thought he just rolled the dice when it came to us.'

Paula smiles again, but the expression is short-lived.

She continues in a serious tone, hugging her baby to her chest. John yawns and closes his eyes, ready for a nap.

'Every individual affects the world, but it is difficult for so many to go forward, the way we would wish them to, when there is so much evil in the world.' She pauses. 'Yet this evil is there for a reason. It plays its part. You remember Ory?'

'Yes. How could I forget? I just killed him last month. Why do you ask?'

But Paula is evasive, as Suzama often was. 'He played his part' is all she says.

'Paula,' I say. 'I described to you what happened to me that night in the desert, when I confronted Ory. It seemed as if for a time I was not physical, that the very matter of my body had changed into light. Is that related to this harvest you describe?'

'Yes.'

'But when I changed, it seemed that I entered a spaceship from another world. But it wasn't a spaceship. I don't think anyone could see it but me, in my changed condition. There were beings aboard. Beings like demons, and I entered the mind of one. At least I think I did. But as time goes by, I begin to doubt that any of this happened, that I didn't just dream it all. Does that make sense?'

Paula nods. 'That is why I can't describe what is to come next. It would just be a dream to us, the way we are now.'

'But were these beings from a negative harvest?'

She touches my knee. 'Sita. You want to understand

everything with your head. You ask me to describe what you call my visions with words. But neither thing is possible. Even your brilliant mind cannot reach beyond concepts. Even your vampire eyes cannot see beyond this world. I don't know who they were, these friends of Ory. I don't know who this Heidi was. I only know that she did not lie to you when she said she met you long ago.' Paula pauses and she raises her eyes to the water, to Lake Tahoe beyond the sheltered bay. 'And that it was long ago things went wrong.'

'Went wrong? For whom?'

'For all of us.'

'I don't understand,' I complain.

'Did Suzama ever just explain things to you?'

'Sometimes.'

'No. She would take a lesson only so far because she was not omniscient. She saw a portion of the mind of God, but no mortal can see all of it. Suzama was not infallible.'

'Is John?'

The boy sleeps soundly. Paula speaks with love. 'John's a baby.'

'But who was he in the past?'

Paula pauses. 'I don't know.'

'Suzama said this child would be the same as the others: Jesus; Shankara, Krishna. She wrote that – I saw her words with my own eyes.'

'Then why are you asking me?'

'To know if it's true.'

'Ah. That is the question, isn't it? What is true? But

didn't Suzama also write that faith is stronger than stone?'

'But I ask you these things so I will know what to have faith in.'

'Have faith in yourself, Sita. These strangers have come for you for a purpose. It does not sound as if they have the welfare of mankind at heart. You must seek them out, learn what they want and how they hope to accomplish it.'

'You have seen this in a vision?'

Paula turns her head away. 'I have seen too many things.'

I have to wonder if she has seen my death.

'You can tell me,' I say carefully.

'No.'

'I am not afraid to hear what is to be.'

Paula lowers her head. A tear runs over her cheek.

'I am afraid,' she whispers.

'Suzama,' I say, and stop myself. But Paula is already looking at me and shaking her head.

'I didn't call you as I promised I would after I fled from Kalika,' she says. 'Do you know why?'

'I meant to ask you. I assume you had a vision that it would be better to keep your distance. At least for a time.'

'No. I didn't talk to you because I began to understand your destiny – destiny itself. It can only be lived, it cannot be explained. It is like a mystery, which ceases to exist the moment you explain it. The same with a magic trick. When you are told how it works, it loses all its charm.'

'What you're saying is that you'll tell me no more of what you've seen?'

'I have seen no more, and for that I am glad.'

'You look more sad than happy.'

Paula smiles sadly. 'Because I know you'll be going away soon.'

I thought the same thing. I am anxious to return to Los Angeles to trace Heidi's background. 'But I will keep in touch,' I say. 'I will see you soon.'

Paula doesn't say anything more. She glances at the vase containing Kalika's ashes.

'Why did you bring that here?' she asks.

'To put the ashes in the water.'

She nods. 'It is time to move on.'

Sorrow washes over me. 'I still think of her all the time.'

'She lived the life she was born to live.' She pauses. 'I never told you what she said to me when she burst into my house and grabbed hold of John. She said, "Hello, Paula. I have no friends but I am a friend of your son's. Tonight everything will come together in a wave of blood. But don't worry, he is stronger than this night."'

Now I am close to tears. 'Her life was so short.'

Paula comforts me, rubs my arm. 'She couldn't stay too long. She was a star that burned too bright. The strength of her soul would have made us all go blind.' Paula gestures to the vase and stands, John still asleep in her arms. 'Say your goodbyes. I will wait for you at the house.'

I ask weakly. 'To say goodbye?'

'Yes.'

My voice cracks with emotion. I need her to understand why. 'I loved Suzama. I loved her with all my heart. When she died, I almost died.'

Her voice is soothing. 'You were younger then. You are stronger now.'

I look up at her. 'Will I see you again? After today?'

Suzama stares at me for a long time. It is Suzama, yes, and she stares with the eyes of humanity's greatest clairvoyant. Her eyes are dry now; she has no tears, as she slowly shakes her head.

'I don't think so, Sita,' she says.

She turns and walks away.

I am left alone with my daughter's ashes, and soon these are gone, too, on the gentle ripples of the bay. I poured them from the vase without words, but with great nostalgia and love. True, she was an avatar, a creature of the divine, yet even Kalika's ashes dissolve in water. My memories are strong then, my pain nailed to a bloody past. But strong also is my vision of the future. It is true what Suzama says. I will leave this place, leave my few friends, and confront an enemy I know will kill me. Kill me because I crave love instead of power. But this I have lived five thousand years to learn. Power is as cold as forgotten ashes. Only my love can keep alive the memory of my daughter, the stories of Ray, Arturo, Yaksha, and most of all the grace of Krishna.

My blessed Lord – how he must laugh at me when I sing him to sleep in the middle of the night. Sing him songs from the holy Vedas that he himself wrote when he walked under the trees of ancient India. It is the divine child I will miss the most. Not to see him grow old, to hear him speak wisdom. I fear I will be ash before he even utters his first words. And I have to wonder who will remember me when I am gone. I worry that even Suzama and Seymour will forget me. Me – Alisa, Sita, or a thousand other names that I have been called by strangers who became friends or lovers. I fear it will be as if I never was. Never a vampire. The last vampire, whose long life now comes to a close.

Death does not scare me, but oblivion does. There is a difference. In my daughter's ashes I see my own bright star sink beneath the surface and go out. My end will erase my beginning. I don't know how but I know it is true. And I must choose that end because it is my destiny.

3

The wallet and the passport from Heidi's pockets identified her as a certain Linda Clairee. I know her address, her bank account number, even her supposed birth date. She is supposed to have lived in a house not far from where I lived when I gave birth to Kalika. I am very curious as I drive to her house after flying into LAX.

The place is modest, nondescript even, stucco walls with a wooden fence surrounding an uninspired yard of grass and a few bushes. Slowly I walk towards the front door. There is someone inside watching TV and drinking what smells like beer. The sounds and odours drift out through a torn screen door. I knock lightly and brace myself for instant death. Yet I have a matrix in my pocket, and I have finally figured out how to operate the ray gun. It is a totally cool weapon.

A bearded fellow in a frayed T-shirt answers the door. He looks as if he's on his second six-pack. Twenty-five, at most, his gut hangs over his belt like a sausage off the side of a breakfast plate. But I warn myself that Heidi – Linda – appeared to be very ordinary until her psychic force field went up. This guy might be more than he appears, but it's hard to believe.

'Hello,' I say. 'Is Linda home?'

He burps. 'She's out of town.'

At least he doesn't know she's missing her head.

'My name is Alisa,' I say. 'I'm an old friend. Do you know when she'll be back?'

'She didn't say.'

'OK.' I catch his eye through the screen door and squeeze his neuron currents. 'Would it be OK if I come in and search through her personal things?'

His brain is soft mud, easy to impress – I think. 'Sure,' he says, and opens the door for me.

'Thank you,' I respond.

I leave him in the living room, watching a baseball game. But my ears never leave him. If he tries to sneak up on me, he'll fail. But I won't kill him, if he shows strange powers, not right away.

Linda's room is neat and tidy. She seemed to enjoy sewing and the Dodgers. And if I begin to think I have the wrong house, there are pictures of her and Brother Bud on the mirror on top of the chest of drawers, cheap Polaroids shot with a camera with a dusty lens. Heidi is Linda and I am in the right bedroom. In each of the pictures Linda smiles as if someone just told her to.

I search the drawers and find nothing important. Even the closet is boring – clothes and baseball caps, shoes and socks. And this is the creature who said we all have powers? Talk about a double life. I am on the verge of leaving when a stack of papers under the bed catches my eye.

They are all about UFOs.

Specifically, newsletters from a UFO foundation.

FOF – Flying Objects Foundation.

What happened to the unidentified? I don't care. All the newsletters are addressed to Linda Clairee. She was definitely a member of this group, and it is the only wrinkle in her ordinary life that I have found. Holding the papers in my hand, I return to the living room and Bud. He is, in fact, finishing a can of Budweiser as I walk in. I turn off the TV without asking his permission and sit down across from him.

'Hey,' he says, annoyed.

I catch his eye and burn a tiny hole in his frontal lobes. It will probably do him good, in the long run.

'Where did Linda say she was going?' I ask.

He replies in a flat voice, staring straight ahead. 'Phoenix.'

'What's in Phoenix?'

'A convention.'

'A UFO convention?'

'Yes. FOF.'

'Did Linda often attend such conventions?'

'Yes.'

'Why?'

He could be hypnotized. 'She likes UFOs.'

'Why?'

'I don't know.'

'Are you interested in UFOs?'

'No.'

'Does Linda believe UFOs exist?'

'Yes.'

'Is she an alien?'

'What?'

'Is Linda an alien creature?'

'No.'

'Are you sure?'

'Sure, I'm sure.'

'When did you meet Linda?'

'Three years ago.'

'Where?'

'In a bar in Fullerton.'

'What does Linda do for a living?'

'She works as a secretary.'

'Have you ever been to her place of work?'

'Yes.'

'Where is it?'

'In Fullerton. On Commonwealth and Harbour. Crays DP Office.'

'What is Linda like?'

'Nice. Boring. Sexy.'

'What is it like to have sex with her?'

'Fun. Always the same.'

'What's your name?'

'Bill.'

'What do you do for a living, Bill?'

'Drive a truck.'

'Have you ever noticed anything unusual about Linda?'

'What do you mean?'

'Besides attending UFO conventions, does she do anything else odd?'

'Yes.'

'What?'

'She stares at the sky at night a lot.'

'How often?'

'Every night.'

'Does she tell you why?'

'No.'

'Do you ask?'

'No.'

'When do you expect her back?'

'In two days.'

'The convention runs until then?'

'Yes, I think.'

'Does Linda have any family?'

'No. They are all dead.'

'Every one of them?'

'Yes. Everyone.'

'Bill, I am going to leave now but I might be back later. Until I return, I want you to forget I was ever here. I never existed. If someone should ask you if a stranger was here, just say no. Do you understand?'

'All right.'

'Also, if Linda should fail to come home, don't worry about her. Get yourself another girl. She is not so important. Understand?'

'Yes.'

'Good.' I stand and step over and turn the TV back on. 'Goodbye, Bill.'

He glances up from the game. He doesn't even realize I interrupted it. 'Goodbye,' he says.

There is a plane leaving for Phoenix in fifty minutes and I get on it. Linda's newsletters have told me where the FOF convention is being held – a Holiday Inn beside a busy freeway. Once in Phoenix, I rent a Jeep and drive to the hotel, but all the rooms are taken. Taking a room at a nearby hotel, I shower and then go for a walk in the desert. Perhaps the UFO freaks took a hotel near the edge of town so they could look at the night sky. It is late – I study the stars as I walk, but nothing flies down from the sky to whisk me away. Yet I feel no pleasure beneath the heavens. A past I cannot remember haunts me.

'We are of an ancient tradition Our line is mingled with yours, and with that of others. We hold all powers.'

Still, Linda wanted more of my blood, if she had any of it to begin with. Yet she must have had something unique. She was fast and strong, more powerful than virtually any vampire Yaksha made. Plus she had technology that put the government's most secret toys to shame. But so many of her answers had made no sense. What did she want to initiate me into?

'But to join us you must sacrifice him. It is part of your initiation.'

It was almost as if she wanted to introduce me to the black mass.

I know about such things, sexual magic, from the past.

The torture and the blood, the sudden awakenings.

But I have not thought of them in a long time.

I find a sandy bluff and sit atop it to mentally survey my life, trying to find a point where my blood could have been taken without my knowledge. But except for Arturo and his alchemy, I think, my blood has always been mine to do with as I chose. Yet a faint feeling of dread sweeps over me as I look back. My shadow is long and dark. In it could lie secrets, hidden from even me, where blood was exchanged and vows were pledged that my conscious memory never recorded. It is as if I sense a blank spot, a place of reality that wasn't real after all. But I only sense its existence – I don't see it. I have to wonder if my imagination leads me to a wall of illusion. My thoughts are never far from those I left behind in Tahoe: John, Seymour, Paula. But Paula swears they are safe there, for now, and she should know. She who has deep visions.

A shooting star crosses the sky and I make a wish.

'Krishna,' I whisper, 'don't let me die until I have set right what I made wrong.'

Suzama's words are with me. God's plan.

Somehow I know it was me who messed it up.
Maybe that's what she had been trying to tell me.
Maybe that was why she sent me away.

4

The next morning I am at the FOF convention in the Holiday Inn, milling around the many booths, poking my head in on lectures. The attendance is substantial, at least two thousand people. The crowd is pretty evenly divided between males and females, but otherwise the cross section is peculiar. There are, for want of a better expression, a lot of nerds here. Many are overweight and wear thick glasses. These are true believers, no doubt about it. The saucers are coming and they are prepared. In fact, they believe they are already here. Eavesdropping on their jumbled thoughts, I soon get a headache.

I sense no superbeings in the vicinity, yet I don't drop my guard. If this convention was important to Linda, there is somebody significant here. If only I knew who. Besides thoughts, I listen to heartbeats, trying to find physiologies that mimic mine. But there is nothing here but pure humanity.

The talks are boring, discussions of different sightings that have about as much credibility as reports of Santa Claus or the Easter Bunny. As I sit through one, yawning, I think about what I should have done with my life. Retired to a remote spot to spend a year building toys and baking goodies, which I would deliver once a year to the needy. At least then I could have given vampires a better name.

Yet there is a lecture at the end of the day that catches my eye. It is entitled: 'Control Versus Anarchy – An Interstellar Dilemma.' The speaker is to be Dr Richard Stoon, a parapsychologist from Duke University. He has a list of impressive academic credentials beside his name, but it is really the buzz of the crowd that draws me to the talk. They have been waiting for this guy. I hear them whispering to one another. Dr Stoon is supposed to be brilliant, charismatic, unorthodox. It is the last lecture of the convention, and I take a seat at the back of the audience and wait for Dr Stoon to enter.

Beside me sits a pale blonde woman, with a waist as small as my own, and clear blue eyes. She has a kind smile and I quickly scan her mind, detecting nothing more than a day job at a boring office, and a husband who has just been laid off. She appears to be in her early twenties but could be older. Noticing my scrutiny, she glances over and brightens.

'Hello,' she said with a southern accent. 'It's been a fun convention, hasn't it?'

'I haven't been here for the whole thing. I just caught today.'

'Have you heard Dr Stoon speak before?'

'This will be my first time. What's he like?'

'Very forceful, opinionated.' She pauses. 'He's interesting but to tell the truth he is awfully arrogant.'

'Why don't you leave then?' I ask.

She makes a face. 'Oh, I couldn't do that. I'm one of those people who has to see everything.' She pauses and studies me. There is a sparkle in her eyes; she is far from stupid, but she doesn't want people to know. She offers her hand. 'I'm Stacy Baxter.'

I shake. 'Alisa Perne. Pleased to meet you.' I give one of my more common aliases because I'm no longer trying to hide. I want to draw the enemy out.

'Very pleased to meet you,' Stacy replies. 'I don't think I've seen you around before?'

'This is my first UFO convention.'

'So what do you think?'

'It's all very interesting.'

Stacy laughs. 'No, you don't! You think we're all crackers.'

Crackers. I haven't heard that expression in twenty years.

I have to smile. 'I don't think you're crackers, Stacy.'

She's pleased. 'Maybe we can have coffee together after Dr Stoon's talk.'

'I'd enjoy that.' I reply.

Dr Stoon enters a short time afterwards. He is a big burly man, of Slavic descent, with dark piercing eyes. His age, like Stacy's, is difficult to pinpoint. He could be thirty-five, or ten years older. He moves as if he owns the room, as if every eye should be on him. After a brief introduction, he is at the podium, overpowering it with his bulk and attitude. His voice, when he speaks, is gruff and unpleasant. Yet he sounds smart, like someone who knows more than he is saying.

And his words sound strikingly familiar.

'There are two kinds of beings in this creation,' he says. 'Those who strive for perfection and those who submit to chaos. It is the same in outer space as it is on this world – there is no difference. We either choose to be masters of our destinies, or we let the fates rule us. I am speaking now about power, and you might wonder what power has to do with a lecture on UFOs. I tell you it has everything to do with our space brothers. Each night we look to the heavens, waiting for them to arrive. But why should they come if we haven't made a choice in our own lives? But when we do make the choice, the right choice, to be important in the galactic scheme of things, then they will know. They will come to us at the most unexpected time, and fill our hands and minds with knowledge we cannot begin to imagine.'

Stacy leans over and speaks in my ear. 'Sounds like a bit of an evangelist, doesn't he?'

'Yeah. He talks without saying anything specific.'

Stacy nodded. 'But look at the people in this room. They are spellbound. Dr Stoon doesn't have to say anything to have the effect he wants.'

Stacy misunderstands me, but her point is well made. Dr Stoon is one of those people who draws others in, smothers them. Even though he's not being specific, he touches on issues Suzama – and that's who she will always be to me – also explained. Yet his bias is from the other side, even though nothing he says sounds intrinsically negative.

He continues in a loud voice.

'We have to open our minds fully to the truth that we control our own futures, while at the same time we must accept that there are powers above us that are willing to help us if we align our thinking with theirs. Who are our space brothers? They are us a thousand years from now. They are strong. And for us to be strong we must cut off all that weakens us as a people. Here I have to speak on a matter that is almost considered a blasphemy in our society, and yet it is the single most important issue regarding our survival. We are literally drowning in the shallow end of our gene pool. Who is reproducing at the most rapid rate in our world? The uneducated and the foolish. But how did our space brothers reach their exalted state? By casting out the foolish. Our genes are our only treasure. We must plan their use, and use the plan – the plan our brothers are waiting to give us.

Again Stacy leans over and whispers in my ear.

'Sounds like Hitler to me,' she says.

I smile. 'But he's not blaming any specific group for mankind's woes.'

'Isn't he?' Stacy asks, and her question is worth contemplating.

Dr Stoon speaks for another half hour, and at the end of that time he doesn't accept questions – probably because no one would know what to ask him. I certainly wouldn't. Yet his words have affected me, not so much by their content, but by their resonance. I don't know, however, if the effect is a good one. His lecture was divisive; nothing he said could be used to bring people together for the common good. Another might say that was not true. Such was the strength and weakness of his talk.

When he finishes I wander towards the front, where he stands chatting with what appear to be old friends. But when his eyes meet mine, he momentarily freezes, and then quickly turns away. He excuses himself from his group and walks briskly toward the exit.

I walk after him.

In the parking lot he climbs in his car and races out onto the road, heading for the desert. Naturally I follow him. He must know I am tailing him. At this time of day, a half hour after dusk, we are the only ones on this narrow road that runs perpendicular to the main highway. Within twenty minutes we are deep in the desert, with the city only a glow on the horizon. The stars come out. Dr Stoon is driving fast, but now it is possible he may not know I am behind him. I have turned off my headlights. I don't need them, of course, but maybe he doesn't either.

Ten minutes later he suddenly swerves off the road

and drives across the sand towards a massive hill that is more reminiscent of Utah's Zion National Park than Phoenix's backyard. The hill is more a stone cathedral, built around a symmetrical interior. The rough terrain is hard on Dr Stoon's BMW but my Jeep loves the challenge.

He drives his car as close to the hill as he can, then stops and gets out.

What do I do? I realize I could be walking into a trap. If he has a matrix, as I have, he could incinerate my Jeep from a distance. I have experimented with the weapon – it has a substantial range. The way he fled from me, for no apparent reason, indicates he is more than he seems. Yet his exit was obvious as well. But I sense no one else in the area, and I can hear a snake slither at a distance of five miles in such a desert.

I decide to risk direct confrontation.

Dr Stoon stands with his arms at his sides as I drive up. Slowly I climb from my Jeep, the matrix in hand. I do not wish to waste time on pretence. If he is like Linda, he is going to do some talking. If he is human, he has a funny way of showing it. Either way I believe he will die in this desert tonight. I may even drink his blood, although I have not fed from anyone since Kalika brought me back from the edge of death. My hunger simply seems to have vanished. I gesture with my weapon. A million stars shine down on us. I see them all, more than a mortal can see with a medium sized telescope.

'Move away from the car,' I say. 'Put your hands in the air.'

He does as I command. 'What do you want?' he asks in a much softer voice than he used at the convention. I step closer.

'I should ask you that question, Dr Stoon,' I say. 'What do you want?'

He does not hesitate. 'We told you.'

'You told me little. Who are you people?'

He smiles slightly, cocky bastard. 'Who do you think?'

'Extraterrestials.'

'You are partially right, and partially wrong. We have been here a long time.'

'How long?'

'Don't you remember?'

His question disturbs me, his voice. I realize he is trying to overpower me with his eyes. His are at least as strong as Linda's. Try as I might, I cannot pierce his aura to read his mind.

'I remember nothing of you. Answer my question.'

'Over a thousand years,' he says.

'Where did you come from? Originally?'

'There is no simple answer to that question. We move in space and time, through dimensions and distortions.'

'Are you here to distort humanity?'

'We are here for the harvest.'

'For which side of the harvest?'

'There is only one side – the expansion of the self, the growth of self-awareness.'

'Sounds nice. But at whose expense?'

He snorts. 'The expense of all those too weak to move forward. Why do you ask these questions? We know you are a vampire, the most powerful vampire on Earth. We have watched you for centuries. You do what you wish; we do as we wish. We are brothers to you, sisters. Why don't you join us?'

'It doesn't sound like you want me as a brother or sister. It sounds like you want me as a blood bank.' I pause. 'Or do you already have some of my blood?'

He makes me wait. 'We do,' he says finally.

I stiffen. The confirmation wounds me.

'When?' I ask. I feel violated.

'Over a thousand years ago.'

'When?' I demand.

He gloats. 'Kalot Enbolot. Chateau Merveille.' He pauses before he says the next words. 'The Castle of Wonder.'

I tremble, not just in my body, but in my very soul.

In all my long life, there had never been darker days.

Yet I thought I had escaped his aerie unscathed.

'Landulf,' I whisper. 'Oh God.'

Dr Stoon grins. 'Landulf took the best you had to give, now we will take it again. With or without your assistance.'

I back up involuntarily. 'You lie!' I gasp. 'He never touched me!'

Dr Stoon speaks with scorn. 'He did more than touch you. He bled you, used you, and then twisted your mind so that you didn't know. But don't you remember now, Sita? As you swam through the waves away from his castle? Swam to what you thought was freedom? Even the ocean water could not wash off the contamination you felt then. Yet you thought you had won, defeated him. Just as you think you will defeat us now.'

I cannot stop shaking. The images his words invoke – I cannot bear to see them in my suddenly shattered mind. Landulf and his sexual magic, satanic practice that used terror and pain for fuel. The human sacrifices, bodies split open with dirty knives, and worst of all the spirits that would appear at his bidding, vicious creatures from an astral hell buried beneath unheeded cries. From the Temple of Erix at which the Priestess of Antiquity had once guarded the Oracle of Venus, in southwest Sicily, he sent forth these unclean spirits and dominated the minds and hearts of men and women throughout southern Europe. Inviting the hordes of invading Moslems, showing them the weaknesses in the Christian world's defenses and so betraying his own race, Landulf had changed the course of history in the ninth century. And so he had changed my life, putting a stain on it that more than ten centuries had not totally erased. I tremble for many reasons, all of them unbearable. Landulf had indeed touched me, I remember, kissed me even, with lips that often enjoyed raw human flesh.

Yet I still thought I had tricked him.

'I will defeat you,' I whisper without conviction. 'If you have anything to do with him, I will not rest until all of your kind are wiped out. Landulf was a demon, and you use his name as if he were a hero. Your power is a travesty.' I aim the matrix. 'You will all die.'

Dr Stoon grins and lowers his hands. 'We are not alone.'

I glance left and right, see nothing, hear only the desert.

Yet I sense the truth of his words, sense a presence.

'Tell them to show themselves,' I say carefully. 'If you want to live one second longer.'

'Very well.' He bows his head slightly.

Suddenly there are three figures in red robes, one on each side, another at my back. Each carries a matrix in his or her hand, although their faces are shadowed, as are their minds. They are humanoid but that is all I know about them. They have me in their sights. There seems to be no escape. Dr Stoon sticks out his hand.

'The matrix, please,' he says.

I shake my head. 'I will vaporize myself before you will have my blood.'

He is amused. 'Try.'

I try the weapon on him. But it doesn't work.

'We neutralized it at the convention,' he explains.

I throw the weapon aside. 'You don't want me dead.'

'True,' he says. 'But we will kill you before we allow you to kill us. Lay facedown on the sand.'

'I hardly think so,' I say, and my attention goes to the figure on my right, the one whose hand shakes ever so slightly. This person – I cannot even see his eyes – but I know it is a male, weaker than the others that guard me. Even though I cannot read his mind, I can sense the general character of it. This is an important assignment for him, one that he has had to struggle to win. If he completes it successfully, captures the vampire's blood, he will receive some type of advancement. But if he fails, he will be killed. Indeed, he is especially fearful of Dr Stoon. He wishes the doctor dead. That is the chink in his psychic armor. He does not care for his associates, hates them in fact, wishes they all were dead so that all the glory could be his. My eyes fasten on his hidden face, my thoughts drill into his cranium.

Kill them. Burn them. Vanquish them.

The man's arm trembles more.

'It is not wise to refuse us,' Dr Stoon says.

'Do you still give me a chance to join you?' I mutter, stalling for time. Never before have I focused so hard, called upon the depths of my will. The strain is immense. For even though this one is the weakest, he is still strong beyond belief.

'Perhaps,' Dr Stoon says. 'Lay facedown or die. Now.'

'Die,' I repeat softly, to the man. 'Die.'

His aim shifts slights. The finger on the button on his matrix twitches.

Dr Stoon is suddenly aware of the danger. He whirls on the man.

'Kill him!' he screams.

There are two bursts of red light, one from behind me, one from my left. My victim vaporizes on an earpiercing scream. But I do not pause to mourn the sound. I am already in the air, flipping backward in a curving arc, my legs going over me, carrying me over the assailant at my rear. There is another burst of red death

– the one on my left tries to shoot me out of the sky. But already I have landed, behind the one who moments earlier stood behind me. In a matter of micro-seconds I seize his matrix and break his arm. Without speaking, I blow away the red robe on the left. Dr Stoon reaches into his coat pocket but I caution him to remain still.

'Don't,' I say.

The figure I have disarmed groans, moves.

I shoot him and he is no more.

Dr Stoon has stopped grinning.

'How many more of you are there?' I ask.

He pauses. 'There is just me.'

'And when you die, you die?'

He hesitates. 'We prefer not to surrender this form.'

I chuckle. 'I do believe there is a not of fear in your voice, good doctor. For a moment there, you know, I thought you were Landulf himself. But Landulf was never afraid.'

'Not even of you,' he says bitterly.

'Yes,' I say sadly, thinking of what he has told me. 'Perhaps I was tricked. What did he use my blood for?'

'Is it not obvious?'

'Only your death is obvious. Answer my question so that death won't catch you asking.'

He is defiant. 'I will not be your puppet. We are alone for the moment, but others of my kind are coming. And if you should slay me, their treatment of you will be that more hideous.'

I shake my head. 'Nothing can be hideous to me. Not after Landulf.'

He speaks arrogantly. 'You will not escape us.'
'Really? You thought I wouldn't escape you.'
He doesn't have an answer for that.
I shoot him and he troubles me no more.

5

I return to my Jeep and drive back towards the road. When I reach it there is another car waiting for me, another person. She stands by the side of the road looking up at the stars. She hardly seems to notice my approach, and only glances over as I park and walk toward her, the matrix in my hand.

Stacy Baxter. She finally glances at me and smiles.

'Hello, Alisa,' she says, and the southern accent is gone.

My finger is on the fire button. 'What are you doing here?' I ask softly.

She shrugs and gazes back up at the sky. 'Just enjoying the night. Isn't it beautiful?'

'Yes. Did you follow me out here?'

She pauses. 'Yes.'

'I see.' I am a moment away from killing her. 'Do you have anything else to say, Stacy Baxter?'

She looks at me again, not smiling now, just watching me, very closely. 'No, Alisa Perne,' she replies quietly.

I shift uncomfortably. This death does not feel right.

'Are you one of them?' I ask finally.

She shakes her head. 'Not me.'

'Who are you?'

'A friend.'

'No. I don't know you.' I shake the weapon. 'Why are you here?'

'To help you, if you want my help.'

'What's your real name?'

'Alanda,' she replies. 'Sita.'

My heart pounds. 'And you are another incantation of Lundulf's?'

Sorrow touches her face. 'You suffered there.'

I bite my lip. 'Yeah, I suffered. But what's it to you?'

She lowers her head. 'Everything you have experienced – it means a lot to me.'

My voice is hard. 'Why? Because you know me from long ago?'

'Yes.'

I fidget on my feet. I want to kill her. Logic dictates that I should. This desert is filled with monsters. Chances are she is one, too. Certainly she is not normal, and knows too much about me. Yet she does nothing to defend herself, even to plead her case, and I find it difficult to strike down the helpless.

'Do you know this weapon I carry?' I ask.

'Yes.'

'I know how to use it.' I pause. 'I will use it.'

Alanda is staring at the stars again. 'Then use it.'

'You are impossible. I will kill you, just as I killed the others out there minutes ago. You saw that, didn't you?'

'Yes.'

I am sarcastic. 'Why didn't you come to my aid? Friend?'

'It was not allowed.'

'By whom?' I demand.

'You had to refuse them. To offer to end your life before they would take it from you.' She adds, 'You did these things.'

'I did nothing but kill. Because they answered me the same way you do, with vague mumblings.' I pause and sweat over the trigger. 'I think you are one of them.'

For the third time she looks at me, and for the first time I really see her. Her blue eyes – they are very much like my own. I could be staring into a mirror. Yet it is more than a physical resemblance. The person behind the eyes, the soul within the body, seems to reach out and touch me in a way I cannot explain. For a moment – from this unassuming person I am threatening to destroy – I feel profoundly cherished. Suddenly she is more than a friend to me, she is a part of me. Sometimes when I looked at Suzama, I would feel this way. Occasionally, gazing at the divine child, I would sense this same expansion of consciousness, as if my mind were only a portion of a much greater mind. It is only in that moment that I realize Alanda is a spiritual being of great stature, someone who loves me more than I am able to love myself.

The matrix slips from my fingers, lands in the sand. A tear rolls over my cheek and joins it in the dust. I don't know why I cry, perhaps because I am happy. Alanda *is* an old friend.

Yet I don't remember her.

As I don't remember Landulf stealing my blood.

'I don't understand,' I whisper.

She comes to me and hugs me, stroking my face. 'Sita,' she says over and over again. 'My Sita.'

But I am not a child. I am a monster. I cannot be comforted even if the space between us is suffused with the vitality of reunion. I cannot turn to this creature that I do not know for help or solace. In a swift move, I brush her off and step away, turning my back on her. If she wanted, she could pick up the matrix and vaporize me. But I know that is not her intention. She lets me stand silently alone. Nothing is hurried in her, I realize. She has waited long for this encounter, and I feel I have as well. Yet I feel exposed before her, and that is a feeling I have never enjoyed. I have always been the master of my own destiny, and now this angelic being comes to me in the night to tell me that I have been fooling myself. Truly, she is an angel to me, a being of light from a distant world I cannot imagine.

'There is no need for imagination,' she says quietly. 'Those worlds belong to you as much as to me.'

I draw in a tight breath. 'You are telepathic then?'

'Yes. As are you.'

'No. I cannot read your mind.'

'You can. You're just afraid, Sita.'

'How do you know my name?'

'Because I know you.'

'From when? From where?'

'From before. From the stars.'

A smile cracks my face, involuntarily. Turning, almost mocking her, I say, 'Where's your spaceship?'

'It's coming.'

That remark makes me take a step back.

'Are you here to take me away?' I ask, and I hear the hope in my own voice. For five thousand years, I have lived a glorious life, yet there has been too much pain. Alanda's love seems to flow to me in waves. The desert is dry, her eyes are moist. I cannot help but be mesmerized by them, by all of her. She is shimmering now with a faint blue light.

This blue glow, it reminds me of Krishna.

The stars. How bright they shine above us.

Almost as if they have moved closer to Earth.

But Alanda's face is both blissful and concerned.

'No,' she says. 'You cannot leave this world now, not until what has been ruined has been set right.'

'Suzama said as much. Do you know her?'

'Yes. She is a sister, like you.'

'Suzama is much more than I am.'

'You are fond of denouncing yourself.'

'I haven't been a saint exactly. You must know that.'

'Yes. But that is past. You are here with me now, and I am with you.'

My throat is constricted. 'I feel you with me, yes.'

'Why are you afraid of love, Sita? Because it has hurt you?'

I nod weakly. 'It hurts all of us. Sometimes it seems that is all love is good for.'

Alanda shakes her head. 'Love is good for many things. You have just forgotten. The veil has to be lifted.'

I am curious. 'What is this veil?'

Alanda turns away and walks on the sand, between the weeds. She is barefoot – I only realize that now. The way her soles touch the ground, it is almost as if they caress the Earth. Gesturing at the desert, the stars, and playing with her long blond hair, she enchants me as she speaks. The communication may even be telepathic, her voice is so soft. But it is easy to understand her.

'This galaxy is ancient, as you know,' she says. 'Your sun is old, but the stars at the centre of the galaxy were there first. The planets circling them gave rise to civilizations. So life evolved. First plants, then animals and finally, what you would call people arrived. Some of these people looked like us, but not all. They became conscious. They knew all that the people of this world know, and more. For there was at that time no veil between the conscious and the unconscious, no loss of the awareness that we are all a part of the creation. The gods of those suns did not desire this veil to confuse their children, and therefore everyone on those ancient planets lived in light and peace. Do you understand?'

'I'm not sure,' I say. 'Continue.'

'Suzama has told you about the coming harvest, on this world. These ancient people also arrived at a point when it was important for them to move on, to move into another realm, a fourth dimension if you like. But then there was a problem. All these beings from the central suns of this galaxy were positive – what you would call good-hearted. But because they had always lived in bliss, they had no incentive to grow. Therefore, for many billions of years, from the third dimension to the fourth, there were few harvests. Such people were a rarity.' Alanda pauses. 'Do you understand?'

'Yes. The source of pain for us – here on this world – is the veil between the conscious and the unconscious. Yet this pain acts as a catalyst for us to grow.'

'Precisely. People of your world often speak of good and evil. But what you call evil goads you onto the greatest good. This is necessary for you, and all people of your world. That is why it is there. That is why the great being within your sun allows the veil to exist. The story from the Garden of Eden – the knowledge of good and evil that your ancient ancestors received – that was not a curse but a blessing. It only seems a curse to you at times like this, when you are in doubt.'

'But to some extent we live our whole lives in doubt.' I pause. 'So you're saying the devil wasn't such a bad guy after all?'

'No. I am saying there is a place for negativity – as much as there is a place for goodness – in the great scheme of things. There is no hero without a villain, no peak without a valley. But our path, the path of love, demands that we overcome negativity. But we do not overcome it by resisting it. That is an illusion. What you resist will persist.'

'Why are you telling me this?' I ask, and there is suddenly fear in my voice. But I know what she will answer. For I knew, personally, the greatest evil that ever walked the Earth. Still, Alanda's words chill me to the bone.

'Landulf cannot be overcome by force,' she says.

My lower lip trembles. 'Landulf is dead. He died a long time ago.'

'Perhaps. Perhaps not. But certainly his work lives on. You met a sample of it tonight in the desert. There are more of them emerging at this time, and they possess a sample of your blood.' She steps towards me, looks at me. 'Do you know what that means?'

I snort. 'Yeah. It means they're tough sonsofbitches.'

Alanda is serious. 'Yes. They are tough. And it was never intended that the negative side of harvest should possess such a powerful army of warriors. In the coming years they will overwhelm your people, turn virtually everyone towards fear. This will be the downfall for all who aspire to the light. This fear will cause the negative harvest to be larger than it would have been. In other words, your world is out of balance.'

'And I caused this imbalance?'

Alanda sighs. 'This must be difficult for you to hear.'

'The truth is always better than illusions.' I pause. 'Is it true?'

'Yes. You are the ultimate source of this cancer, and it must be rectified.'

'Are you so sure?' I ask, trying to deny what I just heard. It's too much for me, to be told that I am the scourge of mankind. I feel as if I must run away. Only my irrational love for her makes me stay.

Alanda is gentle. Her next word is not. 'Yes.'

'But how can you be sure?' I demand.

'Because my old and dear friend, I am from your future.'

I take a moment to absorb her statement. 'What is it like?'

Now she stutters. 'In ruins.'

I am shocked. 'This world?'

The life leaves her voice. 'This entire sector of the galaxy. When so much of Earth fails, much else fails later.' Alanda steps close to me, puts her hands on my shoulders, her eyes in my soul. 'We have come back for you, Sita, to ask you to help us. To ask you to go back to the days of Landulf. To relive those days, and keep him from doing to you what he desired.'

The prospect fills me with horror. 'But I can't remember what he did to me!'

'You will, I promise, when you travel back to that time.'

'No.' I shake my head, feeling my guts turn to ice. 'That is one thing I cannot do. Ask anything of me but that.'

Alanda strokes the side of my face. 'You are afraid.'

Again I brush her off and turn aside. 'Yes,' I say in a shaky voice. 'And I don't understand why. I can't understand why the simple thought of seeing him again overwhelms me.'

'It's because of what you can't remember.'

I whirl around. 'Then tell me what happened?'

'I cannot. You must face the memory when you are once more in his castle. It is the only way. It is why he was able to block your memory in the first place. At that time you refused to face what happened.'

'Did he torture me? Did he mutilate me?'

She nods reluctantly. 'In his own way. But there is more than that to the puzzle – you will see.'

I am sick at the prospect. 'Is your spaceship a time machine as well?'

Alanda glances up. 'Not exactly.'

'But how can I go back to those days? How can I meet myself?'

She stares at me. 'Physically you will not journey in time. Only your mind will go back.'

'I don't understand?'

'As our ships approach light speed, we are able to jump into a realm that exists outside time and space. In that realm we can cross many light-years in a moment. The enemy also has this technology, and that is how they were able to surround you in the desert tonight. In that realm, the laws of physics as you understand them do not apply. For a few seconds you will cease to exist in a particular time and place. Therefore, you will have the freedom to be where you wish to be. If you focus all your will on that ninth century vampire, you will become her. Do you see?'

'No. Will both our minds be in the same body?'

'No. There is only one of you. You will become her, and she will become you. There is no question of two.'

I am still confused, but dread continues to dominate my mind. 'I can't see him again,' I plead. 'You don't know what he was like.'

Alanda is sad. 'But I know his kind well. He is not from the dimension beyond this one, but from the one even beyond that. He is negative fifth density – not merely a sorcerer, but a master of sorcerers. Above his head the vipers hiss, and before his vision all wills turn to stone. Those you met tonight are only his minions. But he is not greater than you, Sita. I know you, old friend, know of your extraordinary origin. You cannot directly resist him when you confront him, for in doing so you will become him. That is his special power, the spell he cloaked you in before. Yet you can defeat him.' Quoting Suzama, she adds, '"Faith is stronger than stone."'

'But you will not tell me how to defeat him?'

'No. You must find the way. It is your destiny to do so.'

I don't want to ask the question but I do anyway.

'Is it also my destiny to die? Alanda?'

She shakes her head. 'I cannot say.'

'But you come from the future. You know. Tell me.'

'I know that you will rewrite our future. Please do not ask me to say more.' Her eyes return to the heavens and she points. 'Behold, Sita. Our ship comes for you.'

6

The funny thing is, I don't see anything. Alanda explains that the ship will land deep in the desert, beside a clear pond. She offers to drive me there, but I prefer to take the Jeep, so she goes with me instead. We cut directly across the sand, murdering more than a few tumbleweeds in the process. Yet the ground is not excessively bumpy, and we soon reach the pond. After parking, I climb out and stare at it in amazement.

The pond appears to be natural – Alanda assures me it is even though it is a perfect circle. A hundred feet across, the water lies so still that it could be a polished mirror set to reflect the stars. Indeed, as I approach the edge of the pond, I see more stars in the water than I do above. I see the approach of the saucer in the water before I see it in the sky, quite a few seconds before. It makes me wonder, yet I say nothing.

The saucer is blue-white, and the light from it slowly begins to flood the area and my eyes, wiping out any chance of my making out the details. If I weren't dreading seeing Landulf, I would be thrilled by this moment. But I can only think of Landulf's devishly handsome face, his deep laugh, and the way he would make an incision in an abdomen with his long sharp nails and slowly pull out the victim's entrails while the victim watched. I feel I must resist Landulf with every fibre of my being. Yet Alanda says that is the way of failure.

I have no idea what I'll do that is different from what I did the last time.

I stare up at the saucer.

'This is incredible,' I whisper.

'This is but a beam ship,' she says. 'Our mother ships are a thousand times this size.'

'And I have been on these before?'

'Yes.'

'When?'

'Another time.'

'Are you sure the brakes work? The ship looks as if it's going to land on us.'

'It will land over this pool.'

'Then we should move?'

'No. We're fine. It will move right over us.'

The light grows dazzling, and I have to shield my eyes.

'This must be visible from a hundred miles away,' I gasp.

'No one sees it but us,' Alanda replies.

I glance at her. 'Is it physical?'

'What is physical in one density is not physical in another.'

I have to laugh. 'One of these days, Alanda, I am going to ask you a question and understand your answer.'

The water of the pond seems to glow as the spaceship settles over us. One moment it is above us, the next we are inside it. The translucent floor, I assume, now covers the pond. During the move to the interior, we have had our clothes changed. We now wear long white robes. I don't even bother asking – the night is so weird already.

A gentleman waits for us inside. He is tall and bearded – like a child's drawing of a Biblical character. His robe is the colour of the outside of the ship, blue-white. The interior of the vessel is in various shades of gold, and the ceiling is a clear dome, that opens to the sky. There appear to be no controls. Alanda introduces her friend as Gaia. He smiles and bows his head but doesn't say anything. His eyes are liquid green and very lovely.

'Gaia is from a race that doesn't speak,' Alanda explains. 'But he understands your thoughts.'

I nod in his direction. 'I appreciate your coming for us, Gaia. I hope it was not too long a journey.'

He smiles and shakes his head. No, not too long.

There is a faint humming.

'What is that?' I ask.

'Our engines,' Alanda says.

'Will we leave soon?'

'We have already left.' Alanda motions with her arm. 'See, we are in orbit.'

The floor of the craft turns clear as glass, and I jump slightly, momentarily afraid I am going to fall. Below our feet is the black-blue Pacific, and the glittering coast of California. I spot Lake Tahoe, and think of my friends. We seem to be moving westward, at considerable speed. Yet the hum has stopped, and all is quiet. The view takes my breath away, it is so beautiful, and yet it also makes me sad. To see the Earth from such a vantage point, to realize it is all I have known. Never before did I realize how much I thought of the Earth as my mother.

'She is a strong woman,' Alanda says softly, reading my mind. 'But delicate as well.'

'Can a planet be alive?' I ask.

'Can a sun?' she replies. 'I told you that it was the god within your sun that decided that humanity should live with the veil – until this time.'

'Are you from a world that experienced such a veil?'

'Originally, yes.'

'Can you tell me about that world?' I ask.

'Not at this time.'

'But I lived there before I came to Earth?'

'Not precisely. Before you came here, you existed in a realm of great glory.'

'You're saying that I was in a higher dimension?'

'Yes,' Alanda says. 'A higher density.'

'Why did I decide to come to Earth?'

'To serve, to grow. The two are the same in the creator's eyes.'

'Why did I chose to be a vampire?'

Alanda hesitates. 'When you came here, you were not a vampire.'

'I had a life before this one?'

Her voice is abruptly filled with melancholy. 'Yes. Very long ago.'

She is trying to tell me something without saying it.

'I made a mistake when I returned?' I say. 'Is that why I had to be reborn as a vampire?'

Alanda reaches over and touches my face. 'You returned to this third density out of love. If you made a mistake, Sita, it was only out of love. You mustn't blame yourself.'

Already we are over India. I nod to Rajastan, desert meeting green.

'I was born there five thousand years ago,' I say. 'I am sure you know that. But what you might not know is that I feel I never left that tiny village. I am still that young girl spying on the Aghora sacrifice that invoked Yaksha into Amaba's dead womb.' I pause. 'I held him as an unborn infant in my hand. He was just a trace of movement beneath the hard skin of a corpse. I had a knife in my hand, and my father gave me the choice of ending his life before it could begin.' A wave of weariness sweeps over me and I lower my head. 'But I couldn't kill Yaksha.'

Alanda hugs me. 'Because of love, you see. You must let go of the past.'

'But you are sending me into a past I want to let go of.'

'But this is the only way you will be able to be finished with it. Trust us, Sita. We do this for you as much as for ourselves. Our futures are entwined.'

I look up and smile. 'Just because I almost killed you doesn't mean I believe you would lie to me.' I pause. 'You risked your life meeting me like that.'

'It was the only way to meet you.'

'It was a test?' I ask.

'In a manner of speaking.'

'You could have defended yourself from me.'

Alanda turns back to the view. 'I counted on your compassion.'

'The compassion of a murderer?'

'Of an angel.'

I have to laugh. 'You are as bad as Seymour. He sees me that way, no matter what I do.'

'He is wise.'

I sigh. 'I would love it if he were with us now.'

Alanda is thoughtful. 'In a sense, he is. He is always with you.'

Her remark strikes deeply into me. 'Why is that so true?'

Alanda stares at the Earth, India. 'You will see.'

A short time later the Earth begins to shrink as we

pull away from it at a tremendous velocity. Soon it is only a blue ball, falling into a well of blackness. The floor turns solid as the sides become clear. The rays of the sun stab through the saucer's view acceleration, however. I see the moon, but only for a few seconds, and then it is lost in the glare of the Earth. But then that planet, the only home I can remember, is also lost in the rays of the sun. The sun begins to diminish in size and brilliance. Alanda turns away and strolls to the centre of the craft. But my eyes are gripped by the stars ahead of us.

'I've had these dreams,' I say to Alanda and Gaia both. Gaia stands at a respectful distance, silent, peaceful, absorbed in a contemplation I cannot imagine. Yet I know he watches me and listens to my thoughts. I continue, 'In them I would be in a spaceship flying through the galaxy toward the Pleiades. Ray would usually be with me, but sometimes it would be my husband, Rama. Never were both with me, but I think that's because – in my dreams – they were always the same person. Anyway, we would be excited and filled with a sense of adventure. We would know, when we reached the Pleiades, that all our friends would be waiting for us. We even knew that Krishna would be there, to welcome us and to heal the many injuries we had received living on Earth. Most of all, in these dreams, I would be happy, and it would be hard to wake from them.' I pause. 'Were they just dreams, Alanda?'

'Or were they real?' she asks. 'Maybe they were a little of both.'

I look at her. 'Are you from the Pleiades?'

'It is a place I know.' She shrugs. 'We are each from God.'

I listen to the silence. 'It's time, isn't it?'

'Yes. In a few minutes, we will make what you might call a hyperjump. At that time, as I explained before, it is important that you focus your entire being to a time just before you traveled to Landulf's castle.'

'It was Dante who led me to the castle,' I say, stepping toward her. 'Should I think of him?'

Alanda pauses. 'The moment you reappear is entirely up to you.'

I force a smile, although the dread weighs on me like a stone in my heart.

'It will be good to see Dante again,' I say. 'A little comic relief before I descend into hell.' I gesture to the centre of the floor. 'Should I sit down and close my eyes?'

Alanda takes my hand. 'Lie down and close them, Sita.'

I do as she says, but she continues to hold my hand. I open my eyes and smile at her. 'Don't worry,' I say. 'It is just my mind that is going back in time.'

She shakes her head slightly. 'But if you die back then.'

I understand. 'I won't exist today?'

She sighs. 'There is something else. These fifth density negative beings – they can imprison you.'

'I'm pretty good at breaking out of most prisons.'

'They can imprison your soul, in their realm.

Make you one of them.'

Somehow that doesn't sound fair. 'For long?'

'Billions of years. You would only be set free when they are set free.'

'Negative beings attain freedom?' I ask.

'Yes. Far up the ladder of evolution, the negative path meets the positive. In the end, all find God.' She squeezes my hand. 'But you could be lost for the life of this universe.'

I cannot conceive of anything worse.

'How can he trap me?' I ask.

'He is subtle, and we cannot penetrate his mind. But he acts much as a mirror does. He stands before you. He shows you what you are. But only the parts of you that can be used to destroy you.'

'He can cause me to destroy myself?'

'Exactly. Be wary. He can kill you without your permission. But he can only pervert you to his cause if you enter into an agreement with him out of free will.'

'But I would never do that.'

Alanda seems unsure. Her expression is anxious. She leans over and kisses my cheek. There is a tear on her face and I reach up to wipe it away but she grabs my other hand.

'You are loved,' she whispers. 'Don't forget that.'

'I know. I know you.' I close my eyes. 'Goodbye, Alanda.'

'Sita. My Sita.'

She lets go of me. The ship darkens.

I hear the strange hum again, a shift inside.

But inside, outside – they have lost their meaning.
We are beyond space and time, and I am falling.
Into horror unspeakable, yes, and maybe hope unimagined.

7

The collage of colours and shapes that I now see is my life. Yet the different scenes from it are not arranged in a linear fashion, more in the form of a hologram, a pictorial dimension of time that encircles me like a living sphere. I have only to focus my attention on a particular event and I am there. But perhaps because my mind is used to dealing with sequential events, I take myself back in order. This is my deliberate choice, not the choice of the creation. To the creation, I realize, everything is happening in the same eternal moment.

I am with my daughter, Kalika, holding her as she bleeds from devastating chest wounds. Her smile is gentle and I am crying. She tells me she loves me. Then I cry over Seymour, beside his funeral pyre, because Kalika has killed him. Yet a few drops of the divine child's blood and he is alive again. Then I am laughing. Tears are connected to laughter in my life. One seems to bring the other, and that in itself is a great mystery to me. Blood, also, is everywhere. I see the night my daughter was born, in pain and love. The opposites of all life fly before my expanded vision, yet they now seem to be in harmony with one another.

Arturo and Joel are beside me. They tell me they love me. There is a flash of blinding light. They die, their love kills them, I destroy them. But a moment later I am saving Joel by making him a vampire, and a moment before that I am reviving Ray by the same process. Then I take a leap and I am sitting beside Ray's father as he dies from a ferocious blow I have struck to his chest. He perishes with the fear that I will harm his son, the son I love. Again and again, my love brings danger and death.

The hologram of my life seems to spin. In quick succession I see Hitler screaming at his troops, Lincoln ordering General Grant to take up the Union's moral cause. Then I am in a castle in the highlands of Scotland, defending it from an evil duke. Once more my lover dies, and in the next instant I stand before the Inquisition, condemning Arturo to death. Arturo, who has meant more to me than practically anyone I have ever known. I see his eyes as I curse him, but I do not see his heart, do not know that he has already tricked me. I ensure his death but he does not die.

Finally I am walking in the dry hills of Sicily outside Messina, eating a bunch of purple grapes and wondering where I am heading. It is the ninth century and even the evening air is hot. This is my first visit to Sicily; the previous day I took a sailboat across the straits from Italy. Something about the land has drawn me to this spot in particular, but as of yet I don't know what. My long blond hair is pulled up under a cap, and I wear gray hose and a short linen tunic. I could be a pretty young boy, with my baggy white shirt and long steel knife tucked in my belt. The sun is in the sky, but it bothers me just a little.

Then I am not watching this other self.

I am her, and it isn't easy for either of us.

There is a moment of duality. She does not know me.

I feel as if I bump heads with a shadow, and yet my shadow thinks she is the real one, and that I am the ghost. It takes me a moment to explain, and the moment almost cracks open into an insane fissure of delusion. This Sita does not have a volume of my memories, and certainly does not know about flying saucers and the possibility of mental time travel. I am forced to impress these possibilities on her through a wall of internal resistance that threatens to explode both our minds. Then I realize it is hopeless, that I cannot force myself on myself. I relax, and back off, and then suddenly she is curious about me. She knows me even when she doesn't know all of me. I was always one for a new experience, and meeting myself along an empty road is about as weird an experience as I have ever had. My younger self calls to me.

'*Ritorna da me,*' she says. Come back to me.

'*Fa bene,*' I reply, aloud. All right.

Sita is startled. Who is talking to whom?

Her curiosity is greater than her fear.

I am able to get inside and there I stay.

Finally she understands. The duality ceases. I am Alisa Perne of the twentieth century, in the ninth century, here in Sicily to defeat a monster. There is only me but I am now of firm resolve. Landulf had better beware.

Around the bend of the next hill, I hear cries. Dante.

Before I had not known I would meet him, but now it is as if he is calling my name. Tossing aside my grapes, I run to an appointment I have with the past. Yet already I am not thinking of myself as from the future. Perhaps the other Sita is there as much as I. Yet I do notice that I am not nearly so fast as I was before. This body has not had the last infusions of powerful blood. I am just an ordinary vampire – I can't even read minds. All that I have, that I didn't have before, are memories of things that have not yet happened. They are my only new weapons against Landulf.

As I come around a hill, I find Dante naked and bleeding, strung up to a skeleton of a tree by a rope tied to his right arm and right foot. Gathered around him are two men and a woman, the two men holding swords and poking at poor Dante, encouraging him to sing. There is another rope around Dante's neck. The meaning is clear – if Dante stops singing, they will cut the other ropes and he will be hung.

Dante is not in good shape. At a glance I realize he has severe leprosy of his left arm and leg. The disease has actually eaten away portions of his bones, and I know he must live in terrible pain. He has also been castrated, but by the sweetness in his voice I recognize that he is no ordinary eunuch. He is a castrato, perhaps of the Holy Father in Rome, whom I despise. The castrati make up the greatest choirs in the Catholic Church. Their manhood is sacrificed to maintain their magical voices in a preadolescent range. There are few things the Church will not do, I realized long ago, to petition the angels in heaven. Dante cannot be more than twenty years old.

'*Ciao!*' I call as I stride up. '*Che cosa fai?*' What are you doing?

The men hardly look over, they are having so much fun. But the dark-haired woman with the cleft palate eyes me suspiciously. '*Stai zitta!*' she calls. Shut up. 'He is a leper. He is to be killed.'

'*Penso di no.*' I don't think so. I slowly draw my knife as I move near. 'Release him now, and I will spare your lives.'

Dante stops singing and the two men with swords now give me their attention. One is a clumsy brute, dark featured, the other, the fair young one, appears quick on his feet. They eye my long narrow knife and chuckle to themselves. But the young man spreads his feet slightly, readying himself for combat. He is an experienced swordsman, although he is not sure yet if I am a boy or a woman. My skin is darker than usual from the sun, the gloss of my red lips partially hidden by my tan. Hanging half upside down, Dante stares at me in wonder, his face a mess of blood and tears. Incredibly, he has hope that I will be able to set him free. Naturally I will, in a few minutes. The brute gestures with his sword.

'*Vattene dia*,' he says. Get away. 'Or it will be you we string from the tree.'

'It won't happen,' I reply, and in a fast move I step forward and cut the top of the woman's left arm. The wound is not serious, it will heal, in time, but I want it to serve as a warning that I am skilled with a blade. Blood springs from her flesh and soaks her peasant clothes. The three hardly saw me move. Yet I know they will need more persuasion than this to back off. Of course I have been here before. A part of me knows that even though it is becoming easier to forget that I have. Surely I will kill them all, for the sake of poor Dante.

The woman screams in pain. 'She has cut me! Kill her!'

'You foul creature!' the brute shouts as he dashes forward and tries to run me through. But I have sidestepped his lunge, and tripped him. As he tries to raise his head from the ground, I kneel beside him and pull his head back by the hair. My blade rests across his exposed throat, and I speak to the ugly woman and the fair man, who at least has had the wits to wait to see what I can do.

'If you leave now,' I say. 'I will let this man live.'

'He is no friend of mine,' the fair man says. 'Do with him what you wish.'

'No!' the woman cries. 'He is my husband!'

'Then you agree to leave?' I say.

The brute, my knife scratching his trembling throat,

is agreeable. 'We will be gone,' he says.

'*Bene.*' Good. I smash his face in the dirt and then release him. But he is no sooner back on his feet than his dull eyes flash with anger and he makes another try for me. Once again I sidestep the thrust of his sword, but this time I sink my blade deep into his heart and withdraw it before he can take it with him to the bloody ground. His wife cries as he lands facedown. She jumps towards me, her arms flailing, and I kill her as I killed her mate. Now there is only the fair-haired man left. Dante is muttering prayers to heaven and drooling all over his wretched face. Wiping off my knife on the sand, I stand and pull off my cap, letting my blond hair fall. It shines in the last rays of the evening sun. Fair head smiles and nods in appreciation.

'My compliments,' he says.

But since he now knows I am a woman, he cannot walk away. Sicilian pride – he finally draws his sword and points it in my direction.

'I have been trained by the Vatican guards,' he says. 'You may submit to me now, or I will have your head.'

Pointing my knife at him, I laugh. 'I have been trained by far more experienced teachers. Leave here this instant or I will cut you badly.'

He takes a step closer. 'My name is Pino. I would take no pleasure in killing such a beautiful woman as you. Drop your knife, and let us take pleasure in each other.'

'No,' I say. 'I would rather kill you.'

He moves closer still. The tip of his blade dangles three feet from my face – I could almost reach out, without moving my feet, and take it from him. But I am too much the good sport, and I don't want Dante to see me as a supernatural being. Then I might have to kill him as well. It is funny, how I know Dante, without even being introduced to him.

'You are young,' Pino says. 'Why make such a rash decision?'

'You are proud,' I say. 'You have seen my skills. Why not withdraw? Your death will prove nothing here.'

He smiles but I have angered him. He takes a swipe at me with his blade, trying to cut my left shoulder. But he misses, and another smooth swipe also fails to draw blood. He appears more puzzled than worried.

'You move well,' he says.

'Last chance,' I say. 'Leave or die.'

'All right, cold woman,' he says as he turns to leave. 'I am no match for you.' But he has hardly turned his back on me when he spins and tries to take off my head with his sword. Ducking, I thrust forward and plant my blade in his abdomen. There I leave it as I back off a few steps. He is still regaining his balance from his failed attack. He stares down at my knife in amazement. I don't know if he understands yet that his wound is fatal.

'What have you done?' he gasps as blood begins to show around my knife. Dropping his sword, he reaches down and pulls out the knife with both hands. Bad move – now the blood spurts out, over his hands and onto the ground. He still cannot comprehend that I have defeated him. 'You witch!'

'I am not a witch,' I say casually. 'I am a good

Samaritan. This man you torture has done nothing to hurt you.'

Pino drops to his knees, bleeding over everything. 'But he is a leper,' he gasps.

'That is better than a corpse.' I come closer so that I stand above him. I stick out my hand. 'May I have my knife back please?'

He stares at me, incredulous. But he hands me back my knife, as if I might now help him because he is cooperating. But he is beyond a cure. I take a step toward Dante, whose head bobbles like that of a puppy dog.

'Oh, my lady,' he gushes. 'God has sent you.'

I begin to cut him down. 'Somebody did,' I say.

Pino cries out to me as he slumps to the ground. There is great sorrow in his words, but I have heard it all before over the centuries. '*Non voglio morire.*' I don't want to die.

Dante answers for me, giving me a future favourite line.

'Then you should never have been born,' he says.

8

Later, at night around a fire, I muse to myself that I killed the two men and the woman exactly as I had killed them before. The knowledge that their deaths were certain did not affect my actions in the slightest. Not even a single word that was exchanged between us was different. It makes me wonder whose future I'm from.

Dante sits across from me, wrapped in the swordsman's finery. He has washed out Pino's blood. My new friend is busy gloating over a rabbit I caught for him. A stick skewered through it, the meat hangs in the fire growing more tasty by the minute. The dripping grease crackles in the flames. Dante licks his diseased fingers and his dark eyes shine with joy. He has been muttering prayers to himself since I saved him.

'Tis a wonderful eve, I know,' he says. 'The light of

heaven follows our steps. There can be no other way of explaining how a helpless maid was able to rescue me.'

I laugh. 'Dante, please don't call me that. Or I will show you again just how wrong you are.'

He is instantly apologetic. 'I meant no offence, my lady. I intended only to praise the grace of God. You are his instrument in this world, I know that in my heart.' He adjusts the rabbit in the fire and licks his cracked lips. 'We can eat soon.'

'You can have it all,' I say. 'I have already eaten today.'

He is offended. 'If you will not feed with me, my lady, I myself will go hungry. It is not right that I should keep taking from you.'

I continue to smile. 'There is one thing you can give me – information. I have never been in Sicily before. Tell me about this land?'

He brightens. 'It is a beautiful land, my lady, filled with sweet orchards and tall trees that cover the hills. You stay around Messina and wander not too far from the well-travelled roads, and you will have a pleasant visit.'

'If I had not been far off the well-travelled roads this evening, I would not have been there to rescue you. But I am curious why you say I should stay close to Messina. Surely the Moslems have not landed on Sicily's southern shores?'

His face darkens. 'But they have, my lady. A force of them is camped on the beaches in the southwest. Have you not heard?'

'No. I heard that the Duke of Terra di Labur is strong in the south, with many armed knights.'

Dante trembles. 'Do not speak that name, my lady, for he no longer goes by it. He has turned against the Christian God, and has murdered his own knights. It is by his power and with his protection that the heathens have managed to land their forces on Sicily.'

I am surprised, even though I know all these things deep inside. Yet the future becomes more a dream to me with each passing hour. I know it exists, I know I am from there, but I have to focus to maintain this knowledge. Yet this does not worry me. It seems entirely natural that I should be one hundred per cent in the present moment, with Dante, and the cooking rabbit, and his stories of the evil duke. But I have spoiled Dante's appetite by asking about the latter. Dante stares miserably at the fire as if he were staring at a picture of hell. He scratches at his lepered arm and leg – my questions bring him pain. Yet I know I must ask all about the political details.

'What does the duke call himself now?' I ask.

Dante shakes his head. 'It is better not to repeat it in the night lest he hear us talking of him. For the night is his cloak, and shadows flow around him.'

I laugh again. 'Come on, he can't be that bad. I must know his name.'

Dante is adamant. 'I am sorry, my lady, I will not talk of him. To do so is a sin to your good company.'

'My good company will not be so good if you do not answer me. What is the Duke's name now?'

Dante speaks in a whisper. 'Landulf of Capua.'

I have heard the name before, of course. But now it

rings in my ears with less potency and more harmless connotations. Myth surrounds the title, not remembered agonies. Yet I know Landulf is the one I have come for – from the stars, for the stars – even if the flames that sparkle before my eyes blot out most of the night-time sky. I do not want to focus on future facts – it is another choice I make. I am more intrigued than scared. Capua is tied to Landulf's name because he was originally from there.

'I know this name,' I say. 'Even in Italy, the farmers in the countryside speak of him. They say he is an evil wizard, capable of performing magical acts.' I pause. 'Dante, why are you crying?'

He is really devastated. 'It is nothing, my lady. Let us talk of another person.' He pokes at the rabbit with another stick he has found. 'Or we can just eat, you can have some meat. You must be hungry after such a long day.'

There is something in his tone that catches my attention. 'Do you personally know this Landulf of Capua?' I ask.

He stiffens. 'No.'

'You must know him to be so frightened of him.'

He rubs at his leper arm. Actually, the disease has spread so far, he has only a stump left. His left leg is also little more than a stump; he walks with the aid of a wooden brace I found not far from where he was strung up. His sores are open and fluid oozes from them. He must be near death, yet he has energy. But now his strength is in a whirlwind of constant motion. His eyes are moist and he cannot stop shaking.

'I cannot talk about him,' he begs. 'Please do not force me to say his name.'

'Dante,' I say. 'Look at me.'

He raises his head. 'My lady?'

'Stare deep into my eyes, my dear friend,' I say gently, carefully bending his will to mine. 'You need not be afraid to speak of this duke. He cannot harm you now.'

Dante blinks and his tears begin to dry. 'He cannot harm me,' he whispers.

'That is true,' I say. 'Now tell me about him, how you came to know him.'

Dante sits back and stares at the fire again. He has forgotten the rabbit. He is half in a trance, half in a dream. I know I am asking him to repeat a nightmarish section of life. For even though I have calmed him with my power, his withered leg and arm continue to twitch. It is almost as if his leprosy was given to him by the duke, but that I find hard to believe.

Yet I do believe it. I *know* it.

What do I know? The stars are far away.

Dante's face holds my attention.

'My duke was not merely a duke, but an archbishop and a special friend of the Holy Father,' Dante says, in a clearer voice than usual. 'It was to Rome my duke brought me at the age of ten to serve as his personal attendant and to sing in the Vatican choir. The Holy Father said my voice was a sacrament, and I was allowed to join the privileged castrati and sacrifice my manhood to the Church. This I did not mind, as long as I was

271

allowed to stay close to my duke. For five years I was at peace within the holy walls, and I thought of nothing but my duty and my vows.' He pauses and sighs. Even though he is partly hypnotized, his pain comes through. 'Then, it happened, one terrible day, that my duke was falsely accused.'

'What was he accused of?'

Dante hesitates. 'I thought it was a lie.'

'Did the pope accuse him?'

'Yes. The Holy Father himself.'

'Of what?' I repeat.

Dante pauses before he answers. 'Of invoking the spirit of Satan.'

I do not believe in such nonsense, nevertheless, his words are chilling. 'Was he cast out?' I ask.

Dante coughs. The smoke of the burning logs has entered his lungs. The agony of remembering suffocates him, too. 'There was a trial,' he says. 'The cardinals and the Holy Father were present. Accusations were made, then witnesses were called – I had never seen these people before. Each one came forth and stated how my beloved duke had poisoned their minds with demonic spirits. Even I was called to denounce him. The Holy Father made me swear to tell the truth and then – in the same breath – told me to tell lies.' A tear rolls over Dante's ruined face. 'I did not know what to say. But I had never seen my duke commit any of these sins. I was afraid but I knew in my heart I could not lie.' A hysterical note enters his voice. 'Jesus never lied, even when he stood before his accusers.'

'Be calm, Dante,' I say soothingly. 'That was long ago. None of it can hurt you now. Just tell me what happened.'

He relaxes some, but shifts closer to the fire, as if chilled.

'The pope grew angry at me, and accused me of being in league with Satan and my duke. I was chained to my seat and more witnesses were called, more people I had never seen before. These spoke against me as well as my duke, while the cardinals whispered among themselves. I was very afraid. They were talking about burning us. I did not know what to do!'

'Peace, Dante, peace. Continue.'

Dante swallows thickly before continuing. On top of everything else, he seems to have trouble breathing. A frown wrinkles his features and he blinks, trying to remember where he is, or where he has been. Yet his voice remains clear.

'We were led away, my duke and I, and thrown into a stone cell where criminals were normally taken. We spent the night together in that stinking place. My fear was great – I knew we were about to be killed. But my duke acted pleased. He said nothing could harm us, that the Holy Father would be forced to release us.'

'Were you released?' I ask. My knowledge of the inner workings of the Vatican is extensive. No one accused by the pope of consorting with Satan ever survives. Such mercy would set a poor precedent. Yet Dante nods in response to my question.

'The next morning the jailer came and opened our door. There stood the Holy Father. He said the judgment of the holy council was that we were to be let go, but to be banned from the city of Rome. My duke's titles and properties were not confiscated, and I was amazed. My duke knelt and kissed the pope's ring before we were led away, and then he stared into the pope's eyes, and for the first time I saw the Holy Father afraid.' Dante pauses. 'I was afraid as well.'

'Of your duke?'

'Yes.'

'Why?'

He gestures with a stump. 'Because it was as if a black snake reached out from his eyes and touched the Holy Father between the eyes. A snake the others could not see.'

'But you saw it?' I ask

'Yes.'

'How?'

He speaks with conviction. 'It was there!'

'I understand.' I have to calm him again, not allow him to come out of his trance. 'What did you and your duke do next?'

'Traveled to Persida.'

The name is not familiar. 'Where is that?'

'Not far.'

'Where?'

'Near. Hidden.'

I find it strange he is able to avoid answering me directly, and wonder if powerful hypnotic powers have already been brought to bear on his memory.

'What is special about Persida?' I ask carefully.

He coughs painfully. 'It is where magic was first invented.'

'By your duke?'

'Yes.'

'Why did you stay with him in Persida?'

Dante struggles. 'I had to.'

'Why?' I insist. 'Did he use magic on you?'

He bursts with memories. 'Yes! He called forth the great serpent! The living Satan! He invoked it in pain and blood and it poured forth from his navel. I saw it again, the snake – it grew from his intestines and screeched when it saw the light of the world. He poisoned my soul with its filthy powers, and then he poisoned my body.'

'That's when you started to get sick?'

He calms down, so sad. 'Yes. In Persida, where magic lived, I began to die.'

'Why did he make you sick?'

'For his pleasure.'

'But you were a loyal subject?'

More tears. 'He did not care. It pleased him to see me eaten away.'

I want him to go on. 'What did he do next?'

'He went to Kalot Enbolot. That is the door to Sicily. He has a castle there. It was given to him by the Holy Father. He wanted to open the door to the heathens.'

'To let the Moslems overrun the Christian world through Sicily?'

'Yes.'

'And it was there he took up the name Landulf?'

'Lord Landulf of Capua.'

'How did he slay his knights? At the castle?'

'He made them slay one another. The demons summoned by the sacrifices always demand betrayal.'

'You keep saying he invoked demons, that he summoned them. What proof do you have of this other than the snakes you thought you saw?'

'I did see them!'

'Fine. But what was Landulf able to do with these demons?'

'He used them to torture men. To control their wills.' Dante stops and glances away from the fire, into the dark, and his whole body shakes. 'Distance does not matter with these demons. They can cross water and bring death. In the fair land of England, my duke boasted, knights in search of the Holy Grail wander lost because of the spells he cast over them. They will never find the Grail, he said. Forever, they will be lost.'

I was familiar with this mystical quest. But it was hard for me to imagine that Landulf had a hand in it. 'Why does he bother with these knights?' I ask.

Dante speaks with pride. 'Because they are righteous, and the light of God shines before them.'

'But you say Landulf is stronger than they are?'

Dante hangs his head, as if ashamed. 'I am afraid that he is the strongest.'

'But you are a Christian. Your Lord Jesus Christ says no demon can stand before the name of Christ.'

Dante continues, dejected, 'Landulf cannot be defeated.'

'Surely he is not all powerful. You escaped from him. How did you manage to do that?'

But Dante shakes his head. 'I did not escape. He sent me away.'

'Why?'

Dante looks me straight in the eye, and I believe my power has finally failed. He is no longer in a trance, but he is still frightened, more so than ever – terrified of what he has already told me, what I may do with the knowledge.

'My lady, he told me to find him an immortal ruby beyond all worth. And bring her back to him.'

An immortal ruby? My vampiric blood?

It sounds as if Landulf of Capua already knows about me.

That is fair. I intend to know a lot more about him.

I will go to his castle, I decide.

Dante will lead me to the black wizard.

9

It takes a week to walk to Landulf's aerie, which stands in the heights of Monte Castello, in southwest Sicily, where, Dante tells me, the Oracle of Venus, the Goddess of Love, once stood. Dante knows a tremendous amount of Roman and Greek history and mythology. He is much more educated than I would have guessed. I begin to understand that one of the reasons Landulf kept him around was because of his powerful story-telling abilities. Even the evil duke loved a good tale, and when Dante starts on a story, his whole demeanour changes, as if he were hypnotized, and he speaks with great eloquence. But the moment the tale is over, he reverts. The sudden personality changes are disconcerting, but I am sympathetic to him because he was obviously been warped by his exposure to Landulf.

I feel guilty that I am manipulating him further. Only by dominating him with my eyes, by soothing him several times a day, am I able to persuade him to lead the way to the castle. The thought of the place fills him with dread and he must be wondering that his legs continue to carry him in that direction.

Yet he doesn't seem to wonder about me. His affection for me is genuine; it pains me to use him so. And it is obvious that he is more concerned about me than about himself. When my influence on him wanes, he begs me to turn back. The human sacrifices he tells me about as being commonplace at the castle fill me with doubt. It is hard to believe there could exist such evil as he describes. Of course that is Dante's point. Landulf is no longer human. He has become a beast he invoked. The devil lives and breathes on a peak once considered sacred in ancient Rome. Before resting each night, Dante recites the entire mass in Latin, praying to a small copper cross he hides during the day in the wooden brace that supports his leper's stump. At night I see him scratching at his sores, and his suffering weighs on my heart. Only a devil, I think, could have cursed him so.

Yet I still do not believe in his Christian demons.

But what draws me to meet Landulf is the chance to witness his magic, whether it be white or black. Although I know for a fact it will be black, that I have visited the cruel wizard already. But what I remember of the future grows more abstract with each passing day. The dirt paths of old Sicily are my only guides. I remember Alanda's name but I cannot imagine her face. At night, though, I stare for hours at the stars, trying to convince myself that I was once there, in a mysterious ship, with creatures from another world.

And perhaps with the gods of ancient myths.

Dante wants to tell me about Perseus as we walk.

I am familiar with the mythology, of course, having lived in ancient Greece for many years. But Dante insists I have not heard it properly, and it seems to be one of his favourite stories, so I let him speak. But talking as he walks is a luxury Dante can ill afford. Often he must stop to lean on me for support, but now he is remarkably energetic. He has found a stout walking stick that helps him walk as he speaks with loving enthusiasm about the ancient hero. Obviously Dante worships such characters, and wishes he were one, instead of the crippled leper he is. A handsome young god who could sweep away a beautiful princess such as me. I know Dante is more than a little in love with me.

'Perseus was the son of Zeus and Danaë. His grandfather was Acrisius, a cruel king, who visited the oracle at Delphi and learned that his daughter's child was destined to be the instrument of his death. Perseus and his mother were therefore locked in a chest and set adrift on the ocean. The chest floated to Seriphus, where it was found by a fisherman and brought to the king of the land, Polydectes, a generous man who received them with love. When Perseus had become a young man, Polydectes sent him to destroy the Medusa, a terrible monster that was laying waste to his land and turning men to stone. History has it that Medusa had once been a beautiful maiden whose hair was her chief glory. But she dared to compare herself to Athena, and in revenge the goddess changed her wonderful curls into hissing snakes and she became a monster,' Dante pauses. 'But that's not what happened.'

I have to smile It is only a story.

'What *really* happened, my friend?' I ask, a mocking note in my voice.

Dante is not dissuaded. 'The Medusa never compared herself to anyone. She thought she was beyond comparison, beyond all the gods and goddesses. It was only her hair that became monstrous – her face remained beautiful.'

I laugh. 'That is good to know.'

'It is an important point. One never knows if it was her beauty or the serpents on her head that were able to turn men and other creatures to stone. But I must continue with the tale. Perseus, given a divine shield by Athena, and winged shoes by Hermes, approached Medusa's cave while the monster slept. Perseus took special care not to look directly at her. All around him in the cavern were the stone figures of men and women and animals who had chanced to gaze at the evil creature. Guided only by the Medusa's image reflected in his bright shield, he cut off her head and ended the threat of the monster.'

'Then he gave the head to Athena?' I knew the end,

I thought. Dante shook his head and spoke seriously.

'That is not true. He kept it for himself. It was with the Medusa's head that he was able to defeat Atlas, and steal the gods' golden apples. It was only with the Medusa's head that he was able to turn to stone the Titan that was threatening to eat Andromeda, who would later become his wife.' Dante shook his head again. 'Perseus never gave up the severed head of the Gorgon. It was too valuable a weapon.'

I continue to smile, even though I know we draw close to Landulf's castle. The forest has changed, become wilder and darker, filled with trees that have twisted arms for branches, sharp nails for leaves. A gloom hangs over the land and it depresses even me, me who is usually not affected by subtle elemental vibrations. Even the sun's rays are dimmed by a gray overcast that appears made more of dust than water vapor. There is a constant odor of smoke, and I believe I detect the stench of burnt bodies. Still, I think I am an invincible vampire, no easy victim for Landulf and his black sorcery.

'That is only one version of the story,' I say.

Dante regards me with disappointment.

'It is the correct version, my lady,' he says. 'It is an important story. Hidden within it are many great truths.'

'You will have to explain them to me another time.' I pause and survey the land ahead. We are in rugged mountains made of hard rock and dry river-beds. In the distance hangs a black mist that even my supernatural vision cannot pierce. This unnatural cloud clings to some kind of massive stone structure, but I cannot discern the details. I point and ask, 'What is that?'

Dante is suddenly the cowering fool again. He clings to my arm and the fluid from his open sores stains my white shirt. 'It is our death, my lady. There is still time to turn back. Before his thralls come for us in the black of night.'

'Who are his thralls?'

Dante speaks in a frightened whisper. 'Men who have no hearts, and yet still live. I swear to you I have seen these creatures. They see without eyes and have no need to breathe fresh air.'

'How many men does Landulf have at his command?'

Dante is animated. 'You don't understand, my lady. His power is not in strength of arms. Had he not one man, he could still hold off the full might of Rome, and the Moslems for that matter. Even they fear him.'

I grip Dante's shoulders. 'Tell me how many men he has under his command. Even an estimate will help me.'

Dante is having trouble catching his breath. 'I never counted them. It must be several hundred.'

'Two hundred? Eight hundred?'

Dante coughs. 'Maybe five hundred. But they are not important. It is the spirits that haunt this land that will kill us. They are in the trees, the rocks – he sends them out to spy on those who dare to challenge him. He must already know we are here. We have to go back!'

I am gentle, but I do hold his eye. 'Dante, my friend, you have done me a great service. I know you didn't want to come here but you have. And I know it was out of love and respect for me. But now you have repaid your debt to me. You are free to return the way you have come. I want you to return to Messina, and save yourself. There is no need for you to go any farther along this road.'

To my surprise, my power over him is outweighed by his love for me. He shakes his head and pleads with me. 'You do not know what he will do to you. He has powers you cannot imagine. A lust for cruelty and pain that cannot be spoken. He rips the eyes from his victims and stores them in jars to later feed to caged rats he keeps in his personal quarters. He pulls the bones from slaves before their very eyes and munches on them at gruesome suppers. All this he does to set the stage for his satanic invocations. But when the spirits come, there is nowhere to hide.' Dante weeps and grips my arm fiercely. 'Please don't go there, my lady! In God's holy name I beg you!'

I kiss him, stroke his face, and then shake my head.

'I must go,' I say. 'But I will go in the name of your God, if it comforts you, and the name of my God as well. Wish me luck, my dear Dante, and take care of yourself. You are a precious soul, and I have known so few in my life.'

He is in despair. 'My lady?'

'Goodbye. Do not worry about me.'

I turn and walk deeper into the gloom.

I do not hear him follow.
Yet all around me darkness deepens.
The sun still shines.

10 ～

This castle and its enclosure are built at the top of a cliff. Coming within a mile, I am able to see through the mist enough to know that the rear of the castle is unapproachable. The drop down the back is virtually straight, a thousand feet easily. Unable to see beyond the drop, I know that the ocean must lie not far beyond that – two miles at most. With such a commanding view of the sea and coast, Landulf would be able to spot enemies approaching at any point along southern Sicily. His home is strategically placed – as Dante said – as a doorway to the Christian world.

Outside the castle proper but still within the high stone wall are many small houses, some for living, others military structures where horses and arms are stored. Soldiers with swords wander around small fires, cooking meat, talking among themselves. Over them hangs the bulk of the castle – much larger than I had imagined it. These fires, I see, could not be responsible for the strange mist. Yet I no longer smell cooking human flesh and have to wonder if I imagined it.

I glance behind me. The shadows have grown long, the day is almost over. Dante is nowhere is sight. Yet I hear horses approaching from behind me, where I left Dante. They have a cart of some kind – its wheels creak on the rutted path. Above, a thick branch hangs over me and in a single leap I am cloaked within the leaves of the tree. The castle will have to wait for a moment. I want to see what these men are up to.

Minutes later I receive partial verification of Dante's wild tales.

On the cart is a cage, with metal bars. Three desperate females are locked inside. They are naked, but the four soldiers who have captured them are in full battle gear. Two drive the horses, while the other two are on horseback, one at the front, the other at the rear. The men are young but appear strong and battle tested. The females are each about eighteen. There is, of course, no way I can allow them to be taken into Landulf's castle, even if my intervening might upset my plans.

Vaguely, I remember I have rescued them before.

My plan of attack is simple.

As the first horse passes beneath me, a hundred feet in front of the cage, I drop down and land on the animal right behind the soldier. He is surprised to have company. I don't give him a chance to experience the wonder. Reaching up, I grab the back of his head and twist his skull. There is an explosion of bone and cartilage in his neck. He sags to the side, dead, and I shove him from the horse. Behind me, the two horses pulling the cage rear up. My horse I bring to a halt, and turn to face the others.

Already my long knife is out. Whipping my arm through a blinding arc, I let go of the hilt and plant the blade in the forehead of one of the drivers. The other driver draws his sword. I am forced to run towards him empty-handed. But I receive unexpected help from one of the females. As the soldier raises his sword to strike me, a girl with long hair gives him a swift kick in the back. He loses his balance and topples toward me. Before he hits the ground I relieve him of his sword and cut off his head.

There is still the fourth soldier, the one bringing up the rear. He has drawn a bow and arrow and is taking aim at me. He is an excellent shot. In the blink of an eye I see an arrow fly towards my head. Ducking, I realize that even though it will miss me, it will strike one of the girls. I am reluctant to show too many of my powers, but I have no choice. As the arrow flies by, I reach up and grab it and then break it over my knee.

The fourth soldier is worried.

'I am going to release the women,' I say to him, staring. 'They will ride back the way they have come.'

The soldier just nods.

There are keys to the cage tied to the belt of the

soldier who has my knife in his forehead. I relieve him of these and open the cage, marveling at the intricacy of the lock. The craftsmanship is far beyond anything I have seen before. But the keys work fine and a moment later the women are free. I give the reins to the one who assisted me, and throw the cloak from a dead soldier over her.

'Ride fast from here,' I say catching her eye. 'Do not speak to anyone about me.'

She nods. I step from the cart as she turns it around. In seconds the women in the cart are out of sight. Slowly I walk toward the remaining soldier, who has moved aside to let the women pass. I admire his courage, that he has not tried to bolt. But he is still a kidnapper, and I am thirsty. The soldier draws his sword as I approach but I shake my head.

'You are going to die,' I say. 'It is better not to resist.'

He swings at my head, misses. Stepping forward, I grab the hand that holds his sword and look up into his frightened eyes. 'Who sent you to capture those women?' I ask. 'Was it Landulf?'

He shakes his head. 'No.'

'Who then?'

He refuses to answer me, even though I press him with my eyes. He continues to shake his head, and I am puzzled. I finally pull him from his horse and throw his sword aside. Drawing his face near, I let him feel the warmth of my breath.

'What is he like?' I ask.

The man is resolute. 'He is my lord and my master.'

'Is he evil?'

He sneers. 'You are evil!'

I have to laugh. 'I suppose I am – to you.'

He dies, in my arms, from blood loss. Afterwards, I feel refreshed, ready for more action. The bodies I hide in the bushes beside the path. The blood, even, I cover over with mud. I wash and dress like a young boy again, my hair under my cap. Then I walk towards the castle and boldly knock at the iron gate that guards the entrance in the wall. A host of soldiers answer and I am stern with them.

'I am here to see Landulf of Capua,' I say in a powerful voice. 'Bring me to him.'

They lead me through the courtyard filled with soldiers and smoke to the castle door. A servant comes, and then another. They all seem fairly normal, although I obviously make them nervous. Finally the woman of the house arrives, Landulf's wife, Lady Cia. A striking woman, she wears a high-necked, tight-sleeved, long tunic belted at the waist. Many jewels adorn her hair and elegant fingers. Her hair is black and worn up and her eyes are dark. She is not Mediterranean but English. Her smile is welcoming, yet it doesn't reach her eyes. She is exceedingly thin, and holds herself under rigid control. I cannot say I warm to her, but she is anything but threatening. Certainly she does not seem afraid of me. I have left my long knife with the bodies of the soldiers.

Lady Cia invites me in without many questions. I don't ask why a man who used to be an archbishop now has a wife. Since the pope doesn't want him, I think, he may have decided to enjoy good company.

'It is seldom we get visitors from Greece,' she says, when I explain where I have just come from. 'But that is not your home, is it, Sita?'

Removing my cap, I shake out my blond hair. 'No. Like you, I am from England.'

She is pleased. 'You are perceptive. But surely you are not travelling through the country by yourself?'

I act sad. 'No. I was with my uncle. But there was an accident on the road, and he was killed.'

She touches her heart. 'I am so sorry. What was the accident?'

'His horse threw him. His neck broke.'

She shakes her head and leads me deeper into the castle. 'You poor dear. You must be devastated. Let us give you food, shelter.'

'Thank you.'

The castle is magnificent, and although my eyes strain to detect anything odd, the only unusual thing I see is an excess of wealth, even for a Sicilian aerie commanded by a duke. Landulf has sculptures from all along the Mediterranean. The marble on his floor is inlaid with gold, and the plaster ceilings are warmed by wooden beams. Everything is tasteful, not an offense to the eye. I compliment Cia on her home.

'My husband prides himself on his collections.' She points to a marble statue from ancient Greece. 'Since you were just in that part of the world, I am sure you would appreciate our hero.'

I approach the statue, touch it, think of Dante, and pray he is all right. Perseus holds the head of the Medusa in one upraised hand, a sword in the other. His head is slightly bowed; his great exploit has not made him proud. But the face of the Gorgon is a horror; even in death she finds no peace. A feeling of disquiet sweeps over me, but I push it away. I have seen this statue before, of course I have. Lady Cia stands by my side.

'Can I have a servant show you to your room?' she asks. 'You can rest and wash. Then perhaps you can join us for supper.'

'You and Lord Landulf?'

She does not flinch at the name. 'Yes. We would both enjoy the company.' She snaps a finger and a chubby maid appears. 'Marie will show you to your room.'

I grasp her hands. They are cold, although the castle is warm, with fires burning in most corners. She trembles at my touch but I steady her with my strength. Staring deep into her eyes, I notice nothing supernatural.

'You are most kind,' I say.

Marie leads me up three flights of stairs before we come to my quarters. Along the way we pass a window covered with iron bars, and I see that night has firmly arrived. Marie is dressed in a long black tunic over a white chemise. With a rosary around her neck, she could have been a nun. A few of Landulf's walls are covered with frescoes, paintings done directly on fresh plaster. Most of these have a spiritual theme. He seems to have an obsession with the Old Testament. The God that looks over his household is often angry.

Marie opens a door onto a small room. There is linen on the straw mattress and a bowl of water. Marie lights a row of candles and asks if I need anything else.

'No thank you,' I say.

She leaves and I am alone. Washing my hands in the water provided, I am at a loss to explain why I keep looking around for a faucet with running water. Then I remember there are such niceties, in other places. The water is cold but seems fresh. I drink some and it rinses away the blood in my mouth. I do not understand how the soldier was able to resist my questions.

11 ⌁

A short time later I am at Lord Landulf's supper table. An old spear is fastened to the wall. It is this spear that the room seems to be designed around. From the massive stone fireplace logs crack and shoot showers of sparks out into the room as I am introduced to Lord Landulf by Lady Cia.

'This is the young woman I told you about,' she says. 'She came to our door not more than an hour ago, seeking asylum. Her travelling companion, her uncle, has just been killed on the road. Sita, this is the duke and my husband, Lord Landulf.'

He is not a tall man and looks frail, which surprises me, after all the gruesome stories I have heard of him. Yet his delicateness is not necessarily a sign of weakness. He appears to be physically agile, and I suspect he is an

294

accomplished swordsman. He wears a neatly trimmed black moustache and a pointed greying beard. He has oily smooth skin, and is dressed impeccably in a dark red silk chemise with long, tight sleeves, black hose, and a red and gold embroidery tunic, which comes down past his knees. His hands, like those of his wife, are decorated with many uncut gems and pearls. A ruby on his left middle finger is the largest I have ever seen. His voice, when he speaks is cultured, educated and refined. His large dark eyes are warm but shrewd. He clicks his soft, heelless leather shoes together and bows in my direction.

'Lady Sita,' he says. 'It is a pleasure.'

I offer my hand. 'The pleasure is mine, Lord Landulf.'

He kisses my middle finger, and glances up at me. 'Surprise visitors are always the most enchanting.'

'Hidden castles are always the most exciting,' I say with a smile.

We sit down to a vegetable soup. Lady Cia leads us in a brief prayer. There are only us three at the table; we have four servants waiting on us. The soup is finished when Landulf inquires about my travels. Considering the expansion of the Arab World, it is impossible to talk for more than a few minutes without the subject turning to the invading Moslems. At this Landulf's mood turns foul.

'Six of those heathen ships tried to land on a beach not five miles from here,' he says bitterly. 'They came in on a wave of fog, but my scouts were wary. We were able to set fire to their sails before they reached land. All their people were lost in the tides.'

His remark stuns me. 'You fight the Moslems here?' I ask.

'Of course,' he says, and there is a gleam in his eye as he studies me. 'Have you heard different?'

I lower my head. 'No, my lord.'

'Come,' he says with force, 'we are sharing food. Why have secrets between friends? You have obviously travelled far and wide with your uncle. You know more of Greece than I do. What have you heard of my relationship with the Moslems?'

I hesitate, then decide I may as well dive in. 'The word is that you are in league with them.'

He does not lose his temper as I fear. But the air chills. 'It is only in Rome they would speak such lies,' he says.

'I have been in Rome,' I say. 'Not three months ago.'

'Oh dear,' Lady Cia mutters anxiously. 'We did not know you had been exposed to such matters.'

Landulf raises his hand. 'It doesn't matter. In the short time I have known Sita, it is obvious to me she is not taken in by every story shared by every frustrated priest and nun.'

'That is true, my lord,' I say.

Landulf pulls his chair back from the table and sighs. 'It is true that the Holy Father and I have gone our separate ways. But our differences were and still are more political than spiritual. Nicholas believes we should fortify our defences, and wait for the Moslems to break against our walls. But I know this foe too well. I have met these bloodthirsty monsters on the battlefield. If we do not attack, push the war back into their own lands, they will see us as weak and never leave us in peace.' Landulf stands and steps away from the table. 'But all that is a question of strategy, and in my own land I pursue my own counsel. But to hear the talk in Rome I have denounced the Church and turned against Christ himself.' He pauses. 'Is that what you have heard, Lady Sita?'

I have already taken the plunge. The wild tales I may as well validate, or else put aside. 'I have heard worse, my lord,' I say. 'The peasants say you conjure evil forces. That you are a master of the black arts and able to raise demons from the depths of hell.'

Landulf is momentarily struck, then laughs long and hard. His wife joins him after a tense moment. 'I would like to meet one of these peasants and ask him where he gets his information!' he exclaims. 'That is the trouble with lies. They are perpetually pregnant. At every turn they give birth to more lies.'

'There was a peasant I met along the roads,' I say carefully. 'He acted as if he knew you. His name was Dante. You've heard of him?'

Lady Cia gushes. 'Dante? My lord has known him since he was a child. Pray tell us where you met him?'

I am evasive. 'When I was lost in the woods, after my uncle died. But that was three days' journey from here.' I add, 'Dante seemed lost as well, and I shared food with him.'

'I pray you did not share anything else with him,' Landulf says darkly, referring to Dante's leprosy.

'I was careful always to keep a safe distance,' I say. 'But when he spoke of this place, it was with fear. I couldn't understand why.'

'Surely you must know,' Lady Cia says. 'It is his illness. Since he became ill, he has spoken of nothing but demons that chase after his soul.'

Again Lord Landulf raises his hand. 'It is not so easy as that. I am partly to blame for his condition. When I brought him to Rome, as a boy, the Holy Father became enamoured of his singing voice. Without my consent or knowledge, the pope had him castrated, so that his voice would remain high. Dante took the loss of his manhood badly, and I think he never ceased blaming me for the disfigurement. Since I was the cause of one physical aberration, when the illness came over him, he blamed me for that as well.'

'But we tried to keep Dante here, and comfortable,' Lady Cia says. 'It was just that our servants feared his illness and he himself felt he needed to be free to roam the world.'

Landulf shakes his head. 'It pains me to know that my own friend has joined the chorus against me. Very well, leadership has its price. I cannot turn from the task I have set before me, to protect the underbelly of the Christian world. If I go to my grave cursed by every cardinal in the Vatican, at least I will still be able to hold my head up high when I meet my Lord in heaven.'

'That is all that matters,' I mutter.

Landulf steps closer to the fire, to the spear, and points out the aged iron tip to me. 'Sita, do you know what this is?'

I stand and join him near the object. There is a single crude nail bound to the spear by circles of wire. The black shaft, I see, has more recently been joined to the tip – it is not nearly so old. Landulf touches the metal spear tip lovingly, running his fingers over the tapered edges, which are surprisingly sharp given the spear's obvious antiquity.

'I have never seen it before,' I say.

He nods. 'Few people have, except those who have been chosen to lead the fight against unrighteousness. This is the Spear of Longinus, sometimes called the Maurice Spear. It is this very spear that Gaius Cassius, a Roman Centurion under the command of ProConsul Pontius Pilate, used to pierce the side of the blessed Lord himself. Thus he put an end to Jesus' suffering on the cross. The final prophecy from the Old Testament that Jesus had to fulfill to prove that he was the true Messiah was that of Isaiah, who said, 'A bone of Him not be broken.' You see, Sita, at the time Jesus suffered on the cross, Annas and Caiaphas, high priests of the Sanhedrin, were trying to convince the Romans to kill Jesus before the Sabbath began. It was the priests' hope that the Romans would mutilate Jesus' body, and therefore prove that he was not the chosen one. But Gaius Cassius, although a Roman soldier, was devoted to Jesus and his teachings, and did not want to see Jesus' body defiled. He took up this spear of his own free will, and in that moment all the prophecies of the world were held in balance in his hand. But at the moment this spear pierced Jesus' side, all the prophecies were fulfilled. For that reason, it is said that whoever holds this spear commands the destiny of the world.' Landulf paused and smiled slightly. 'It is the story that is told about it.'

And a fascinating one, too. I reach out and touch the spear, and feel a strange power sweep over me. It is unlike anything I have ever experienced before, at least none that I can remember. But vaguely the thought of a brown-skinned child comes to my mind. The spear is a weapon of war, yet somehow it comforts me. I touch the tip and think of the blood that once spilled over it. The blood that supposedly had the power to wash away all sins. Standing beside Landulf, I feel the weight of all the people I have murdered for their blood. He seems to sense something odd because he stares at me intensely.

'Sita?' he says.

'But you believe this story?' I say in an unsteady voice.

He continues to watch me. 'I do, but then I am a romantic at heart.' He leans close and whispers in my ear. 'What do you feel when you touch it, Sita?'

I momentarily close my eyes. 'I feel the child,' I whisper.

'The baby Jesus?'

'John.'

He moves back. 'The Baptist?'

I open my eyes, confused. For an instant the face of

Suzama flashes in my mind. But she had no children, I think. Suzama was celibate. Yet the name of John haunts me, as does the face of a child I cannot quite pinpoint.

'I was not thinking of the Baptist,' I say.

'What then?' he insists.

In that moment, in that castle, I cannot remember.

'I don't know,' I say.

He gestures to the table. 'Why don't we finish our meal?'

'Thank you.'

He takes me by the hand and leads me back to the meal.

12 ~~~

Later, in my room, I feel dull and tired. I am four thousand years old, I do not normally need much sleep. Yet my vision is now blurred with fatigue. Staring in a mirror surrounded by candles, I feel as if my face changes into that of a person from another time and my blonde hair turns dark red. The candles grow to the size of the flames that burned in the fireplace. Splashing water on my face, I feel some of the illusions leave me, but they do not go away. There is an unpleasant taste in my mouth that the water cannot wash away.

Then it strikes me.

I have been drugged.

Landulf, perhaps with his wife's knowledge, had something put in my food. There is no other explanation for my lethargy. But it is unlikely that the drug was administered for my benefit – a good night's sleep in a castle rumored to be filled with demons. If he has drugged me it is because he wants me unconscious so that he can do something awful to me. All of Dante's tales come back to me in a haunting wave, and I am amazed at how I have dropped my guard. But could my carelessness have something to do with Landulf's magic?

For all I know, his drug was poison and I am already doomed.

I force myself to vomit. Then I drink the water left in the bowl and vomit again. Within seconds my head clears, but I am still far from being at full strength. Moving to the door, I find it locked by a device as sophisticated as the one I found on the cage that held the young women. The metal parts are made of a peculiar alloy – stronger than anything I have ever encountered. Fortunately the door, although thick oak, is only wood. Leaning hard on it, and taking deep breaths to clear my system of the lingering effects of the drug, I am able to break it open without much noise.

Marie stands outside my door.

I grab her and pull her inside.

'What are you doing here?' I demand.

She is frightened. I have a strong grip on her neck.

'I was coming to see if you needed anything, my lady.'

'You lie. You were waiting outside my door. Why?'

She wiggles her head. 'No, my lady, I am here to serve you.'

'You are here to spy on me.' I choke her. 'Did Lord Landulf send you?'

She gasps. 'No. Please? You are hurting me.'

I tighten my grip and she begins to lose colour. 'You feel how strong I am? I have the strength of a dozen men. Tell me the truth now or you will die in pain. Were you spying outside my door?'

She can hardly get the word out. 'Yes.'

'You had been told I was drugged?'

'Yes.'

'Who told you?'

'Lady Cia.'

'You were waiting by the door for me to pass out?'

'Yes.'

'What were you going to do with me then?'

Marie turns blue. But she has enough will left to struggle.

'No!' she gasps.

I dig my fingernails into her neck, drawing blood.

'You answer me or I'll rip your head off!'

She moans. 'I was to take you to the sacrifice.'

I loosen my grip and frown. 'What sacrifice? Where?'

She struggles for air. 'It is below – in the hidden chambers.'

I point my finger at her. 'You will take me there, through a back way. I want to see this sacrifice but I do not want to be seen. Do you understand?'

She coughs weakly. 'I don't want to die.'

I am grim. 'You keep thinking that way.'

Marie leads me through a dark passageway unconnected to the hallways and rooms of the public castle. We hardly leave my bedroom when we enter a narrow tunnel opened by touching a stone with a series of special pressures. The entrance closes behind us, and I wonder if I would have the strength to reopen it. The effect of the drug continues to plague me. Coloured lights flash and trail at the corners of my vision. My heart pounds in my head and I cannot stop yawning. Cramps grip my spine. The power of the poison stuns me. Ordinarily, my system is immune to any kind of abusive substance.

We reach steep stairs and start down. The walls continue to press in on us. The stairs are seemingly endless. I carry a torch in one hand, grip the back of Marie's neck with the other. 'If you cry out at any time.' I say, 'that cry will be the last sound you hear in this world.'

'I won't betray you,' she whispers.

'I can see you are very loyal.'

We continue to go down for the next twenty minutes, and I begin to believe Landulf has fashioned his castle over a natural cave. It is ridiculous to think he could have carved away so much stone with human hands. Yet somebody must have built this passage-way, and I have to wonder if it is older than I imagined. The surrounding stones appear ancient. I remember Dante's remark, that this spot used to shelter the Oracle of Venus.

Eventually I detect a red glow ahead. At the same time the temperature increases sharply. Putting out my torch, I stop Marie and question her.

'Lord Landulf performs sacrifices down there?' I ask.

'Yes.'

'What kind?'

'All kinds.'

I shake her. 'Does he kill humans? Torture them?'

'Yes. Yes.'

'Why?'

She weeps. 'I don't know why.'

'Then why do you stay here? Are you not a Christian?'

She trembles beneath my gaze. 'If I do not serve, I will be sacrificed.'

'Is that the law?'

'Yes. Please let me go.'

'Not until I am finished with you. Is there a place from where we can watch these sacrifices? And not be detected?'

She glances in the direction of the red glow. It is as if the light of hell beckons us. I smell burnt flesh again, and it has the odour of fresh meat. Marie is having trouble breathing.

'There is a passageway off to the side and above,' she whispers. 'But it is not all stone.'

'What do you mean?'

'It is a metal grill, set in the ceiling. If they look up, they will see us.'

'Why should they look up?'

'The eyes of my lord are everywhere!'

'Shh. Don't call him your lord. He is a perverted human.' I grab her by the neck again. 'Come, you will see.'

The passageway Marie speaks of comes well before we reach the cavern. I feel and hear the hot tension in the cavern, the sound of many people whispering among themselves, the moans of a few unfortunates, the faint clash of metal. Even before I see, I know Landulf has brought his devotees as well as his soldiers to this accursed hole. I have to wonder if they're not all Satan worshippers.

Marie leads me into a tunnel where we have to get down on our hands and knees and crawl. The way is hot and soon I am drenched with sweat. But below our hands and knees the stone finally turns to wire mesh. We have reached the grills from which we can peer down at what is to be.

The ceremony is about to begin.

We are directly above the altar. It is circular, surrounded on all sides by rows of pews that lead up and back one hundred feet. There are approximately six hundred people present. Each person wears a red robe, except for a few soldiers at the doors, who have on metal breast plates and helmets. The altar is black and polished; it appears to be made of marble. Inlaid is a silver pentagram. The five tips of the stars dissect the room into five sections. Landulf sits on the floor with his wife. He is the only one wearing a black robe, and I can't help but notice the small silver knife resting in his lap.

Candles surround the altar. They are black and very tall, but what is most remarkable is that they burn with purple flames. The sober light spills over the marble and the silent participants like a glow from an unearthed volcano. The tension in the air is palpable and it is not something I would wish to touch. I sense that Landulf strives for tension in his rites.

Landulf stands and walks to the centre of the pentagram.

He raises his hand with the knife.

The group begins to sing, and for a moment I am bewildered. For it sounds to me as if they are singing the Catholic Mass in Latin. But then I realize they have started at the end, and are working their way towards the beginning, moving verse by verse through the litany. And the knife Landulf holds – the handle is shaped like a crucifix, yet he grasps it by the blade, upside down.

Everything they are doing is backwards.

Landulf's grip is tight on his blade. Blood runs down his arm as his worshippers sing, but he doesn't seem to mind. In all of this, the most amazing thing is that their voices are quite beautiful. They remind me of Dante, who never went to sleep without reciting the Mass. Yet their motives are clearly the opposite of Dante's. He implored God for forgiveness for sins he had never committed. These creatures implore another power to accept their sins and reward them for them.

After forty minutes the twisted mass ends. A wooden cross is brought out by soldiers and laid in the centre of the pentagram. Clad in a white robe, a bound female is carried out next. Her mouth is tied, she cannot cry out. But I see it is one of the girls I thought I had saved. That must mean the other two did not escape either. The girl is spread out on the cross but her white robe is left on. Finally the material stuffed in her mouth is removed and she cries out weakly. Landulf stands over her like the Grim Reaper, or worse. He has exchanged his knife for a small hammer and a bunch of nails. His intention is painfully obvious.

He is going to crucify the young woman.

I cannot watch this. I cannot let it happen.

But I have to watch. And I know I can do nothing.

Landulf holds nails and hammer up for all to see. So far the group has been fairly sedate, but now they leap to their feet and start screaming and jeering. I cannot tell if they are experiencing pain or pleasure. It seems a perverse mixture of both. Landulf kneels beside the girl and the soldiers who hold her down as the noise of the group reaches a frenzy. The very air is now vibrating. I find myself panting hard, on the verge of vomiting. I am a vampire who has killed thousands, yet I cannot bear that they should do this *thing* to such innocence, and enjoy it, and still remain human. It doesn't seem as if God should allow it.

I have to remind myself that God allowed it long ago.

Landulf begins to hammer in the nails.

The blood flows over the silver pentagram.

The girl's screams rend my soul.

Then I cry out, and the group falls instantly silent.

Plump, frightened Marie has stabbed a knife in my lower back. Put it in deep, cut a few arteries and important nerves. My blood seeps over the wire mesh and spills onto the altar below. Directly on to Landulf's face. He stares up and hungrily licks it as it drops – rain from hell. There is poison on the tip of Marie's blade; it mingles with the drugs already racking my system and causes havoc with my reflexes. Straining to pull it out, I feel my wound being licked by this docile servant girl. She has been told something about my blood, and thinks it will grant her immortality and great powers. She is like a giant insect sticking a needle in my vital organs. But apparently she takes the feeding ritual too far. Landulf suddenly shouts at her.

'It is for me!' he yells.

I am in such agony. Without wishing it, my weight and Marie's weight sag onto the wire mesh. It breaks. We fall like creatures cast down from heaven. Marie lands on her head and her skull explodes in a grey mass. I land on my back and the knife rams so deeply into me that it pokes through my liver and out my front. I have crashed beside the half-crucified woman, and Landulf steps over her to get to me. His face is smeared with blood, yet incredibly he appears sad, as if he wished it could have ended another way. I feel I have reached the end. My strength ebbs rapidly; I cannot get the knife out of my back, so that I may heal. The tortured girl screams at me as if I were a demon. Her mind is shattered. On the cold black altar our blood mingles and flows over the silver star as the crowd cheers. All this had been entertainment to them. Landulf puts a foot on my bloody hair and stares down at me.

'How do you feel, Sita?' he asks with feeling.

I cough blood. 'Wonderful.'

'You have come to where I always wanted you to be.'

I try to roll on to my side, still trying for the blade.

He steps on my free arm with his other foot.

'I am happy for you,' I gasp.

He grins slowly. 'You are very beautiful, your body, your spirit. This agony is unnecessary. Join me, I will remove the knife and you will be better.'

The pain is unbearable. 'What do I have to do to join you?'

He presses hard on my arm, grinding the bone into the floor.

'A small thing,' he replies. 'Just finish nailing these stakes in this young woman you foolishly tried to save.'

I think about it for a moment.

A long moment considering my situation.

'My lord,' I say. 'Go to hell.'

He laughs and raises his foot and puts it over my face.

Darkness comes. It is especially dark.

13 ~~~

When I come to, I feel as if I am being crucified. There is pain in my arms and chest, and I can hardly breathe. Opening my eyes, I find myself chained in a cell, deep in a black dungeon. My arms are strung above me, spread out like the wings of a bird, pinned to a dripping stone wall with locks similar to the ones I saw on the cage. This metal is a special alloy that I am unable to break, at least in my present condition. I struggle with the binds and only end up exhausting myself further.

Naturally, I can still see in the dark. From head to foot, I am covered with blood, but I see that it is not my blood, but that of the girl they were sacrificing. The knife has been removed from my spine and that wound has healed. But there is no relief for me. Crucifixion brings death by slow suffocation, and the position of my arms and legs mimics that of the Roman style of execution. My feet are also bound to the wall, but they are slightly above the floor so that all the pressure of the metal anklets is on my calf bones. Remnants of Landulf's poisons continue to percolate in my system. I have to wonder if he siphoned off large amounts of my blood while I was unconscious.

Yet I do not think so.

How long I have been hanging there, I do not know. But steadily my pain grows so great that I begin to cry quietly to myself. Yes, even I, ancient Sita, who has faced the trials of four thousand years of life and survived, feel as if I have at last been defeated. Each breath is an exercise in cruel labour; the air burns my chest as it is forced in, and each time I exhale, I wonder if I will have the strength to squeeze in another lungful. My cries turn to feeble screams, then moans that reverberate deep in my soul, like the solemn laminations of the dammed already sealed in hell. I feel I have been forced beneath the earth, into a place of unceasing punishment. Landulf's face swims in my mind and I wonder if I see a vision of Satan.

Yet in my suffering, on the verge of final unconsciousness, something remarkable happens. My mind begins to clear, and I remember Alanda and Suzama, Seymour and the child. I see the stars and recall how I floated high above the Earth, and swore to do everything I could to protect my mother world. I am five thousand years old, not four thousand. I am from the future and I have returned in time to defeat

Landulf. And I will defeat him, I tell myself. He will come for me, I remember he did before. I just have to hang on a little while longer.

I remember other things as well.

The Spear of Longinus.

I remember it from twentieth century Europe.

In Austria, in the year 1927, in the capital city of Vienna, I saw Richard Wagner's opera *Parsival*, which portrayed the adventures of King Arthur's knights in search of the Holy Grail, in a mythological setting. Historians claimed at that time that there was no historical basis for the events in the opera. Still, Richard Wagner's masterpiece was very moving, the powerful music, the tragic plot of how the knights struggled against the evil Klingsor, who obstructed them at every step from behind the scenes. Most of all, I was intrigued by Wagner's use of the Spear of Longinus – which I had seen in *my* past – as a magic wand in the hands of the evil Klingsor.

It made me realize, *then*, that Klingsor might have been Landulf.

There could be historical accuracy in the opera, after all.

After leaving the theatre, I researched Wagner's source material and read Wolfram von Eschenbach's *Parsival*, upon which the opera was based. I was intrigued to see that the spear played an even more central role in the actual tale, and was stunned to learn that Eschenbach had lived eleven generations after the time of Arthur and Parsival, and yet had managed to write a thrilling story even though he was supposedly an illiterate imbecile. From what could be gleaned from the old texts, it seemed that Eschenbach had simply cognized – out of the thin air – the mystical tale.

Even then, in the twentieth century in Austria, that fact had made me wonder if perhaps Eschenbach's story was symbolic of deeper truths. Because by the twentieth century, history had all but forgotten Landulf. Yet even Eschenbach, a wandering Homer of little reputation, a *minnesinger*, had named him the most evil man who had ever lived. Who knew better than I why Eschenbach should condemn the duke so? Chilled by my own memories, I became convinced that Klingsor was indeed Landulf.

In the story, Klingsor, had been an archbishop who lived at Kalot Enbolot, in southwest Sicily, where he summoned demons and sent them forth to torment the world. But most important, Eschenbach had described Klignsor's most important identifying mark and the basis of his evil.

Yet, in Landulf's dark prison, I cannot remember that mark.

From far away, as I become more delirious, I hear a sound. Knights and lords approaching from above, slowly winding down to my black cell. My torment is unbearable – for it to end, it seems, is all I can hope for. Yet I force in a shuddering breath and steel myself to fulfill my promise to those who sent me back in time. I recall Krishna's promise to me, that his grace shall always be with me. But I do not ask God to save me, only to give me the strength to save myself.

The door opens and in strides Landulf.

Alone. His men wait outside.

He brings a clean damp towel and wipes at the blood that has dried on my face. Then he touches my cheek, and before I can react, leans forward and plants a kiss on my cracked lips. I try to spit in his face, but there is not enough moisture in my mouth. Landulf stares at me with such compassion that I have to wonder if I have slipped into a dream where demons are angels and the future is already burned to ash by our ancestors' sins. For a moment I am in more than one time, but then Landulf slaps me hard on the cheek, even as he pretends to bemoan my torment, and then I am alone with him, only him.

'Sita,' he says with sympathy. 'Why do you do this to yourself?'

I strain to moisten my swollen throat. 'I could swear, my lord, that I did not climb into these chains while I was unconscious.'

He enjoys my gusto. 'But these chains are of your own making. I have offered you another way. Why don't you take it? What is the sacrifice for one such as you? We are already old partners in this war.'

'I didn't know that this was a war?' I say honestly.

He is serious. 'But it is – a battle far older than even your nonperishable body. It goes back to the birth of the stars, to the dropping of the veil, and of the opening of the two paths back to the source. You see me as a monster but I tell you I am God's greatest devotee.'

'Aren't you exaggerating just a little?'

He slaps me again. 'No! It is the truth you refuse to see. Will is stronger than love. Power lasts longer than virtue. My path is left-handed, true, but it is the swiftest and the surest.' He pauses and comes closer. 'Did not your friends tell you that all roads lead to the same destination?'

His question stuns me, the implications of his insight. 'What friends are those?' I ask innocently.

He nods to himself as he studies my eyes. 'I have seen you before on the path.'

I force a smile and know it must more closely resemble a grimace. 'Then you must know I will never join you. Because although I may be a sinner, I am also a servant. I love virtue, I love human love, even if I am not human. These are the things that bring me the most joy. Your path may be swift and sure but it is barren. The desert surrounds your every step and you walk forever a thirsty man. You may leave me to rot in this cell, but I am not forsaken. When I leave this body I know I will drink deep of Christ's and Krishna's fathomless love, and I will be happy while you crawl on your hands and knees to invoke your miserable demons. Whom you send out to perform deeds you are too frightened to perform in person. You sicken me, Landulf. Had I a free hand, I would tear your tongue from your face so that you could no longer spew lies in my direction.'

He is unmoved by my speech.

'You will beg for my mercy, Sita. You will kill at my bidding.'

317

I snort. 'You will not live long enough, my lord, to see me do either.'

He holds my eye. 'We shall see.' He raises a hand and snaps a finger and two armour-clad soldiers with torches, a prisoner between them, waddle into the cell.

They have brought Dante.

'My lady!' he cries when he sees me and tries to run to my side. But he trips and falls facedown on the damp floor, and is only able to rise when Landulf pulls him up by his hair. The black lord shoves my friend in my direction and Dante cowers and prays at my feet, weeping to see me in such a desperate condition. I would weep for my friend if there were any tears left in my body. But all I can do is sigh and shake my head.

'Dante,' I say. 'I told you to go back to Messina. Why are you here?'

He clasps my foot. 'I could not leave you, my lady. I will never leave you.'

Landulf is grim. 'We caught him outside the castle walls, groveling like an animal.' He grabs him by the neck and picks him all the way up off the floor with one hand. The demonstration of strength disturbs me. Perhaps he did take my blood, and put it into his veins, while I was unconscious. Yet Landulf does not show the signs of being a true vampire. He dangles Dante in front of me. 'Will you not beg, Sita?' Landulf asks me.

I am fearful. 'For what?'

'You know, my proud ruby.'

I sneer. 'Why beg for that which does not exist?'

In response Landulf throws Dante down in a heap

and takes a torch from one of his men. Knocking out the flame on the damp wall, he steps towards Dante with the embers of the torch top still glowing. Seeing what Landulf has in mind, Dante tries to scamper to me but is kicked aside by Landulf. The evil lord kneels by my friend and points out to me Dante's sores.

'These wounds are infected,' Landulf says. 'They must be cauterized and sealed. Don't you agree, Sita?'

I stare in horror. 'He served you loyally for many years.'

Landulf eyes Dante, who trembles in anticipation. 'But he betrayed me in the end,' he says. 'And it is only the end that matters, not the manner of the path.'

'Landulf!' I cry.

But he ignores me, and then Dante is crying, screaming for me to save him as if I were his mother. But even though I have returned in time with the wisdom of the ages, I can do nothing – cannot keep Landulf from pressing the embers into Dante's oozing sores. Landulf first does my friend's deformed hand, and then he moves towards Dante's leg, where the damage is even more extensive. Dante howls so loud and hard it seems as if his skull will explode. Certainly the sound threatens to rupture my own heart. As Landulf moves forward with the torch again, I hear myself cry out.

'Please?' I yell. 'Please stop!'

Landulf pauses and smiles up at me. 'You beg me?'

I nod weakly. 'I beg you, my lord.'

Landulf stands. 'Good. You have passed the first step

14 ～～

More time goes by and with each passing minute I die a little more inside. Crucified alone in the dark, I could imagine no crueller torture, yet I had not known the half of it. Dante is largely unconscious, but still he moans miserably. For a time I pray that he does not wake again, that he simply dies, and so ends his suffering. But then the curse of all who suffer comes to me.

I glimpse a faint ray of hope.

I have to wake Dante, bring him back to the nightmare.

Calling his name softly, he finally stirs and raises his head and looks around. It is so dark; it is obvious he cannot see a thing. But I can see his ruined expression and it pierces my heart. He is hung up on the wall right beside me.

'Sita?' he whispers.

'I am here,' I say gently. 'Don't be afraid.'

He is having trouble breathing. Landulf's knights have tied him up like me, his arms pinned by unbreakable chains. Yet his feet are not bound; they manage to touch the floor. But I know soon he will begin to smother. He coughs as he tries to speak.

'I'm sorry, my lady,' he says. 'I disobeyed you.'

'No. You have nothing to be ashamed of. You are a true hero. Even when the situation appears hopeless, you plunge forward. Perseus himself, I would guess, would be envious of your stout heart.'

He tries to smile. 'Could it be true?'

'Oh yes. And you might yet save us both.'

He is interested. 'How, my lady?'

'I need you to shake free of your leg brace and push it over here.'

'My lady?'

'Your tiny copper crucifix, the one you pray to before sleeping each night. I need it.'

He is worried. 'What are you going to do to it?'

'I am sorry, Dante, I am going to have to ruin it. But I think I can form the cross into a narrow instrument that I can use to pick these locks.'

'But, my lady, your hands are bound!'

'I am going to use my toes to mould it into a proper shape. Don't worry about the details, Dante, just push your brace over here. Is it easy to slip out of?'

'No problem, my lady.' I see him struggle in the dark. 'Are you on my right or on my left?'

I have to smile. 'I am on your left, two feet away.'

'I feel you near,' he says with affection as he slips out of the brace and pushes it towards me with his stump. 'Do you have it?'

'No. My feet are pinned together. You will have to give it a shove, but not too hard. The brace must come to rest against the side of my legs.'

'But I can't see your legs.'

'They are pinned to the wall. Lay the brace against the wall and just give it a slight nudge forward.'

'Are you sure this is a good plan?'

'Yes.'

'I am not sure.'

'Dante?'

He suddenly hyperventilates. 'I am afraid, my lady! Without my brace I will be a cripple!'

I speak soothingly. 'I will not damage your brace, Dante. Only the cross you keep hidden in it. When I am free, you will have your brace back and we will escape from here.'

He begins to calm. 'We will go back to Messina?'

'Yes. Together we will travel to Messina, and there we will stay in the finest inn, and order the best food and wine. You will be my companion and I will tell everyone how you rescued me from the evil duke.'

Dante beams. 'I will be like Perseus! I will slay the Gorgon!'

'Exactly. But let's get out of here first. Push the brace closer to me.'

'What if I push it too far?'

'You won't, Dante. You are a hero. Heroes don't

make mistakes.'

Dante pushes feebly at the brace with his leper stump. 'Is that all right, my lady?'

'Harder.'

'I am trying, my lady.' He strikes the brace with his stump and the wooden leg bumps up against my calf. 'You have it?'

'I have it,' I quickly reassure him. 'You relax and catch your breath. You don't even have to speak to me. I will concentrate on getting us out of here.'

He groans. 'Hurry, my lady. I am in some pain.'

'I know, my friend.'

Even for a vampire, what I plan to do next is not easy. First I have to let the top of the brace slide down to where I can reach it with my toes. This I do without much effort, but Dante's cross is not stored at the top of the brace. It is fastened somewhat deeper inside the wooden stump. After fishing for it with my toes for ten minutes, I am no closer to reaching it, and even more weary, if that is possible.

Then it occurs to me that I must invert the brace. This is tricky, because if the copper cross slips past my toes, it will land on the floor and be out of reach. What I do to add a safety margin to my plan is to raise the brace up with just one foot, catching it between my big toe and the toe next to it. Then I plug the end of the brace with the bottom of my other foot. Shaking the brace upside down in the air, at a ninety-degree angle to my calf, I feel the cross touch the sole of my free foot. In a moment my toes have a grip on the crucifix and I let go of the brace.

'My lady?' Dante cries.

'Everything is all right.'

'My brace is not broken?'

'It is fine. Be silent and conserve your strength. We will soon be free.'

'Yes, my lady.'

Both my feet grip the copper cross. I will keep plenty of toes wrapped around it at all times, I tell myself. There is no way it is going to spring beyond my reach. As I work to mould the copper, I pray Landulf's *soon* did not mean in the next few minutes. I have prayed many times since entering the castle.

The crucifix is relatively thin, little more than a stamped plate, and this is fortunate. It does not take me long to squeeze the lower portion of the cross into a stiff wire. True, it is a rather plump wire but the key holes in the locks that bind me are far from tiny. Clasping the wire in my right foot, and holding still the key hole with my left foot, I slowly glide the cooper toward the inner mechanism.

'My lady?'

'Shh, Dante. Patience.'

'My hand pains me.'

'We will make it better soon. Please do not speak for the next few minutes.'

The wire enters the lock and I feel around to get a sense of its design. My mind is very alert now. The traumas I have suffered – I put them all behind so I can focus on the inside of the lock. It does not take long before I have a complete mental picture of how it was built, and when I do, I know precisely how to move my wire.

There is a click and the lock springs open.

I kick off the chains. My feet are free.

'My lady!' Dante cheers.

'Quiet. Let me finish.'

He gasps. 'Oh, yes, hurry. I cannot breathe like this.'

Now comes the hardest part. I cannot pull either hand chain down close enough to my face so that I might work the locks with the wire between my teeth, assuming I could get the copper in my mouth. No, I have to reach up with my right foot, stretching my leg to a next-to-impossible length, and attack the *left* lock that way. My muscles are stiff so the task is doubly hard. Yet I can taste freedom now, and it gives me fresh strength.

Clenching the wire in my toes, I kick up.

My hamstring muscles scream.

I fail to reach the lock. I have to kick up a dozen times before I even approach it. But steadily my joints limber, and finally I am steering the wire into the lock that grips my left wrist. Since I already know the internal design of the mechanism, I take only a second to trip it. My left hand is now free, and I immediately transfer the wire from my toes into my fingers. Two seconds after that, I have sprung the right lock and am able to stand and stretch. But Dante has gone downhill. He doesn't even realize that I am free. I step to his side and caress the top of his head. He looks up without seeing me in the pitch black and smiles.

'Are we safe?' he asks softly.

'Almost,' I say, and I use the wire to open his locks. But his arms don't come down when they are free, his limbs are so damaged. I have to draw them down, and this makes him cry out. He buries his face in my chest and I comfort him. 'Dante,' I say. 'This dungeon will not hold us.'

He lets go of me, but he is lost in the dark and he cannot stand without support. 'Where is my brace?' he asks. 'Will it still work?'

'Your brace is here and it is undamaged, as I promised.' I slide his stump back into it but cringe at the smell of his burnt flesh. Taking his wounded left hand, I study the sores. Landulf took his cauterization too far; he burned into the healthy tissue beneath Dante's wounds. Later, I swear to myself, when we have time, I must sprinkle a few drops of my blood on the sores to ease his agony.

'It is best you don't touch me, my lady' Dante says in shame.

I squeeze his arm. 'You are my hero. Of course I will touch you.'

He is happy, for the moment, but he is also close to death.

'My lady,' he gasps as he continues to struggle for air, despite his release from the bonds. 'I know a secret the duke might not even know.' He taps the wall behind his head. 'There is a passageway back here, if we can get to it. The way leads under the farthest wall and out into the woods.'

'Can we reach this passageway from the tunnel beyond this cell door?'

'Yes, my lady. But how are we going to get through the door?'

Good question. After studying the door, I see that it is made of the same alloy as the locks and chains. I cannot break through it. But I have come to this dilemma before. My awareness of the future is still present, but still somewhat cloudy. For several seconds I cannot remember precisely what I did next. Then the water dripping from the wall against which we were imprisoned catches my attention. The mortar between the stones must be weak, I reason, to allow so much moisture to seep through it and into the cell.

'Dante,' I say. 'Is this secret passageway of yours flooded?'

'Sometimes, my lady. At certain times of the year.'

'Is this a certain time of the year?'

He hesitates. 'There should be some water in the passage, yes. But I do not think it will be flooded. I hope it is not.'

'Does the water run out into the forest?'

'The passageway leads in two directions. The water runs out to the cliff, in the direction of the sea.'

'Stand away from this wall, by the door. I am going to work on these stones.'

'Yes, my lady. Where is the door?'

I have to lead him to it. He slides down, weakly, with his back to the exit. He cannot stop moving his left hand, and I can only imagine the pain it must be causing him.

Landulf has removed my shoes, but this does not stop me from leaping in the air and kicking at one of the stones with my right heel. It cracks with a single hard blow, and a series of kicks crush it. I pull out the chunks of stone and mortar with my hands, and soon I have a small river running through my fingers and over my lap. Yet I see the passageway is slightly above us, and that there is not more than a foot of water passing through it. Dante shivers and cries out as the cold water touches him and I have to talk to reassure him. My hands are frantically busy, pulling out pieces of stone. My strength level has gone up another notch. We were both so close to death, everything was hopeless, and now we stand on freedom's door.

Soon there is a hole large enough for us to crawl through. I help Dante into the passageway, and then I follow him. Soon I am standing beside him, steadying him with my hand. The water current is feeble; even Dante is able to stand against it. He grabs my arm and points upstream.

'This way is the woods, my lady,' he says. 'Soon we will be free of this unholy place.'

I stop him. 'I can't go with you, Dante, not yet.'

His exhilaration turns to distress. 'My lady? Why not?'

'I cannot go from here and leave Landulf alive.'

Dante is devastated. 'But if you go after him you will die! He is too strong!'

'I am strong, Dante. You have seen that. But I need

your help to find him. Where does he spend most of his time in the castle?'

Dante is animated. 'No, my lady. I don't know. He is like most people and moves around from place to place. You will not find him before his knights find you. Please, we must escape now while we have a chance.'

I clasp his shoulders. 'But I have to try to find him, Dante. Landulf may have taken something from me, something very precious, and I cannot leave this castle without knowing that he has been destroyed.'

Dante is confused. 'What did he take from you that is so precious?'

'I cannot explain that to you. I just need you to trust me that I speak the truth. Come, you spent many years with him. Where is the most likely place he will be right now?'

'But I don't know when right now is, my lady. All is dark in here.'

I stop and concentrate. Even though I have been unconscious much of the time, my very cells remember the passage of time. 'It is the second morning after I came here, not long before dawn.' I pause. 'Where does he spend his mornings?'

Dante's face twitches. 'If I tell you, will you do what you did last time? Will you go to him?'

I stroke his head and speak in a gentle hypnotic voice. 'You have to tell me. You are my friend. You are the only one I can trust. It is imperative that I destroy Landulf before I leave here. Not merely for the safety of you and me, but for the well-being of all people everywhere. You can see that, can't you? His evil has spread far and wide. I must stop it here at its source.'

My words go deep into Dante. 'He causes much suffering in many lands,' he whispers as he nods to himself.

'And that suffering can stop today. Tell me where in this castle he spends his mornings?'

'But, my lady, if you leave me now, when will I see you again?'

I continue to stroke his head. 'Remember the pool of water where we slept the night before we came to the castle? It was off the road. Do you think you would be able to hike back there?'

He nods vigorously. 'I can do it. I know these woods. When will you meet me there?'

'This evening. I can get there by then. Can you?'

'I am sure of it, my lady. If I do not stop to rest.'

'You can stop to rest. If I get there before you, I will wait.'

He grips my arm fiercely. 'Do you promise, my lady?'

'I promise you, Dante. With all my heart.' I pause and sharpen my tone. I know my next words must feel as if they cut right through him like knives but the time has passed for gentle persuasion. 'Now tell me where Landulf is.'

Dante speaks quickly, startled. 'He is probably not in the castle now. He spends most mornings at the ancient oracle, where Venus was long ago venerated.'

'Where is this spot?' I demand.

'It is a stone circle built into the side of the cliff at

the back of the castle.' He gestures downstream. 'That way opens onto a stream that falls not far from the place. But it is a dangerous spot, my lady. His power is greatest there, and the spirits protect him. You will not be able to get to him. You have to wait until he leaves the circle.'

'We will see.' I pat Dante on the back. 'Before this day is through, you and I will meet again. It will be a time of rejoicing. The evil enemy will be defeated and good friends will be together and free to go where they wish.'

'To Messina?' he asks excitedly.

'Yes, we can go to Messina.' I hug him. 'Take care of yourself, Dante. You are much loved by me.'

He hugs me in return and speaks in my ear.

'You are my love, my lady.'

15 ～

The dark path leads to light, but the sun is not yet up when I exit the underground passageway and stand on the edge of the cliff and look out at the vast panorama. A large section of the south shore of Sicily is indeed visible. The sea is purple and there are few clouds. The closest beach – far below and perhaps three miles distant – is occupied by a large contingent of soldiers. I can see the color of their skin, their black and green flags that wave in the morning breeze.

Arabs. Moslems.

They could not be so near without Lord Landulf's consent.

The duke is not far away, off to my left, down about five hundred feet. As Dante warned, he sits in the centre of a circle of stones – defined by the shape of the ledge and the pointed rocks that enclose it – in another pentagram. This five-pointed star appears to have been drawn by blood, and there is something red and slimy in his hands. He sits on his knees with his back to the cliff and I do not know what thoughts run through his corrupt mind. I only know he will be dead in a few minutes.

I start down the cliff.

Venus shines bright in the eastern sky.

I take her white light as a good omen.

I come within fifty feet of the stone circle before I pause. There is a young woman chained to the cliff just below me, and I see Landulf has the Spear of Longinus with him at the centre of the pentagram. I find it odd that I did not see it at first since I have not let him out of my sight on the hike down the cliff. But the fact does not concern me; the girl does. She is the one who assisted me when I rescued her and her friends from the cage. Like her friend, who was sacrificed at the black mass, she wears a white robe and looks terrified. Yet except for the three of us, I sense no one else in the vicinity. I descend another thirty feet, silently, staring at Landulf's back. I know it is him. The girl sees me and I motion for her to remain silent. Her eyes are suddenly wide with hope, and I have to wonder if that is good. This all seems too easy.

Then I pause again. Something makes me sick.

Lady Cia lies not far from the chained girl.

Her heart has been cut from her chest.

Now I know what Lord Landulf holds in his hands.

He continues to sit with his back to me. Defenseless.

'It was necessary, Sita,' he says softly.

That he knows I am here stuns me.

'Why?' I ask.

He glances over his shoulder.

'The sacrifice demanded the ultimate sacrifice,' he says.

'To achieve what aim?' I ask.

'To bring you here, to this spot.'

I snort. 'I brought myself here, thank you. None of your demons assisted me.'

He stands and stares at me. His wife's heart continues to drip in his open palm. His eyes are so dark 'That's what you think,' he says quietly.

I gesture to the girl. 'Why is she here?'

'For you. For the next step in your initiation.'

I point to my ears. 'I have sensitive hearing. The three of us are alone on this cliff. Not that it matters. You would need an army to protect you from what I am going to do to you now.'

He gestures to the circle, using the heart. 'You say your ears are sensitive. What about your eyes? Can you not see what you are up against?'

Now that he mentions it, I do notice a peculiar vibration in the air. It's as if we're surrounded by a swarm of insects, yet there is no sound. The sensation of the swarm is psychological. Now I feel as if something foul picks at my skin. I start to brush it away, but stop myself. I fear to show weakness in front of him. Yet a faint thread of fear has already entered my mind, and slowly begun to wrap around the centre of my brain. However, I still feel I have the upper hand. I am an ancient vampire of incredible strength. He is just a man. Why, he doesn't even have his spear in his hand to protect himself.

I step toward the stone circle and bump into a barrier.

It is invisible but palpable. A wall.

Or a magnetic force that resists physical contact.

I pound on it with my fist to no effect.

Landulf grins at me from inside the circle.

'To enter,' he says. 'You will have to sacrifice an innocent.'

The girl cries behind me. I silence her with a gesture.

'That will never happen,' I say as I slowly probe the perimeter of the stone circle, seeking for a weak spot. But the force field is uniform, and I am amazed that it even exists. My memories of the future are back again, clearer than ever. I have to wonder if the shield is of extraterrestrial origin. The last time I confronted Landulf on this spot, I defeated him by using his wife as a shield. This is the first event that is being played out differently from the last time. So I know I must have come back in time for this final moment.

Yet I do not know what to do.

Landulf follows my movements and does nothing to thwart me. I complete my inspection of the circle and pause to consider the possibility of jumping into the circle from the side of the cliff. Landulf reads my mind, or perhaps he logically figures out what my next move must be.

'You can try it,' he says. 'I would enjoy watching you bounce off the edge of the cliff.'

'You cannot stay in there forever,' I reply.

'Dante cannot stay in the underground passageway forever.'

I freeze. 'You bluff. You cannot stop him from here.'

In response Landulf raises the heart toward the sky and to my amazement it starts beating. The blood squirts on his face and he licks it. Then he lets out a high-pitched cackle, and I hear a loud shifting of stone far above. Glancing up the way I came, I see that the exit to the cliff has been closed over with a fallen boulder. Landulf lowers the heart.

'That is one end,' he warns. 'I can close the other end the same way. If . . .'

He doesn't finish. He wants me to.

'If I don't come get you,' I say.

'Exactly.' He gestures to the chained girl, who is not enjoying the display of the duke's powers. 'The life of your friend for the life of a stranger.'

I glance at the girl and she shakes her head slightly.

'Don't worry,' I snap at her.

'You need to rip out her heart,' Landulf explains. 'Quickly. While it still beats, you will be able to penetrate the circle.'

'I do not barter in human lives.' But sudden doubt plagues me. If I do not kill him, he will kill the girl anyway. And I will not be able to take her with me down

337

the side of the sheer cliff. Dante's innocent face haunts me, as do Landulf's hypnotic eyes. I just want to get to the duke and scratch his face off to put an end to his circus. He moves to the edge of the circle, comes within five feet of where I stand. Once more I pound on the barrier but my fists rebound against my chest. His dead wife's heart continues to beat and now the sound is in my ears. I do not understand how his palm can animate it. How a wizard, no matter how powerful, can infuse life into what should be dead.

'You will barter,' he promises. 'Fool! There is no part of you I cannot touch. No aspect of you I cannot defile.' He stops. 'Hear something, Sita?'

The beating of the heart grows louder in my ears.

In my head. Even when I cover my ears it doesn't help.

He shoves the heart toward me and I am forced to stare at it.

This is madness – I cannot even close my eyes.

'Kill her and it will stop,' he says.

'No!' I cry.

'Kill her and your friend will live! Kill her and you can kill me!'

The blood of the pounding heart splashes through the barrier and catches my face. I taste the waste of Cia's perverted life on my lips and the pounding in my head increases ten-fold. Surely I will go mad if I do not stop it in the next few seconds. Whirling toward the chained girl, I do not know what she hears except that she suddenly screams. Maybe the sight of my crazed expression makes her scream. What is one human life, I think? In four thousand years I have murdered thousands, ripped the lives from a parade of innocents. I need her heart, just for a second. Her sacrifice is necessary to spare the torment of billions in the future. She should be happy to die for such a noble cause. God should see that I have no choice in the matter.

But he will not see that and I know it.

Because I am five – not four – thousand years old.

I know to murder innocents is to murder my own soul.

But the pounding grows louder.

It is a miracle Landulf's voice can be heard above it.

'You can rip out my heart when you are done with me,' he says. 'And then you will finally be at peace. Peace, Sita!'

My body balls up in pain.

I squeeze my ears between my knees.

The beat of the dead heart. Nothing can stop it.

Tears run over my face. Bloody tears.

The girl swims in my red vision.

My head will explode, I know.

'Kill her, Sita!' Landulf implores.

My mission will fail. Billions will burn.

'Rip out her heart!'

In my head. The pain. The pounding. Please.

'Do it!'

I do it. Finally, just this once, I listen to him.

Leaping toward her, giving her almost no time to react, I thrust my left hand into her chest, smashing through her white gown and her pale ribs. Yet for a fraction of a second, she knows what I am going to do. She feels the absolute horror of the ritual execution. That is what Landulf wants, what he needs, to activate his black sorcery. The battery of the bastard is tied to perversity and pain. The girl's heart is in my hand. I feel its life, and still I yank it from her chest and leap toward the circle. Out the corner of my eye I see her staring at me, and understand the betrayal she is feeling deep in my soul. Her eyes are as blue as mine. Even in death, they could be mine.

I land inside the circle, at the tip of a point on the pentagram.

The pounding stops. The agony in my head.

The dead girl's heart seems to melt in my hand.

Landulf has picked up the mystical spear.

'They are always hungry,' he explains as he nods toward the heart vaporizing in my left palm. In moments it is entirely gone. There is not even a stain of blood left on my hand. Landulf raises the spear and takes a step toward me. He is pleased with me. 'You have passed the second step,' he says.

I ready myself for his attack. I shift to the right side.

My foot touches fire.

I whip my foot back. There are no visible flames.

'You are now in hell,' Landulf says. 'You are required to stay inside the lines of the pentagram. But I am free to roam where I wish, all over the circle.'

He lunges at me with the spear. He is fast.

I leap over to the adjacent star point.

He barely misses me. He flashes me a smile.

'Isn't this fun?' he asks.

'Delightful,' I say.

'There is one other rule you should know. Don't jump or walk through the centre of the pentagram. There is an invisible being waiting there that might consume you alive.'

'You expect me to believe you?' I ask.

'You don't have to. But then, I will lose you forever, and you will be trapped in a dark place forever.' He raises the spear once more. 'But do what you want. You may even try to escape from the circle, but you won't be able to. Once you are in here with me, you will stay in here.'

He makes another stab at me. I leap to the next point on the star. He misses, but I realize that I cannot keep on like this forever. His freedom of movement gives him a devastating advantage. His speed and strength are a mystery to me. But perhaps they come from the sum total of all the demons he carries in his heart. He is not necessarily as strong as I am, but his strength is close. I can tell by the power in his physical bursts. And he has the mystical spear, and I have to wonder if Christ's dried blood is an advantage or disadvantage in this cursed place.

'The spear is neither negative or positive,' he says, maybe reading my mind, maybe guessing. 'The tip is simply a point around which destiny turns. In the hands of a saint, it could be used for great healing. In my hands, it is merely a tool for my immortality.'

'You are not immortal,' I snap.

'But I will be, Sita. In a few moments. As soon as I pierce your side with this spear and channel your blood into my body.'

'You could have done that when I was unconscious.'

'No. To get the full benefit of your blood it is necessary that I drain you in my place of power. And you had to enter here of your own free will, after executing an innocent. Everything that has happened to you has been planned to bring you to this precise point.' He pauses. 'You see, Sita, I know you are from the future.'

He continues to shock me.

'How do you know?' I gasp.

'Because I am from the same future.'

'Did I know you?'

'Yes.'

'Who?'

'Linda's boyfriend. I was the one who sent you into the desert.'

'That fat slob?'

He is not offended. 'I was in disguise.'

I nod in admiration. 'You are clever. More clever than any foe I have ever encountered.'

My remark pleases him. He lowers the spear.

'Thank you. You have also been a worthy adversary. Why don't you let this end with dignity? I will give you that if you stop resisting me.'

I sigh. 'What do you want me to do?'

'Stand still for a moment. I do not need a lot of time.'

'What will you do to me?' I ask.

'I will take your blood. I need your blood. But you will not have to suffer. You have my promise on that.'

I consider. 'All right. I will surrender on two conditions.'

'What are they?'

'I want to open my own veins. And I want to use the nail that was on the cross, the one now tied to the tip of your spear.'

'Why the nail?' he asks.

'Because you say it was pounded into the hand or foot of Jesus. If I am to die, I want that nail to pierce my own flesh.' I add, 'It will make me feel closer to him as I die.'

Landulf is thoughtful. 'That will not save you from what is to follow. You are already in my circle. No works of Christ function here. I am not lying to you.'

'Perhaps. But those are my conditions.' I shrug. 'I don't ask much.'

He is wary. 'You could try to use the nail as a weapon. You could throw it at me.'

'Would you be able to block such a throw?'

'Yes.'

'Then what do you have to fear by tossing me the nail?'

'Nothing. I fear nothing in my place.'

'Then toss me the nail, O Fearless One.'

'You mock me?' he demands.

'Well, in the future it might be called flirting.'

He hesitates. 'I don't have to do this. I will get you eventually.'

'Probably. But you never know.'

'You believe the talisman will protect you? Despite what I say?'

'No. You are wrong there.'

'Then you lie to me. You will not keep your side of the bargain.'

I laugh. 'You call me a fool? You have nothing to lose by trusting me.' This time I catch his eye, and put all my will behind the gaze. 'You will never be successful as an immortal if you live in such fear, Lord Landulf.'

I have pushed the right button.

Perhaps his only button.

He hates to be called a coward.

He began to undo the wire holding the nail in place.

'When you have the nail, you open your veins immediately,' he says. 'I will tolerate no delay.'

'I will not waste your time,' I promise.

The nail is free. He tosses it to me.

'Christian paraphernalia,' he says bitterly.

I place the nail in my right palm, the tip pointed toward Landulf, and stare at it. Neither Yaksha's nor the child's nor my daughter's blood is in this present form of mine. I am strong but still only a shadow of what I will be in the future. Since returning to Sicily I have felt no power of psychokinesis, the ability to move objects with my mind. It was Kalika's blood alone that gave me that ability, and my daughter hasn't even been born yet. Still, my daughter gave her life to save the child, paid for his life with her own. And the child's blood, in an earlier reincarnation, was once on this nail. There is a connection that can reasonably be made here, or else mystically contrived. No doubt a particle of Christ's blood still remains on the metal, deep in the folds of the atoms that bind it together.

It is on this invisible blood I focus. I still believe in the miracle of this blood. My belief is born of experience. I have seen it bring a friend back to life. My belief is stronger than evil incantations spoken to cruel spirits, and bloody pentagrams drawn on forsaken cliffs. I made a serious mistake by stealing the girl's heart, but now I will give my own heart in exchange for hers. And in exchange for my life, for just a second of time, I ask for the power that my daughter already gave to me. I ask it out of favor to Kalika, whom I am sure would not want her mother to go down without a final chance of victory. Yes, I have the nerve to remind God that he owes me for my daughter's sacrifice. But I also have the faith to believe he hears me.

And my faith is stronger than stone.

Landulf lifts the spear. 'You had better hurry.'

I feel my mind touch the nail.

'Yes,' I whisper. 'Hurry.'

I feel my heart touch it. Caress it.

And I know beyond all doubt it once touched Christ.

Landulf shoulders the spear. 'You die now, Sita.'

The nail trembles. My hand remains firm. My gaze.

Power sweeps over me from way beyond the circle.

'No,' I say. 'Evil one, you die.'

Landulf starts to let the spear fly.

345

The nail flies out of my palm and is impaled in his forehead.

Between his eyebrows. He stares at me through a red river.

'You,' he says, and drops the spear.

I leap to his side and catch the spear before it lands. The nail has plunged all the way in.

'I take back what I said a moment ago,' I say. 'You are not so clever.'

I stick the spear in his heart, and his blood spurts out, even into the centre of the pentagram, where it is mysteriously consumed in midair. He tries to speak one last time, probably to curse my soul for all of time, but he is staggering blindly with a long spear thrust through him and a nail in his brain. He makes the serious mistake of stumbling into the centre region of the five-pointed star he has drawn with his wife's blood, and there something truly awful happenes. In a sickenigly wet sound, his clothes and flesh are simultaneously ripped from his body. For a moment he is a carved cadaver risen from an autopsy table. Then invisible claws go around his head, and he is pulled down and backward, into a pit of nothingness. He just vanishes and I am so grateful that I fall to my knees and weep for a long time.

The spear and nail remain where they have fallen from his body. They lie in the centre of the circle. And I know the power of the circle has been broken.

Eventually I climb down the cliff, and walk toward the ocean. I swim away from the hordes of Moslems, who only stare at me as I step onto the beach covered with blood from their dead benefactor. Perhaps they are afraid to touch me, I don't know. But they must have heard stories about Landulf's castle.

The place where magic was performed.

I swim through the waves beyond the invading army.

Beyond reason. The water is clean and stretches forever.

Yet I feel as if I will never be clean again.

16 ~~~

When I reach the clear pool of water that same evening, Dante is not there. His absence hits me like a wall. It was too much to hope, I know. But as I sit exhausted beside the pond and stare at the reflection of the vanishing sunlight and the slow emergence of the stars, I ponder the unfairness of life. Here was Dante, a simple man who would give his life for a just cause, killed out of love for me. And here am I, a monster, who will easily kill, and I am still alive. God had granted me a miracle that very morning, yet I feel I would trade all of his grace just to see my friend for a few minutes.

But the night grows darker and still Dante does not come.

He is dead, I know. Death is all I know.

There is blood on my left hand.

The hand that stole the girl's life.

Funny I hadn't noticed it before. Leaning over the pond, I place my hand in the water and try to wash off the dark red stain.

But it does not come off. I wonder why.

'Good. You have passed the first step of initiation. The second step will come later, and then the final and third step.'

Killing the girl had been the second step.

Or so he said. That Prince of Lies.

He is dead now. He will say no more.

Not to me. There will be no third initiation.

I scrub my hand fiercely. To no avail.

I have never seen a stain like this before.

'But I am sorry for what I did,' I tell the starry pond. 'You know I had to do it. I had no choice.'

If I am explaining to God, he does not answer me.

But once more my memory of the future is clear. Perhaps the pond acts as a catalyst. It is every bit as clear and round as the one Alanda led me to. And as I could at that watery oasis, I imagine that I can see more reflected stars than I can in the sky itself. My sudden grip on reality makes me marvel at how much my memory faltered while I was embarked on my dark adventure. Maybe Landulf had been blocking me. Maybe my deep-seated fears distorted my memory. I could have tricked myself into not knowing the horrors that awaited me. Or perhaps it was all a function of coming back in time.

I feel as if all my powers, the ones I left behind in the twentieth century, have returned to me. Come back just when I no longer need them. I am surprised, now that my mission is complete, that my staring at the stars does not bring me back to Alanda and Gaia and their spaceship. But maybe I don't want to leave yet. I promised Dante I would wait for him and I am determined to wait. I don't care how long it takes, long past hope I will sit here. Or, indeed, I even consider the possibility of returning to the castle to see if he has been taken captive once more. I could free him, save him.

But the latter is all bravado.

I will not go back to that castle.

I swore it once before and I swear it again.

The stars, as they are reflected in the pond, move lazily on the faint motion of the water. They are beautiful and I feel as if I can stare at them forever. Yet my mood is not peaceful. There is music in my head and it will not go away. I hear a strident refrain from Richard Wagner's *Parsival*. It is almost as if, staring at the heavens, I look upon a vast stage where Wolfram von Eschenbach's *Parsival* is still being played out. I see the knights striving to fulfill their quest for the Grail, and then, Klingsor, in the back-ground, always out of sight, obstructing their every move with his magic wand, the Spear of Longinus. I wonder if I should have left it in Landulf's body. The sacred stabbed through the sinful. But I had feared to approach the centre of the pentagram to retrieve it.

Even when he was dead, I was still afraid of him.

It is a truth I have trouble accepting.

I am afraid even now. The stain bothers me.

How was Klingsor stained? What was his mark?
The play explained it all. If only I could remember.
Something about a certain kind of smoothness.
But I cannot remember. No.
Nor can I understand why Dante was so insistent that I understand the meaning of the Medusa story. He was such a simple fellow, full of phobias and goodness, but when he spoke of mythology, he spoke with great authority. Almost as if another personality used his mouth and lips. I keep feeling as if Dante had been trying to warn me of a deeper threat. One that could not be seen because the true power of the wizard was that he was able to control one's will. Capable of turning whomever he wished to stone, so that he or she did not move unless the wizard wished it.

Could that be the real meaning of the Medusa tale?
The Gorgon did not merely kill her enemies.
She placed them under complete mind control.
Doubts continue to assail me. Questions that are more like ancient riddles. What about the snakes in the hair of Medusa? What about her fair face? Dante had emphasized that the latter was crucial. And I had laughed and told him it was time to concentrate on what was real. But I of all people should have known that reality was not always what it seemed.

A profound certainty sweeps over me.
Dante had been trying to warn me of something *unseen*.
Then I see him. And it is a miracle.
He is struggling up the path to the pond, limping

badly, gasping for breath. In a moment I am by his side, helping him to sit down on a large rock not far from the water. He is in worse shape than when I saw him last and is already babbling about how sorry he is that he is late, and why he is late. I can't get a word in, but I am so happy to see him that I weep. Really, it is one of the most wonderful moments of my life. God has heard all of my prayers.

'The passageway was blocked,' he says rapidly, with hardly any air in his lungs. 'There was a large stone. I had never seen this stone before. Never! My lady, I didn't know what to do. I tried walking back in your direction, but I couldn't find you, and I kept slipping in the water. My brace kept falling off, and once it almost floated away. I would have been crippled! Then I took another path that I know but no one else knows and I went back into the castle and by all the saints in heaven I knew I was going to be put back in the prison. But everyone ignored me! The knights were running all over the place and the servants were crying and it sounded as if something horrible had befallen Lord Landulf.' He pauses to breathe and his eyes shine with hope. 'What befell him, my lady?' he asks.

I have to smile. Yet there is no joy in it and I wonder why. My happiness is tempered with regrets I can hardly explain to myself.

'He died,' I say. 'I killed him.'

Dante bursts out with laughter. But then he catches himself and quickly does the sign of the cross. But his relief is not to be contained and a moment later he is howling in pleasure again. He jumps up from his rock and hugs me and shakes like a child. Yet the news is too good for him. He is having trouble believing it.

'Is he is really dead?' he keeps asking. 'Are you sure it was him? Did you see his body? Are you sure it was his body?'

I strive to calm him. 'It was him, I swear it. I put the Spear of Longinus through his evil heart. He died like any other man.'

Dante is smiling. 'Did you burn his body? Did the smoke stink?'

I shake my head. 'No. I didn't burn him. There wasn't time.'

His smile falters slightly. 'But what did you do with his body, my lady?'

I shrug. 'Nothing. I left it. Don't worry, he will not return to haunt us. I am sure of it.'

Dante seems reassured. 'Then we can go to Messina now and tell everyone that the world is safe?'

I force a laugh. 'Yes. We can tell everyone that there is nothing left to worry about.' But my laughter soon dies because that is not the way I feel. I add softly, 'We will tell the whole world.'

Dante is uncertain. 'Is something wrong, my lady?'

I turn away. 'No. I am just worried about you. You need to eat, to rest and regain your strength.'

He stands and steps to my back. 'Something weighs on your heart. Share it with me, my lady. Perhaps I can lighten your burden.'

My eyes are suddenly damp. I am ashamed to look at his face.

But I feel I can tell him. He will understand.

'When I found Lord Landulf,' I say, 'he was in the stone circle as you said he would be. But I did not do what you suggested. I did not wait for him to leave the circle to attack him. I was too impatient. He was simply sitting there – I thought I could just kill him and then it would be all over with.'

Dante speaks sympathetically. 'But you could not penetrate the circle.'

My hands clasp each other uneasily. I cannot stop moving them. 'Yes. There was an invisible shield around it. Landulf had created it, I believe, by employing a sacrifice that required him to cut out the heart of his own wife.'

Dante gasps. 'Lady Cia!'

'Yes. She was dead when I arrived. But there was a young woman chained nearby who was very much alive. Landulf told me if I wanted to get to him, I would have to rip out the girl's heart. At first I refused, but then this pounding started in my head, and it wouldn't stop, and I didn't know what to do. In a moment of pain and anger I reached for her . . .' I have trouble finishing. 'I reached for her and I – I killed her, Dante. I killed her with my own hands, and she had never done anything to me.'

Dante is silent for a long time. Finally I feel his good hand touch my shoulder. 'You did what you had to do, my lady.'

I clasp his hand but shake my head. 'I don't know. Sometimes I think I just did what I have always done in the past – kill. That has always been my ultimate solution to every problem.' I gesture weakly. 'But this girl – she was praying for me to save her.'

'But you saved the rest of us.'

I am emotional. 'Did I? Did I do what I was supposed to do? If I did then can you explain to me why the stain of this girl's blood refuses to wash off my hand?'

Dante grabs my left hand and stares at it anxiously. 'Perhaps we only need to wash it in clean water. Come, my lady, a quick wash in the pond and everything will be all right.'

I take back my hand. 'No, Dante. I have tried washing it a dozen times. The stain will not come off.'

He is confused. 'But why?'

I lower my head. 'I think it is because I listened to Landulf, in the end.'

'No!'

'Yes. I performed the ritual murder of an innocent. That's all that was needed to be initiated by him.' I pause and stare at my left hand. There is only the stars for light, but I see the stain well. It is almost as if I see my whole life expressed in the red of the mark. 'I have become one of them,' I whisper.

Dante is adamant. 'No! You are the opposite of them! You are an angel! You bring light where there is darkness! Hope where there is despair! A dozen times you have come to my rescue! A dozen times I would have died without your courage!'

I turn and force a smile. 'Oh, Dante. I had to keep saving you because I kept putting you in danger.' I raise my hand as he tries to protest. 'Please don't look upon me as an angel. When you get to heaven, you'll see real angels and they'll look nothing like me.'

He pauses and seems to think hard for a moment. But his eyes never leave my face. 'You have too much love in you to be hated by God,' he says finally. 'When we get to heaven, you'll see that.'

I have to laugh and hug him again. 'My friend! What would I do without you? No, wait, don't answer that question. There is something I want to do for you. Something I have been planning to do for the last few days. But before I do it I want you to know that it is entirely safe. That no harm will come to your body or soul by the change I am going to bring.'

He is curious. 'What is this wonderful thing you are going to do?'

I hold his shoulders and stare into his eyes, trying to bring calm and understanding into his excited mind. 'You saw how Landulf was anxious to get my blood? There was a reason for that. Long ago a mysterious man gave me some of his blood, and that blood changed me in a way that made me both strong and resistant to disease. It is impossible for me to get sick. And just a few drops of my blood is able to heal others.' I pause. 'Do you understand what I am saying, Dante?'

He shakes his head. 'I am not sure, my lady.'

'I want to cut myself and sprinkle a few drops of my blood over your sores. I know they hurt you terribly, but when a little of my blood touches them they will close and heal. It will be almost be like you never had leprosy. No one will be able to tell by looking at you.'

He frowns. 'But it is God's will that I am sick. My disease is a punishment for my sins. We cannot change the will of God.'

'Your disease is not a punishment. It is not from God. It is something you caught from another person who had the same disease.'

He blinks. 'From the other lepers in Persida?'

'Exactly. They gave you the leprosy.'

He protests. 'But I never did anything to them. I only tried to help them.'

'But you were around them. You touched them. That is how you got sick.'

His confusion deepens. 'But Landulf wanted to use your blood, my lady. I should not use it. I should not do anything he wanted to do.'

'There is a difference, Dante. Landulf wanted to use my blood to hurt people. I want to use it to heal you.'

His superstitions are deep. His disquiet remains.

'But blood should not be shared,' he says. 'That is what heathens do. When the Holy Father accused my duke, he said that he had been sharing blood with children. I thought at the time that it was lies but it came to pass that it was true. And it was a great evil that from hell. The pope saw clearly.'

'The pope did not see clearly. Good God, Dante, the pope had you castrated.'

His face twitches and his lower lip trembles. I have

wounded him with my words and feel ashamed. He drops his head in humiliation.

'I wanted only to do God's will,' he moans. 'That is all I want to do right now. But I do not know how your blood can make my disease disappear.'

I feel I have no recourse. We can argue all night, and get nowhere, and I believe it is possible that he could die this very night. From the burning and the other abuse, his sores are even more inflamed. Half his body is infected tissue, and I feel without even touching him the fever that cooks his blood. The effort it took him to reach me has drained what reserves he had left. His breathing is a perpetual wheeze. If I do not give him my blood soon, I will not be able to return to the future with a clear conscience.

'Dantè,' I say, meeting his gaze again. 'Look at me.'

He blinks rapidly. 'My lady?'

'Look only at me, my friend. Listen only to me. You do not need to be afraid of my blood. It is a gift from God. Just a few drops of it will make you feel better, and God wants you to feel better after all that you have struggled do in his name.'

He is suddenly dreamy. 'Yes, my lady.'

'Now close your eyes and imagine how nice it will to have your sores healed. How good it will be not to have people run away when they see you because they see you only as a leper. Dante, my dear, I promise you the leprosy will be gone in a few minutes.'

'It will be gone,' he whispers to himself with his eyes closed.

'Good.' I stretch out my hand. 'Now keep your eyes closed but give me your hand. I will lead you to the pond and we will first wash your sores and then I will sprinkle something on them and they will be all better.'

'All better,' he mumbles. But he stiffens when I try to lead him toward the pond even though his eyes remain closed. He is still under my spell, at least I think he is. 'No,' he says.

I have to speak carefully. 'What is the matter?'

'I cannot go in the pond.'

'You will not go in the pond, only beside it. I need to wash you off.'

'I can drown in the pond,' he says.

Now that I think of it, I have never seen Dante wash beside a pond. It is probably one of the reasons he smells.

'I will not let you drown. There is no way you can fall in.'

'No,' he says.

He appears to be under my spell, but he is resisting me as well. I am reminded of an earlier time when I pressed him for information he knew and yet he managed to evade me – even while in the midst of a powerful hypnotic trance. There is still something in his mind, a psychic aberration of some type, that makes it impossible for me to read him clearly. Even with all my powers now at my disposal, I cannot read what he is thinking exactly.

And I should be able to read his mind completely.

'What if you rest on the rock you were sitting on a

moment ago,' I suggest. 'And I bring you water to clean you. Would that be all right?'

He nods with his eyes closed. 'I'll rest on the rock and be all right.'

I lead him back to the stone where he initially rested. As he sits, I stroke his head. 'I will moisten my shirt,' I say. 'Then I will touch your sores gently, to clean them. There will be no pain. You will feel nothing but relief. You understand, Dante?'

'I understand,' he whispers.

I let go of him. 'I will be gone a few seconds. Remain at peace.'

He sighs. 'Peace.'

At the pond the water is very still, more so than ever. Like the pond in the desert, it is a perfect mirror of the heavens. There are so many stars on its delicate surface, so many constellations that it seems almost a sin to disturb the cool liquid. Yet I have stood here before. Last time I also gave Dante my blood and sent him on his way healed of his horrible disease. Like now, and then, I felt moved by love to give him what I could. Certainly he has earned my blood and my trust.

I bend to dampen my shirt and then pause.

I cannot stop staring in the water at the sky. There is the familiar constellation, Andromeda, and I can't remember it ever looking so clear. Why, I can almost imagine that I see Perseus' wife, chained to the rocks as the Titan slowly approaches, bound as a human sacrifice to appease an evil monster. Much as Landulf chained and sacrificed young women to appease his own wickedness. It is incredible, as I look closer, to see Perseus creeping closer to her side, to rescue her, with the Medusa's head hidden in his bag, out of sight. He will only show it at the last moment, when the Titan has exposed himself. Perseus was wise to keep his weapon hidden. It was Dante who suggested that Perseus would have been a fool to part with such power.

Medusa. Perseus. Dante.

'My lady,' Dante whipers at my back.

'Coming,' I say.

I kneel to wet my shirt.

But once again I pause.

Richard Wagner's opera returns to me on the silence of the night air. The music echoes in my mind with rhythms older than man. Again it is as if I am watching the opera, *Parsival*, being staged against the majestic background of the constellations. Each of the principal characters could be a mythological being. King Arthur could be King Polydectes, who sent Perseus after the Gorgon. Parsival could be Perseus, who slew the Medusa. But who would Klingsor be? Why, of course, the Medusa itself. The one who appears fair from the outside, but whose hair – whose *aura* – is filled with hissing snakes. I understand in that moment that the serpents are symbolically placed above the Medusa's head. They are there so her true identity cannot be mistaken.

'Hurry, my lady,' Dante whispers.

I will,' I say. But I cannot move, or breathe.

Klingsor and the Medusa. Klingsor and Landulf.

They had so much in common.

Except for one little thing. The play spoke of this 'thing.'

Wolfram von Eschenbach's *Parsival* told of this 'thing.'

Klingsor had a special mark.

He was smooth – in a delicate spot.

I remember now. Everything.

And I am sick because the truth is horrible beyond belief.

I am turned to stone. Tears cannot help me. They will not come. Not before a pain beyond all measure comes. Because even though I know the truth, I refuse to accept it. My faith may be stronger than stone, but in time all stones are worn away by water. Or tears – it doesn't matter. All I can do now is force my stone body to face what waits behind me.

Wetting my shirt, I stand and spy a lizard that slithers near the side of the pond. In a moment he is in my hand, in my pocket, and I casually walk back to Dante, who sits expectantly on the rock where I left him. A smile springs to his face as I approach even though his eyes remain closed. Leaning over, I begin to gently wipe at his burnt and diseased hand and arm. My touch pleases him.

'Oh, my lady,' he says.

'Just relax, Dante,' I say softly, 'I have to clean you and then I can cure you. You want me to cure you, don't you?'

'Oh, yes.'

'Good.' I momentarily close my own eyes and bite my lower lip. 'That's good.'

Seconds later his hand and arm are clean. I stand

and reach for the lizard in my pocket. 'Now don't be afraid,' I say.

'I am not afraid,' he whispers.

Placing the lizard behind my back, I pulverize it in my hands. I crush it so hard all the blood squirts into my palms. Then my hands are over Dante's leper sores, dropping the reptile's blood over his wounds. The lizard was cold-blooded; its blood is not so warm as mine would have been. But Dante doesn't seem to notice and for that small favor I am glad. I cannot take my eyes off his face. I am looking for something there, a faint change of expression as his system soaks up my blood. An expression I have not seen before. An expression of triumph, perhaps, or maybe even arrogance. I need to see such a thing to dispel all my questions.

But what I see is much worse.

As the blood sprinkles over him, his lower lip curls ever so slightly. Curls in an unpleasant manner, and I believe deep in my heart that he is reacting to my great sacrifice with all but disguised contempt. I pull my hands away.

'Open your eyes, Dante,' I say.

He opens his eyes and beams. 'Am I cured, my lady?'

I grin with false pleasure. 'Almost, my friend.'

Then I grab him by the collar of his filthy shirt and, before he can react, I drag him to the edge of the pond. The water has not completely settled since I touched it, but it is flat enough to show his reflection. No wonder he did not want to stand next to the pond with me by his side. For in the water, Dante's supposedly ruined and pained expression is extraordinary.

Literally, he is more beautiful than a man should be.

He could almost be a goddess.

I leap back from him and tremble.

'Landulf,' I gasp. 'It was you. All along, it was you.'

The other Landulf was just a puppet. Just a disciple of the real master, Dante. The duke in the castle was just a minion.

Dante was the real power behind the throne.

Dante *was* Landulf.

He stares down at his face for a long time before responding. Perhaps he has not seen his reflection in a while – I don't know. When he finally does speak, his voice is remarkably gentle, not unlike it was before, yet with more power, the confidence of a being that has for a long time been master of his own destiny. He straightens as he speaks, as if his physical disease has no real hold over him. But I am not sure if that is the case. He speaks with authority but there is disappointment in his tone.

'I should have guessed you would return with greater wisdom,' he says. 'Last time you were easily tricked. But now I am the one who has been fooled.' He sighs. 'You have grown, Sita, in the last thousand years.'

'Because I chose wisdom over compassion?' I ask.

He glances at me. 'In a sense. It is easier for humans to pass a test of love than a test that requires wisdom. Because even love often obscures wisdom.'

I am bitter. 'You do not have the right to speak to me of love.'

He has been tricked but he still has the ability to smile. 'But I do admire you even if I don't love you,' he says. 'Admiration is the closest my kind gets to love. It serves us well. I never feel the lack of this love you constantly crave.'

'You imply that I need something from you. You're wrong.'

'Yet you cherished Dante's love,' he says.

'I was merely bewildered on the path. You are lost here at the end.'

'Perhaps.' He pauses. 'How did you guess?'

'*Parsival*. I saw it in Vienna before World War Two. The character of Klingsor was Landulf. He had been castrated by the pope.' I mock him. 'In the play, they said he was smooth between the legs.'

A wave of anger rolls over his face but he quickly masters himself. 'You have an excellent memory. No doubt I made other mistakes with you as well.'

'Yes. But I am puzzled. Why did you give me the clue of the Medusa's head?'

'It was necessary. For you to be totally mine, you had to be warned by me in advance. Free will operates on both paths, the right and the left. When you intentionally killed that girl, then and only then were you made ready to meet me here.'

'It was all just a set up? The whole thing?'

'Yes.'

'And had I willingly given you my blood, I would

have completed the third step?'

'Precisely. Then your blood would have been of the most use to me.'

I sigh. 'Well, I guess now you're not going to have it.'

He stares at me. I see him clearly now, his supernatural beauty, even the faint tendrils of black that crawl around the field above his head. Yet I realize he still has leprosy.

'You are wrong on that point,' he says softly.

I take a step back. 'You are still about to die. You need my blood to live even a few more days. Your evil invocations really did give you leprosy.

He takes a step in my direction. 'That is correct. The work has its price. But I need your blood to sustain this physical body, and continue my work in this third density. But unlike last time, I will now be unable to pass my blood onto others. You can no longer be convinced to be my initiate and undergo a shift toward negative polarization. Still, your blood will be useful to me for a long time.' He removes a dagger from under his dirty shirt. It is the same one that the maid stabbed me with. It is stained with my blood. 'There is no point in trying to run from me, Sita, or in trying to harm me. My psychic powers are beyond yours.'

I find it impossible to turn away from him.

Indeed, I cannot even move my arms or legs

The Medusa. My body has turned to stone.

'It doesn't matter what you do to me now,' I say, thankful to be able to use my tongue. 'I have defeated you and the rest of your kind. In the future there will be no army of invincible negative beings to confuse humanity. Your cancer has been cut from society. The harvest will go forward the way it was intended. You have lost, Landulf, admit it.'

He steps to within two feet of me. He brushes my long hair with his knife. Then he licks the tip of the blade, the dried blood, and smiles sadly.

'It is not my nature to admit anything,' he says. 'But I will say that I would have enjoyed your continuing adoration almost as much as your body, and the immortal blood that pumps through it.' He scratches the skin below my right eye and a red drop runs over my cheek. The sight fills him with pleasure. 'A vampiric tear, Sita. Cried for me? I must still be your hero.'

I am defiant, and no longer afraid.

The stain on my left hand has vanished.

'My only regret is the tears I cried for you,' I say. 'Other than that I have none. I am at peace. And you are still a monster. One day you will be forced to look in Perseus' mirror, and you will see your own reflection, and see just how foul you are to behold. And on that day you will turn to stone, Landulf. You will die and rot, and the world will be relieved of a great burden.' I stop. 'Kill me now and get it over with. If you have the nerve, you disgusting creature!'

I spit in his face. He does not like that.

He wipes the saliva away and raises his knife.

'I was going to kill you quick,' he says. 'But now, Sita, it may take all night.'

He moves to slit open my side and then pauses, puzzled.

I am confused as well, for a moment. My body has begun to glow. The pond shines as well, with the light of the heavens. It is as if the constellations in the sky have been awakened, and been inspired to send down their light to Earth. The white light that fills my body comes from the direction of the pond as well as the sky. Landulf seems to recognize the transformation I am undergoing and is filled with dismay. But this stellar current fills me with euphoria. I have experienced it before, just before I rescued the child from the Setians. Landulf is like one of those creatures, I see, only worse. He struggles to cut into my flesh as I grow brighter. His frustration makes me laugh.

'I guess you're going to have to remain a leper,' I say in a voice that grows faint. 'But don't take it too hard. You're not going to be around much longer. Yaksha is still somewhere on this planet and you might try to find him, but I don't think that you'll get to him in time. As far as you're concerned, I am the last vampire. Your last chance, Landulf. How does that feel?'

His rage is incredible to behold. The fair face of the god is transformed into a demon. The all but invisible serpents above his head hiss poisonous vapors. They surround him in a noxious cloud. It is as if his whole body has been swallowed by his leper's sores. He tries to grab me but his fingers pass through me. Seeing his efforts are useless, he strains to regain his pleasant demeanor, to make one last stab at my soul. But he still has the knife in his hand and in either case I will never be fooled by him again.

'Sita,' he says. 'Our offer is still good. We can grant you powers unimaginable. You have only to join us, and we will rule this world together.'

I am practically a ghost but I can still laugh.

'You shouldn't have mentioned the togetherness part,' I reply. 'I can't think of anything more dull.'

17 ~~~

There is a brief moment when I am lying on the floor of the interstellar craft. I feel Alanda and Gaia close. It is possible Alanda even calls my name. She must know I have successfully completed my mission. She must be waiting for me, to smile at me, to take me to other worlds, into a glorious future.

But my battle with Landulf has taken something from me.

Finally I am tired of such adventures.

As Yaksha finally grew weary, I also crave a change.

Before Alanda can call me back to the present moment, I focus my entire being on another page of history. I return to the first vampire, the strange night Yaksha was born, five thousand years ago in India, when I was a girl of seven years. The Aghoran ceremony has ended and the evil priest has been killed by Amba's animated corpse. The corpse finally lies down but there is movement inside Amba's belly, which is still swollen with the nine-month-old foetus she was carrying when she died. My father takes his knife and goes to cut out the unborn child trapped in the womb. I leap from my hiding place behind the bushes.

'Father!' I cry, as I reach for his hand that holds the knife. 'Do not let that child come into the world. Amba is dead, see with your own eyes. Her child must likewise be dead. Please, Father, listen to me.'

Naturally, all the men are surprised to see me, never mind hear what I have to say. My father is angry with me, but he kneels and speaks to me patiently.

'Sita,' he says, 'Your friend does appear dead, and we were wrong to let this priest use her body in this way. But he has paid for his evil karma with his own life. But we would be creating evil karma of our own if we do not try to save the life of this child. You remember when Sashi was born, how her mother died before she came into the world? It sometimes happens that a living child is born to a dead woman.'

'No,' I protest. 'That was different. Sashi was born just as his mother died. Amba has been dead since early dawn. Nothing living can come out of her.'

My father gestures with his knife to the squirming life inside Amba's bloody abdomen. 'Then how do you explain the life here?'

'That is the yashini moving inside her,' I say. 'You saw how the demon smiled at us before it departed. It intends to trick us. It is not gone. It has entered into the child.'

My father ponders my words with a grave expression. He knows I am intelligent for my age, and occasionally asks my advice. He looks to the other men for guidance, but they are evenly divided. Some want to use the knife to stab the life moving inside Amba. Others are afraid, like my father, of committing a sin. Finally my father turns back to me and hands me the knife.

'You knew Amba better than any of us,' he says. 'You would best know if this life that moves inside her is evil or good. If you know for sure in your heart that it is evil, then strike it dead. None of the men here will blame you for the act.'

I am appalled. I am still a child and my father is asking me to commit an atrocious act. But my father is wiser than I have taken him for. He shakes his head as I stare at him in amazement, and he moves to take back the knife.

But I don't give the knife to him.
I know in my heart what I must do.
I stab the blade deep into Amba's baby.
Black blood gushes over my hands.
But it is only the blood of one. Not thousands.
The creature inside Amba's body stops moving.

Alanda turns to Gaia after studying her friend's body. They are not in a spaceship, but stand in the desert at night beside a clear pond. Many stars shine overhead.

'She is not breathing,' Alanda says. 'Her heart has stopped.'

'But she stopped him,' Gaia says, who actually can speak in his own way. 'The path is now clear for many.'

Alanda glances down at her friend. There is sorrow in her voice. 'But she was coming back to us,' she says.

Gaia comforts her. 'She always went her own path. Let her go this way.'

Yet Alanda later sheds a tear as they slide her friend's body into the pond. For a moment her friend floats on the surface of the water, and the reflection of the stars frame her figure. And when Alanda glances up, she sees the same outline in the heavens. For a moment her friend is the constellation and it gives her a measure of comfort. But when Alanda looks back down, her friend has sunk beneath the mirror of the water and is gone.

'It is like she never was,' Alanda whispers.

'It is like that for all of us,' Gaia says.

One moonless night, when I am twenty years of age, I am awakened by a sound outside. Besides me sleeps my husband, Rama, and on my other side is our daughter, Lalita. I don't know why the sound wakes me. It was not loud. But it was peculiar, the sound of nails scraping over a blade. I get up and go outside my house and stand in the dark and look around.

For a long time I stand there, expecting to meet someone.

But there is no one there.

Finally I return to my bed and fall asleep.

The next morning I am playing with my Lalita by the river when a strange man comes by. He is tall and powerfully built. In his right hand he holds a lotus flower, in his left a gold flute. His legs are long and his every movement is bewitching. I cannot help but stare at him, and I am delighted when he comes and kneels beside me on the bank of the river. For some reason, I know he means me no harm.

'Hello,' he says, staring at the water. 'How are you?'

'I am fine.' I pause. 'Do I know you, sir?'

A faint smile touches his lips. 'Yes. We have met before.'

I hesitate. He does seem familiar but I cannot place him.

'I am sorry, I don't remember,' I say.

He finally looks at me and his eyes are very blue. They remind me of the stars at night; they seem to sparkle with light from the heavens. 'My name is Krishna,' he says.

I bow my head. 'I am Sita. This is my daughter, Lalita. Are you new to this area?'

He turns back to the water. 'I have been here before.'

'Is there anything I can do for you? Would you like some food?'

He glances at me, out the corners of his eyes, and I feel a thrill in my heart. There is such love in his glance, I don't understand how it can be so. 'I was wondering if I could do anything for you, Sita,' he says.

'My Lord?' I ask, and I feel he is deserving of the title.

He shrugs faintly. 'I merely came to see if you were happy. If you are, then I will be on my way.'

I have to laugh. 'My Lord, I am not long married. My husband is a wonderful man whom I love dearly and God has seen fit to grace us with a beautiful child. We are all healthy and have plenty to eat. I cannot imagine being any happier than I am right now.'

He nods briefly and then stands. 'Then I will say goodbye, Sita.'

But I jump up. 'You came all the way here just to see if I was happy?'

'Yes.' His eyes are kind as he looks at me for the last time. 'Your happiness is all that matters to me. Remember me, Sita.'

Then he walks away and I never see him again.

But I never forget him. Krishna.

Epilogue

Seymour Dorsten sat at his computer in his bedroom and stared at the words on the screen. It was late, close to dawn, and he had been writing most of the night. For the last six months, in fact, he had worked almost every night without rest. But it didn't matter how much sleep he missed. He could always sleep during the day. Because he was very sick with AIDS, he no longer attended school, or even went out of the house. Indeed, his personal physician thought he wouldn't live out the year, and it was almost Christmas. Yet the tragedy of his early demise did not disturb him, at least not at the moment. Like his imagined heroine, he was happy in the end, to have even reached the end.

He had just finished his story. *Her* story.

About Alisa Perne, his Sita. The Last Vampire.

Seymour felt as if he had taken her everywhere she could go, but at the same time he knew that it was *she* who had led him on the adventures. Lifted him up to heights he could not have imagined if not for his serious illness. For him, the constant experience of his waning mortality had been the greatest muse. She had never said who she was sending her thoughts out to, but it was to him, always to him. But *he* had made her immortal, and himself, so that he wouldn't have to be afraid of his own death. He knew, in the end, that she had not been afraid, and that her only regret had been that she had not been able to say goodbye to him. But at least he could say goodbye to her.

Seymour leaned forward and turned off the screen.

There was a noise outside his window.

He glanced over. Quickly, he always did.

But it was nothing. A cat, the wind.

But such sounds, this late at night, always made him think of her. Ageless Sita coming through the window to give him her magical blood. To save him from his illness. But she had chosen the only destiny worthy of her. She had simply decided to vanish, to exist only in his heart.

Seymour coughed weakly and brushed away a tear that came to his eye. He should be in a hospital. His lungs were half-filled with fluid, and he couldn't draw in a full breath without pain. Still, he thought, it was better to be at home with his computer and his story. He just wished his heart could beat for her forever.

Seymour was going to miss her. Yeah.

'Goodbye, Sita,' he said to the empty screen. He thought he would miss her forever.